Elizabeth was on her way out of the bookstore when she saw Roarke enter with Lady Anne. She darted between two shelves, but wasn't at all sure he hadn't seen her. She was feigning interest in a volume she had plucked at random from the shelves when he found her.

"It seems you've found something to keep you occupied," he observed. "Will you be reading Miss Austen this evening? Perhaps I shall see you later."

"I'm certain you'll be far too involved with Lady Anne to concern yourself with me. In fact, I feel guilty keeping you from her side now."

"I would much rather be here with you." His dark eyes bored into hers, holding her prisoner by their intentness. "Don't you know that by now? Has your father completely poisoned you against me?"

"My father has said nothing that isn't the truth," she shot back, her temper flaring.

"The truth can be viewed from many sides," he continued. "I don't want to fight with you, Elizabeth. At one time we got along quite well, didn't we?"

Elizabeth smiled, remembering their better times. "Very well indeed," she agreed.

"I want it to be that way again," he said, reaching out to brush his finger down the side of her cheek.

Roarke's touch set Elizabeth's skin on fire. Her back was against the bookshelves and she could not move away, but then, she found she had no desire to do so.

"I want to kiss you, Elizabeth." His finger still rested against her lips.

This time she did not fight the urge . . .

If you would like to read the stories
of the other second-sight ladies
mentioned in this book
ask for

A Gifted Lady
and
The Willful Wife

from
Alana Clayton
and
Zebra Books

THE
HEADSTRONG
HEART

Alana Clayton

Zebra Books
Kensington Publishing Corp.

http://www.zebrabooks.com

ZEBRA BOOKS are published by

Kensington Publishing Corp.
850 Third Avenue
New York, NY 10022

Zebra and the Z logo Reg. U.S. Pat. & TM Off.

First Printing: April, 1999
10 9 8 7 6 5 4 3 2 1

Printed in the United States of America

To a very special aunt,

Flossie Puckett

*whose encouragement and friendship
are gifts I greatly treasure.
With love.*

One

The scream pierced the thick mahogany door and echoed down the dimly lit hallway. The solid walls of the town house did little to protect the inhabitants from the horror of the sound as it built in volume. It held the dwelling in its grip for what seemed an eternity before it changed into a pain-racked wail, then dwindled until it faded altogether. A deadly silence fell.

Elizabeth Leighton had finally awakened.

Elizabeth's eyes jerked open. Her heart was racing, and hoarse gasps rasped through her raw throat as she pulled air into starved lungs that had been emptied by the scream. The terror of the nightmare swirled around her; horror and fear hovered over her, trapped beneath the canopy of the bed.

Too weak to sit up, Elizabeth lay stiffly, afraid to close her eyes, afraid the same sight might be locked behind her eyelids, merely waiting for them to shut again. As she regained her breath, another scream gathered itself for release. She pressed her lips together, determined to keep it trapped inside. After all, she was at home in her own bed, with nothing to fear from a bothersome dream. She had nearly convinced herself, when the door burst open and her Aunt Louisa rushed into the room.

"Elizabeth? Dear God, Elizabeth, was that you?" Face pale, hands clasped at her breast, Louisa stared down at her.

Before Elizabeth could answer, her maid came running through the door, joining her aunt by the bedside.

"Oh, ma'am. Was it Lady Elizabeth? I could hear the sound all the way to the kitchens."

"I don't know, Betsy. Her eyes are open, but she hasn't moved or uttered a sound. It might have been merely a reflex."

"Oh, ma'am, and I had so hoped."

"I know, Betsy, so did I."

Elizabeth could stand it no longer. "Why are you talking as if I'm not here?" she croaked, wondering what had caused her voice to become so raspy. She had sounded perfectly fine when she had retired the evening before. Perhaps she had caught a chill during the night; that would explain both the nightmare and the hoarseness.

Betsy uttered a shriek and grabbed the bedpost, clinging to it as if she were adrift in a rough sea. Louisa stared at Elizabeth a moment longer, then dropped into the chair at her niece's bedside as if her legs could no longer hold her.

"Elizabeth, do you know who I am?" she asked hesitantly, in a voice more suited to addressing the elderly than a young woman in her prime.

"Of course, I know who you are," Elizabeth complained. "Having a nightmare doesn't mean I've lost all my senses. Although I must admit I do feel a bit out of sorts." The effort of speaking was strangely draining, and Elizabeth thought the chill she had caught must be a particularly strong one.

Louisa gave a strange strangled gasp of laughter. "I imagine you would," she agreed. "You've been ill, my dear."

"Did I catch a chill yesterday?" asked Elizabeth. "I suppose I was feverish, and that's the reason I'm so hoarse."

"No, you've been ill longer than that."

"Oh, Lady Elizabeth, it's been just terrible," burst out Betsy, still clinging to the bedpost, but regaining her ability to speak.

"Hush, now, Betsy," said Louisa. "There will be plenty of time for that later. At present, we must concentrate on Elizabeth's well-being."

"Just how long have I been sick?" asked Elizabeth, highly suspicious that her aunt was keeping something from her.

"For a while," quibbled Louisa.

"One day? Two?" pressed Elizabeth.

Since she had first crawled across the floor, Elizabeth had been inordinately persistent, and Louisa knew she wouldn't stop until she got the answer she wanted. She had been attempting to break the news gently to her niece, but it seemed that was to be denied her. Taking a deep breath, she said, "Four months. That scream was the first sound you've made in four months."

Elizabeth stared at her aunt. There was no teasing smile on her face to inform Elizabeth this was all a hum. Louisa was watching her closely, her expression full of concern.

"No. It couldn't have been," whispered Elizabeth, overwhelmed by her aunt's announcement.

"I'm afraid it's true," Louisa insisted softly. "You've been unresponsive for so long we had all but given up hope for your recovery."

Elizabeth was speechless; her mind momentarily unable to process the information she had received. She looked around the familiar room, putting off the inevitability of facing the truth of what Louisa had revealed. Her gaze stopped at the window. Only the day before, a warm September sun had shone warmly on her parasol as she strolled through Bond Street with Betsy. But today was gray and dreary with sleet pelting the glass panes. Across the room a fire blazed cheerfully in the fireplace. Surely there could not have been such a radical change in the September weather overnight.

"It's January," said Louisa, noticing her bewilderment.

"This is all part of the nightmare," Elizabeth argued.

"I'm sure it feels that way to you. It may take some time for you to accept what has happened. But I assure you, my dear, what I've told you is true. Neither Betsy nor I are apparitions come to bedevil you," she said, smiling.

"But what of the Little Season, the holidays?"

"All gone. But they will come again very quickly," Louisa assured her, "and this time you will enjoy them all, I promise."

"But I don't understand. What happened that caused me to forget the past four months?"

Louisa leaned forward and placed her hand on Elizabeth's forehead. "You're cool to the touch, but I think we should wait until Dr. James sees you before we explain anything. I wouldn't want to make you sick again by telling you too much at one time."

"Not telling me could be far worse," said Elizabeth, but the warning lost much of its threat due to the weakness of her voice.

"If you'll just be patient," pleaded her aunt, "I'll tell you everything you want to know. It's a difficult situation, and I'm not certain what to do at the moment."

"What could be so complicated about being ill?" Elizabeth asked. But before she could receive an answer, her father, William Leighton, Lord Carvey, appeared in the open doorway. He wore his beaver hat and greatcoat, and leaned against the doorframe for a moment to catch his breath. The flush in his cheeks, Elizabeth decided, was due more to racing up the stairs, than to the inclement weather.

"I just now returned," he said to Louisa. "Marston told me Elizabeth screamed." His gaze shifted to Elizabeth, then back to Louisa, who nodded her head. Tears filled his eyes as he approached his daughter's bedside.

"Hello, Papa," said Elizabeth, addressing him as she had in her childhood.

"Oh, my dear." Tears flooded his eyes as he reached for her hand. "Look, I have forgotten my gloves," he said, attempting to laugh.

"Betsy, take these downstairs," said Louisa, helping her brother out of his coat, and taking his hat and gloves. "Bring hot tea, and something a little stronger for Lord Carvey."

"Is it true?" asked Elizabeth, looking up at her father. "Have I been ill for so long a time?"

"I'm afraid you have," he said, taking her hand, and warming it between both of his. "But you're back with us now, and that is all that matters."

He turned toward Betsy as she was leaving the room with his coat. "Tell Marston to send for Dr. James immediately." Betsy gave a small bob and hurried out.

"What's been wrong with me?" Elizabeth asked, a plaintive note in her voice. "Aunt Louisa won't tell me a thing."

"We're not altogether certain," said Lord Carvey, taking the chair that Louisa had vacated. "We believe you received a blow to the head."

Elizabeth could remember nothing of what had brought her to this state. "How did it happen?" she asked, her bewilderment showing plainly on her face. "Was it a carriage accident?"

"Why don't we wait until Dr. James arrives," suggested her father. "I'd like him to judge whether you're strong enough to hear the whole story. I wouldn't want to do anything that might cause you to slip back into your previous condition."

"That's exactly what Aunt Louisa said," remarked Elizabeth crossly. "I don't feel the least bit like swooning, or sleeping, or whatever it was I was doing," she protested.

"Then you won't mind waiting, will you?" reasoned Lord Carvey. "It shouldn't take Dr. James long to get here. He's taken a great interest in your case."

Elizabeth knew it was useless to argue with her father when he had his mind set. "I've missed everything since last fall," she complained.

"It was not so very much," Lord Carvey consoled her. "The Little Season was dull and the winter has been the worst I can remember. Since we didn't feel festive, we decided to save Christmas until you were better. As soon as you're able, we'll open our presents."

Elizabeth understood the full extent of his sadness, for Christmas was one of his favorite times of the year.

"Now don't overtire yourself," said Lord Carvey, as she opened her mouth to ask another question. "Let us do the talking until the doctor arrives."

Despite her obvious impatience to learn the details of her illness, Lord Carvey kept firmly to his decision. He and Louisa spoke only of lighthearted on-dits which had occurred since the previous September. Neither would say anything about what had caused her to be unaware of her surroundings for such a long period of time.

Elizabeth's patience was at an end, and she was ready to demand an explanation when Dr. James arrived.

"Lady Elizabeth, it's extremely gratifying to see you awake at last," he said, setting down his bag, and reaching for her wrist.

"I can't believe what I've heard."

"Of course, you can't," the doctor agreed. He peered at her eyes, then patted her hand. "It would be exceedingly difficult to accept you've been in a trancelike state for four months, but I assure you that is exactly what has happened. Now tell me how you feel. Are you in any pain?"

"No, none at all. I do feel weak, and I have a terrible headache, but other than that I'm fine. Now, please, tell me what happened."

"I think it would be worse to keep her guessing," said Dr. James, looking at her father.

"Then tell her," said Lord Carvey wearily.

"We don't know everything," began Dr. James. "What we do know is that you were found unconscious. There was a swelling on your head, so we can assume you were struck with an object. We considered the possibility you could have fallen and hit your head, but ruled it out when we found nothing nearby which you could have fallen against."

"But, where . . ."

"Let me finish, then I'll answer any questions I can," interrupted the doctor. "It will save you energy. After you were found, you were brought home, but you never fully awakened. Your eyes would open, but you didn't indicate you saw or heard anyone. A case such as yours isn't unheard-of, but it is fairly rare, and even more so when the patient recovers."

"We are so grateful you did," said Louisa, dabbing at her eyes with a lace-edged handkerchief.

Betsy entered with a tray, and it was a few minutes before the tea was poured and the men had a glass of liquor to chase away the outside chill which had settled in their bones.

Elizabeth was anxious to hear the remainder of the story, but she kept her tongue between her teeth, for Dr. James was not a man to be rushed. Aunt Louisa placed more pillows behind her back, then held the cup while she took a few sips of hot tea. She had never tasted anything so delicious. Its warmth renewed her strength, and she did not resent the pause as much as she had at first.

Dr. James set his glass down on the table, then took up where he had left off. "Now where was I?" he murmured to himself.

"Oh, yes, I remember. We were talking about your recovery. Usually it's difficult to feed a person in your condition, but we managed to get enough food into you to keep you alive. Your aunt, your father, and even Betsy, spent hours at your side talking about anything that might bring you back to the present. As often as possible, we would seat you in front of the window, in hopes it might also help. But everything we did was to no avail; your condition didn't improve."

Despite the proof, Elizabeth was dismayed she could lose four months of her life and remember nothing about it.

Dr. James removed his wire-rimmed spectacles and cleaned them on a large, white handkerchief he had pulled from his pocket. "Betsy said you screamed loud enough to be heard all through the house. Can you tell me what frightened you?" asked Dr. James, replacing his spectacles on his thin, aristocratic nose.

"It was only a nightmare," replied Elizabeth.

"Do you remember what it was about?"

A shiver ran through her. "I'll never forget it, but it was foolish for me to think it was real."

"Tell me, if you can," Dr. James requested. "I promise, no one will think the less of you."

"I was in a strange room," began Elizabeth. "I saw . . ." She glanced at her father, greatly embarrassed.

Lord Carvey leaned toward her. "It's all right, my dear," he assured her. "Tell us exactly what you saw."

"I saw Helen lying on a bed. She was . . . her clothes were disheveled."

Lord Carvey sank back in the chair, his body went slack, and he covered his face with one hand.

Elizabeth reached out a hand to him, alarmed at his reaction to her dream.

"Go ahead," urged the doctor. "Lord Carvey will be fine."

Her father dropped his hand and gave her a weak smile of encouragement.

"Roarke was with her," Elizabeth whispered.

Lord Carvey's and Louisa's faces blanched. Elizabeth admitted that her nightmare was not a pleasant one, but it should not have caused the reaction she observed.

"And . . ." urged the doctor.

"That was when I woke up screaming."

Dr. James looked at Lord Carvey, who gave the doctor a weary nod. "There is something more I have to tell you, Elizabeth. If you don't feel up to it, we can postpone it until you're stronger."

"No, I want to know everything. I will have no rest until I do."

The doctor took her hand, keeping his fingers on the pulse in her wrist. "I'm afraid what you saw in your nightmare was real. When you were found four months ago, you were in a suite of rented rooms. You were lying on the floor and, as I mentioned before, we assumed you had been struck from behind. Helen was found on a bed in the same room. She was dead. Lord Roarke was lying beside her, unconscious and smelling strongly of liquor."

"No," she whispered in horror.

Dr. James felt her pulse increase. "Try to remain calm, Elizabeth. We need your help. Since the incident, we've been waiting." He glanced again at Lord Carvey. "Hoping you would awaken and tell us what happened in that room that afternoon."

"I can't believe it," she gasped. "I thought it was all a horrible dream."

"I know," Dr. James commiserated. "But if you feel strong enough, think back and tell us what you remember."

Elizabeth closed her eyes and forced herself to contemplate what she had seen in her nightmare. It was hazy, but she recalled walking into an empty sitting room, and calling out. No one answered, but there was a lovely bouquet of roses and a bottle of brandy on a table, so Elizabeth assumed the rooms were occupied. Seeing a door standing open on the opposite side of the room, she passed through it. That was when she saw Helen and Roarke on the bed.

Roarke was lying on his stomach, his head turned toward the side. One arm dangled off the bed, and a brandy bottle lay on the floor as if it had slipped from his fingers. His other arm was stretched across Helen, pinning her to the bed. He wore boots and breeches, but nothing else. His bare shoulders seemed inordinately broad on the small bed. Helen lay by his side, the top of her gown pulled down until her shoulders and arms were bared, and much of her breasts revealed. Her hands were folded on her chest, a blood red rose in their clasp. No sooner did the scene register, than Elizabeth's memory went blank. Awakening with her own scream sounding in her ears was the next thing she remembered.

She recounted her dream to the people in the room. When she was finished, tears filled her eyes. "I'm sorry," she apologized. "I can recollect nothing else."

"Consider that day again," beseeched her father. "Helen did not die of natural causes, and her death was not an easy one. I know Roarke is guilty, but I've been unable to prove it. Perhaps he had help. Was anyone else in the room? Did you see anyone as you went into the house?"

Elizabeth moved her head restlessly on the pillow. "No. I remember nothing more than I've told you. Roarke couldn't have harmed Helen; he loved her too much," she objected, her voice rising.

"Just so," replied her father, as if she had pronounced Roarke guilty.

"I didn't mean . . ." she began, realizing how her statement sounded, but grief overcame her and she was unable to go on. The wall of disbelief she had erected cracked, and reality slipped through. Helen was dead. Even though it had happened four months ago, it had been only a few minutes ago for her. The pain struck, fresh and agonizing. She had lost her best friend, and the man she loved. One was dead, the other forever condemned due to the circumstances in which he and Helen had been found.

Tears spilled over her cheeks, and odd strangled sounds came from her throat. There was the clink of a bottle against glass, as Dr. James mixed her a draught of laudanum. He pressed the glass against her lips, and she eagerly swallowed the bitter liquid. Her eyelids soon closed, shutting out the worried faces of her father and her aunt, and momentarily suppressing the anguish that filled her. But in the center of the darkness, the pain was constant; a dull aching reminder that her life would never be the same again.

* * *

Elizabeth awakened the next morning to find Betsy at her bedside with a breakfast tray. "Dr. James left orders you were to have some real food," she said, smiling cheerfully now that her mistress was awake. "Only a little soft buttered eggs, toast, and milk at first, but soon you'll be eating anything you want."

Elizabeth did her best, but the modest amount of food was more than she could manage. She motioned for the maid to remove the tray. "Thank you, Betsy. I'll do better at luncheon," she promised.

Elizabeth had noticed the thinness of her hands as she was eating breakfast. She had always carried a little more weight than she had liked, but not all the walking nor riding she did had changed it. Her father had chided her for worrying so, telling her she was perfect just as she was. When that didn't satisfy Elizabeth, he assured her that her mother looked just the same when she was her age. He continually repeated she would grow out of it, but Elizabeth had often wondered. It seemed he had been right after all; she had finally shed her baby fat, but in a way she wished she could have avoided.

Elizabeth needed something to occupy her mind. It might be cowardly, but she wanted to put off thinking about Helen again for the time being. She needed to conserve her strength until she could think clearly and logically about what had happened.

"Bring me a mirror, Betsy."

"Oh, Lady Elizabeth, you don't want to tire yourself out now," replied Betsy.

"Looking in a mirror is hardly a strenuous activity. Now, bring me my hand mirror or I shall get out of bed and get it for myself." The threat worked, as Elizabeth knew it would, but Betsy took her time in bringing the mirror to the bed. Elizabeth did not look in it right away. Betsy's reluctance warned her that she would not like what she would see. Admonishing herself as a coward, she raised the mirror and stared at her reflection.

Elizabeth could not restrain a gasp, and Betsy reached out to take the mirror from her. "There, now, my lady. I knew you shouldn't be doing too much."

Elizabeth waved her away, staring more closely at her image. She could barely recognize herself as the apparition that was reflected there. She had never thought herself a great beauty, but now she was a pitiful excuse for a young woman.

The rosy-complexioned girl of the past was now all deadly white skin with bones protruding here and there. Her eyes were sunken in her face, with dark, prominent circles making her seem all the more wasted. Her hair, which had not been remarkable either in color or texture since her childhood days when it was blond, was completely covered by a white lace cap. When Betsy attempted to keep her from removing the cap, Elizabeth knew the worst was probably yet to come. She tugged at the white lace and gasped in horror. What little hair that remained on her head was thin and wispy. She reached up to touch it and a clump came away in her hand, leaving her staring at it in dismay.

"It began falling out about a month ago," said Betsy, taking the cap from Elizabeth's unresisting fingers and replacing it on her head. "Dr. James said it was because you couldn't eat what you should."

Elizabeth remained silent, allowing the maid to arrange the ruffled cap to her satisfaction.

"But it'll come back," Betsy reassured her. "Dr. James promised me as soon as you could eat, it would come back."

Elizabeth was touched by Betsy's concern. She laid the mirror facedown on her bed, resolved not to look at it again until her looks had improved. She would not feel sorry for herself; at least she was alive.

"Don't worry, Betsy. I'll eat everything you bring me if I possibly can." She would eat until she was back to her former self, she vowed, if that is what it took to learn what had happened in those rented rooms four months ago. As soon as she regained her strength, she would look into the matter herself, and she wouldn't quit until she found the answer. Elizabeth could not believe that Roarke, the man she admired above all others, except for her father, could kill Helen, then drink until he was oblivious, and lie down by her side.

Although it was painful, Elizabeth forced herself to think about her friend. She had met Helen Northrup during her come-out. Helen was twenty-one, and seemed extremely experienced to a young girl just turned eighteen. Helen helped Elizabeth through her first days in society, and they became fast friends.

Lord Roarke was one of their circle. The handsome earl captured Elizabeth's imagination from the moment they met, but he paid her little more than the common courtesies while Helen was around, and Elizabeth knew she could never hope to compete with her lovely friend.

When Helen and Roarke were together, Elizabeth thought of them as the perfect couple. They were both tall and well formed, with dark hair and eyes. They dressed to perfection, and carried themselves with a confidence that Elizabeth never expected to achieve.

Lord Roarke's continued presence kept Elizabeth from accepting the offers that were made for her. Since she was an only child, her father did not insist she marry. Lord Carvey's wife had died when Elizabeth was only seven, and he had lavished his entire love and attention on his daughter. She would be well provided for if she chose never to wed.

For three years Elizabeth watched Roarke and her best friend go about together. She was encouraged only because they had not yet married, and prayed they would remain only close friends. Then, in a totally surprising move, Helen announced her impending marriage, but not to Roarke. Elizabeth was stunned by the news; but when she sat in church at Helen's wedding, her hopes rose that she might have a chance to attract Roarke after all. The earl sat nearby, his face devoid of emotion, keeping her perplexed about his feelings at seeing Helen marry another.

After Helen's marriage, Roarke began taking Elizabeth about. She suspected it was merely a ploy to be near Helen without arousing comment, but it didn't matter. It was enough she was by his side.

There were occasions when Helen did not accompany them, and those were times to be treasured, for Lord Roarke gave Elizabeth his full attention. She had begun to hope his friendship might become something more, and was in good spirits. On the last day she remembered, she had been anticipating an evening at the theater and a late dinner with Roarke, George and Sylvia Wendell, and a few others.

Elizabeth was pleased with herself. At least, she was regaining her memory, and could now recall something of the day she had been found. Her reminiscing was cut short by a rap on the door.

"Good morning, my lord," said Betsy, opening the door to Lord Carvey.

"Good morning, Betsy. How's our patient this morning?"

"I can answer for myself," said Elizabeth, "and I'm feeling much better. That is, until I looked in the mirror." Her face twisted into a moue of discontent. "I'll never be able to step outside the house looking as I do."

"Don't fret, my dear. Now that you're awake and able to eat properly, your looks will improve. With Cook's meals, you'll fill out in no time at all."

"But my hair," she complained, barely able to keep from wailing in despair.

"That will grow back," he promised.

"You're merely saying that to insure I'll eat," she accused him with a watery smile.

"Perhaps, but you must admit it's a good inducement. Besides, you look charming in lace ruffles," he bantered, returning her smile as he took the chair by her bedside once again.

Elizabeth thought of Helen and winced at the triviality of her grievance. "I'm sorry. I shouldn't be complaining about something so inconsequential after all that has happened."

"None of it was your fault, Elizabeth. And I wouldn't object if you were in high dudgeon every day, as long as you are healthy."

"Father, I know this must be painful for you, but it's necessary I know what happened the day Helen died."

"You should concentrate on getting well, not worrying about what you can't remember," he advised.

"That's exactly why I need to know. I might have been able to have helped Helen; kept her from dying. I can't rest until I'm certain." Elizabeth's voice broke, and she put a hand over her mouth to keep the cries from escaping.

"There was nothing you could have done against Roarke, even if you hadn't been struck down. He could have easily overpowered you, and you might have suffered the same fate as Helen."

"But I saw Roarke on the bed with Helen when I came into the room. How could he have hit me?"

"Perhaps he wasn't lying there at all; or perhaps he got up after you saw him and hit you. You've been unconscious for four months; your memory might not be accurate. Louisa and I talked about what happened many times while we sat with you. You could have heard us and absorbed the information that Roarke was on the bed with Helen." Lord Carvey's hands fisted on his thighs, and Elizabeth could see the pain he suffered when he spoke of the incident.

He rose to stir the coal in the fireplace, before returning to his seat and continuing his thoughts. "He could have had an accomplice. I don't know which is the answer, but there's one thing I do know. Roarke is responsible for Helen's death, and you narrowly escaped the same fate. I don't want you dwelling on it," he insisted. "I want you healthy and safe and happy again."

Despite all she could do to prevent it, tears filled Elizabeth's eyes and spilled down her sunken cheeks. "I will never be happy until I know what happened. Helen was my best friend, and I can't just pretend she didn't die in the manner she did. I must do something to avenge her death."

Lord Carvey's hand tightened on hers until she feared her bones might break. "No one wants revenge any more than I do. Helen was my wife, for God's sake, and I haven't been able to do a blasted thing about making that blackguard pay for what he did to her."

"Are you so certain it was Roarke?"

"Everything points to him and, as yet, he has not proved differently." Lord Carvey examined her pale face and red-rimmed eyes. "Do you feel strong enough to talk a while longer?"

"Of course, don't let my looks deceive you."

"I'd like to ask you something about that day."

"And you must also tell me everything that you know," she insisted.

"Do you remember how you came to be in that room?" Lord Carvey asked.

Elizabeth hesitated before answering. She remembered finding a note in the hall outside Helen's room. It had been from Roarke, asking Helen to meet him, and giving her the time and directions. But if she revealed the information to her father, he would be totally convinced Roarke was the guilty party. She had never lied to her father, but she could not condemn Roarke without learning more.

"Elizabeth?"

"I was trying to remember, but I can't. I don't know how I knew they would be at that particular place, at that time, nor why I was there." She felt ashamed of her prevarication, but it could not be helped for the moment.

"Don't worry. Dr. James says it isn't unusual to be unable to immediately recall everything after what you've suffered."

Elizabeth thought a moment, then reached for her father's hand. "Who brought you the news about Helen?"

"I was there." At Elizabeth's incredulous look, he hastened to tell her the full story. "There's something more you need to know. A few weeks before Helen's death, I received a note telling me she was having an affair. I admit I was jealous. Helen was much younger than I, and she was inordinately lovely. I never understood why she chose me, but I never ceased appreciating my good fortune. When I received the note, I wasn't completely surprised. Perhaps I had been expecting it," he admitted.

"Helen never indicated she was unhappy with you," protested Elizabeth.

"No, but nevertheless I was compelled to search out the veracity of the note. It may have been wrong, but I hired a Bow Street Runner to get to the truth of the matter." He rubbed a hand over his face before he continued.

Elizabeth thought he looked older than his years. The silver strands were more prominent in his sandy hair, and he looked as if he had lost at least a stone since last September.

"On the day of . . . of the incident, the Runner had followed her to the rooms. He was waiting outside when Roarke arrived a short time later and entered the house. He was satisfied Roarke was the man Helen was meeting and was approaching the door when I arrived."

"You? But how could you know where Helen was?"

"I was returning home when a young lad accosted me in front of the house," he said, motioning toward the window. "He handed me a scrap of paper and told me I should immediately go to that house. In the normal course of events, I might have ignored him; however, with the state of affairs with Helen as they were, I decided I should follow the instructions. Thinking it possible the note was from the Runner, I hurried back into the carriage, and went straight to the house.

"As I said, the Runner was ready to go in when I arrived, and I joined him. When we saw the door open, we entered. The room was empty, but there was another door across the room. You were lying just inside the threshold, so white and still I thought I had lost you." His grip tightened on her hand.

"I'm fine now, Father," she reassured him.

"Thank God for that. I don't know what I would have done if I had lost you, too." He took a few deep breaths, then continued his story. "I made certain you were breathing, then I turned my attention to Helen. As you rightly remembered, she was on the bed, but it was far too late for anyone to help her. Roarke was beside her, wearing only his boots and breeches. One arm was stretched across Helen, the other hand was clutching a liquor bottle. He smelled as if he had bathed in brandy. If it hadn't been for the Runner, I would have killed him before he even awoke. We called the authorities and Dr. James. He opined Helen had been smothered by a satin pillow which was found nearby and carried traces left on the silk."

Elizabeth could not keep from uttering a small cry of distress at hearing of Helen's fate.

Lord Carvey reached for her hand, and gave it a reassuring squeeze. "Are you certain you want to hear this?"

"Yes. Please continue," urged Elizabeth.

Her father gathered his thoughts and resumed speaking. "When Roarke finally awoke, he claimed he had received a note from Helen asking him to meet her and giving him the directions to the house. He swore he had no idea what she wanted, but had simply done as she asked. From there on his story sounds very much like yours. When he arrived, there was no one in the sitting room, but there were brandy and roses on the table. He went into the bedroom and saw Helen lying there, but before he could even rush to her side, he was struck down. That was the last he remembered until he awakened after the three of you had been discovered. He swore he hadn't had so much as a single drink that day, and could only assume someone had poured brandy down his throat and sprinkled it over him to make it seem as if he was in a drunken stupor."

"But couldn't that have happened?" asked Elizabeth, clutching at any supposition to prove Roarke innocent.

"Why would anyone have gone to the trouble?" Lord Carvey asked bitterly. "I have searched my mind, and have come up with no explanation for what happened, other than Roarke killed Helen in a fit of jealous rage. You said it yourself; he loved her. I was a fool not to insist she break it off with him when we first married, but she assured me they were merely friends, and I believed her." He uttered a harsh bark of bitter laughter.

"I can't believe Helen could have done anything so cruel," remarked Elizabeth. "She loved you; I know she did."

"Perhaps in her own way," he conceded. "But there must have been something lacking for her to turn to Roarke."

"I won't allow you to demean yourself," said Elizabeth. If she had been standing, she would have stamped her foot in anger. Instead, she squeezed her father's hand as hard as her meager strength would allow. "There is nothing lacking in you that sent Helen elsewhere. She was happy in her marriage," Elizabeth insisted.

Perhaps she was blind to Roarke's faults, but even after seeing the damning proof with her own eyes, Elizabeth could not yet believe he could have killed Helen. Her father's grief made her more determined than ever to find out what had happened in the rented rooms that day.

"Thank you for your conviction, my dear," said Lord Carvey. "You say you don't believe any part of Roarke's story?"

"There's too much against him, but that won't bring him to justice. His family is an old one that can wield a great deal of influence. Roarke swore in a statement his version of what happened. An investigation of sorts took place, but nothing more was learned. Roarke remained free, while you were lying here perhaps never to speak again, and Helen . . . Helen was gone forever."

"I'm sorry, Father. I didn't mean to remind you, but I needed to know."

"You didn't bring it back, my dear; I never forget it. And I never will until that murderer pays for what he's done. I had hoped when you awakened, you could prove him guilty."

"I'm sorry, but I don't remember seeing anything more than I've told you."

"It's nothing you could help. I want you to try to forget it, and concentrate on recovering your health." Giving her a kiss on the forehead, Lord Carvey left the room, his shoulders bowed under an invisible burden.

Elizabeth dried her tears. She would never accomplish anything if she continued being such a watering pot. She would not waste any more time with crying, but would concentrate on avenging Helen's death.

Two

Logan Greeley, Earl of Roarke, stood at his window looking
out into a solid wall of damp, gray fog. It was the worst that had
descended upon London for some time, and it kept the city prisoner in its grip. Not a bush, nor a tree, nor a building, could be
seen through the thick mist. Those venturing outdoors today
would very quickly lose their sense of direction, and find themselves lost in the murky grayness.

Roarke turned away from the window and seated himself before the blaze that flickered in the fireplace. He stared moodily
into the flames, considering the last four months. He had quickly
realized that finding the guilty party in Helen's murder was not
going to be easy. Someone had gone to a great deal of trouble
to draw the two of them, and Lord Carvey, together at the same
time and the same place. Whoever it was had exercised a great
deal of caution, and Roarke's inquiries had not revealed one single clue as to the person's identity.

The owner of the building where the crime had been committed had received a note and money from a boy who knew nothing
except that he was being handsomely paid to deliver the package.
The message was anonymous and informed the owner that a
private meeting was to be held in the rooms. It instructed him to
leave the door unlocked, and advised him not to linger, warning
that if he did so, retaliation would be swift and painful. The
money was more than the owner would have received for a full
month's lodging. He was a businessman, after all, he had explained. In accordance to the instructions, he unlocked the rooms
that morning, and didn't return until early evening when every-

thing was already over. After numerous interviews, Roarke believed the man was telling the truth.

He had questioned the other people living in the building, but no one had seen or heard anything suspicious that day. After weeks of fruitless searching, Roarke had decided to act as if he had given up on the investigation, hoping the murderer would relax enough to become careless.

But, after four months, his strategy had earned him nothing except charges of callousness and indifference from Lord Carvey. If truth be known, Roarke was far from being the carefree spirit Lord Carvey projected. Helen's murder had put an enormous strain on him. Her death continued to occupy a large part of his thoughts, as did Elizabeth, who was lying so still and quiet at her father's home.

When he had first met Elizabeth, he thought her a pleasant enough girl. Helen had brought her along on most of their outings, and he had grown accustomed to her. After Helen's marriage, it had seemed natural that Lord Roarke continue to take Elizabeth about even when Helen was not one of the party.

Elizabeth was undemanding, and her mere presence helped keep away the husband-hunting mothers who somehow seemed to know each time he was not escorting a young lady. He did not need to constantly flatter Elizabeth nor to worry about entertaining her every moment they were together. She could converse intelligently on a large array of topics, or they could spend quiet moments without the urgency of nonstop conversation. Yes, Elizabeth was extremely comfortable.

Roarke had still been reeling from the shock of Helen's death when he learned Elizabeth had also been found in the room. He had been overwhelmed by despair, until he was informed that though she was gravely injured, she was alive. As soon as he was able to walk, Roarke had attempted to see Elizabeth; however, Lord Carvey had turned him away without so much as a word on his daughter's condition. He had sent flowers and notes, but they had all been refused. Roarke was forced to get his information about Elizabeth as it traveled through the gossip mill; a very unsatisfactory and unreliable method.

Once he had met Lady Louisa Leighton in a bookstore, and

she had been generous enough to give him news of her niece, but what she told him shocked him to the core. That evening, he locked himself in the library with a bottle; however, drinking had not eased the pain, nor the guilt he felt in being unable to protect Helen and Elizabeth.

Then approximately two months after the accident, Roarke received a note asking him to call at Lord Carvey's home. He had been met by Lady Louisa and Dr. James. The doctor first explained Elizabeth's condition to Roarke. He went on to say that he had suggested to Lord Carvey that perhaps a visit from Roarke might bring Elizabeth back to them. Lord Carvey had finally allowed himself to be persuaded for his daughter's good, but had left the house, choosing not to share a roof with Roarke for even a short length of time.

Even though he had been warned, Roarke was shaken by Elizabeth's appearance. She had lost a great deal of weight, and her blue-veined hand felt extremely fragile in his. The pallor in her face was made even more pronounced by the white cap she wore. But what was most disconcerting were her eyes; they were wide open, but totally devoid of expression.

Roarke stayed with her for as long as was allowed, holding her thin hand and talking to her. He recounted their past excursions and described what they would do when she was well enough, but she did not stir. He was loath to leave, but was left no choice but to comply when Dr. James tapped him on the shoulder. Elizabeth's image, and her empty blue eyes, had haunted Roarke since that day.

Roarke renewed his vow that he would find the person responsible for Helen's death and Elizabeth's injury, but again he had been unable to discover a clue as to what had happened. It was then he began searching for the motive behind the crime.

He did not know how or why Elizabeth was at the scene, but he couldn't imagine anyone would have a reason to intentionally harm her. She had led a very sheltered life and, in his estimation, could have done nothing to warrant being hunted and struck down. No, Elizabeth must have somehow blundered into whatever was happening, and fallen victim to it merely because of her presence as a witness. But they would not know for certain

until she awakened. If she awakened, he amended, feeling a fresh
jolt of pain at the reminder.

  If Helen had been the intended victim, then it was possible he
knew the reason behind the attack. During the early part of their
acquaintance, Helen had confided she was hiding from someone
who had once been close to her, and that she lived in fear of
being found. However, she had not disclosed the person's name.
Since her marriage to Lord Carvey, she had felt safe and told
Roarke that she meant to explain everything to her husband, then
confront the person whom she had feared for so long. But Helen
could have been wrong about her safety, thought Roarke. Her
marriage might have merely forced the person she feared to take
a more indirect approach.

  When Roarke had received the note from Helen asking him
to meet her, he thought she had finally decided to reveal everything, then ask his advice and perhaps his assistance. That pre-
sumption had left him careless and he had walked straight into
a trap. He was disgusted that he had been so easily duped, and
vowed his revenge.

  So Roarke had a mysterious suspect, but he did not have a
name or a face to go with the person yet. He needed to find out
more about Helen's background. She had always been so secretive about her life before she had met him, that Roarke was certain the answer to who hated Helen enough to kill her lay in her
past. However, the harsh winter weather had closed in around
London earlier than usual, and had not released its icy grip long
enough for him to search further afield.

  Then again, Roarke could not overlook the possibility that *he*
had been the focus of the murderer, and that Helen had merely
been used as a disposable lure. He had made enemies, he was
sure, but none stood out in his mind as being serious enough for
murder. Although it was possible that embarrassment, not murder, might have been the intention. The plan could have been to
have Lord Carvey catch Helen and Roarke in a compromising
position. But such a scandal would have affected both Roarke
and Helen, so again he was left feeling unsure which one of them
had been the target of the plot.

  It had been months now since the murder, and he had forced

himself to go about his regular activities in a normal manner. If the animal who had killed Helen and injured Elizabeth was watching, he wanted him to think he was safe.

The Season was beginning, and Roarke would have neither Helen nor Elizabeth by his side. For that, there could be no forgiving.

"Don't tell me you are already pining for the outdoors," said Lord Carvey as he entered the drawing room and spied Elizabeth sitting by the window staring out.

"It seems winter is reluctant to loosen its hold," replied Elizabeth.

It was mid-March, and even though it was still cool, the few warm days they had experienced were bringing buds to the trees. It had been difficult for Elizabeth to accept that she had missed last fall, and the holidays. She had always enjoyed the colors of autumn and the traditions of Christmas. She consoled herself by reflecting on the wealth of brightly colored leaves and Christmas carols in her future.

This thought reminded her that Helen would not be there to experience them with her, and she felt the sadness begin to creep in again. She straightened her shoulders and pulled herself out of the doldrums. Helen would not want Elizabeth to continually plunge herself into grief.

"No matter, spring will be here soon enough," replied Lord Carvey. He studied Elizabeth for a short time. "You're looking more the thing. I trust you're feeling better as well."

"I'm nearly good as new. My strength would return more quickly if I could walk about," she complained, "but the weather simply refuses to cooperate."

"Don't be too eager to go out in this changeable air. You could catch a chill and reverse all the progress you've made," he warned.

Elizabeth merely smiled at his concern.

"There's something I want to discuss with you, my dear." Lord

Carvey indicated a chair near the fireplace. When Elizabeth was seated, he joined her.

"You know I've been extremely worried about you. So much so, that I seldom left the house before you awakened. But now that you're looking so much better, there are some things which need my attention. I've talked to Dr. James and he feels it would be safe for me to be away for a short time."

"Of course it is," Elizabeth reassured him. "You must see to your obligations."

"I would not do so if I didn't feel it was necessary. I haven't been to the country estate since . . . since before the incident, and there are matters which must be seen to."

"Then you must go," insisted Elizabeth. "I have Aunt Louisa and Betsy to pamper me, and Dr. James to advise them on just how to go about it. You may trust they will allow no harm to come to me." An impish smile touched her face.

It was the first hint he had seen of her former self, thought Lord Carvey. She had put on weight, and while she had changed a great deal, she was looking much better than she had two months before when her scream had brought them all running. It was true that he had sadly ignored his country home, and was beginning to feel uneasy about leaving it much longer, but he had to be certain that Elizabeth was well before he left town.

Despite her outward bravado, Lord Carvey knew his daughter still grieved for Helen, and for not being able to remember more about that day in order to help bring her murderer to justice. Before he had approached Elizabeth, he had talked to Dr. James about raising his daughter's spirits. They had agreed the best thing for her to do would be to get out and about as soon as possible. It was that, more than anything, he wanted to talk about with her.

"Elizabeth, since Helen was only your stepmother, I believe that six months of mourning is more than sufficient."

"But I didn't know about it until January."

"I think we can overlook that; you've paid enough through suffering. Dr. James feels a change of scene would do wonders for you. I want you to think about joining the Season's activities."

"I don't think I'm ready," said Elizabeth.

"Of course you are."

"It's impossible to consider a Season without Helen."

"She wouldn't want you to shut yourself off from society, Elizabeth. Even though she was your stepmother, the two of you were closer than sisters. She wouldn't want you to suffer because of her."

Elizabeth began to object again, then realized she would be unable to find out anything about Helen's death if she remained locked away at home. By the time a year of mourning would pass, the trail would be very cold indeed.

"Perhaps you're right," she said, agreeing with her father. "But I'm afraid it will be expensive for you. Nothing I have suits me any longer." She smiled, looking down at the gown that hung loosely on her figure despite the alterations Betsy had made.

"Spend as much as you want, my dear. This is one time I'll be truly happy to pay your bills," he teased, rising from his chair.

"Father?"

Lord Carvey looked down at her.

"Even though six months of mourning are acceptable, would you object if I continued wearing black in honor of Helen?"

Lord Carvey looked into his daughter's eyes and saw the sadness she usually took pains to hide. "You may wear what you like, Elizabeth. I don't think anyone will take it amiss." He strode from the room before she could see the tears in his eyes.

The next day, Elizabeth awakened from an afternoon nap, her mind still fuzzy with sleep. She deplored giving in to such a childish habit, but had to admit she was not yet strong enough to endure a full day's activities without rest. She ultimately gave in to the daily struggle, thinking the sooner she regained her health, the sooner she would be able to discover what had happened to Helen. She heard a slight noise, and Betsy tiptoed into the room.

"I'm awake," Elizabeth said, her voice still heavy with sleep.

"You have a visitor below, Lady Elizabeth."

Elizabeth slid her legs off the side of the bed and sat up. "Who is it?"

"Lord Stanford," replied Betsy. "And he has a lovely bouquet of flowers with him."

"Then I'd better go down before he decides someone else is more worthy."

"Oh, my lady," said Betsy smiling. "You know he would never do that."

It was at least ten minutes before Elizabeth reached the drawing room where Andrew, Viscount Stanford, waited for her.

"Time you showed up," he said, taking her hand and giving her an appraising look.

"I told Betsy I should hurry or else you'd take your flowers elsewhere," she teased, happy to see him.

Drew looked the same as ever. His unruly sandy hair still verged on red, and light freckles scattered across a slightly crooked nose that had been broken more than once. His face nearly always wore a good-natured smile, which had caused many people to underestimate the intelligence it hid.

"Didn't have a chance. Your butler took them."

Elizabeth laughed, as she had been meant to, at his sorrowful expression. "I daresay he is having them arranged in a vase, and hasn't made off with them."

"Anyway, kept these," said Drew, offering her a box of her favorite sweets. "Thought you needed a little more weight on your bones."

"Drew! How unflattering. I'll have you know my slimness is the height of fashion."

"Humph! Too scrawny by far," he objected.

Elizabeth merely laughed, offering him a sweet, and taking one herself. Drew was an old friend and could say things that others would never think of voicing. They had met one summer when Drew had visited her father at the country estate. Elizabeth had been a young girl then, but he had treated her kindly, and they had been friends ever since. He had been there to request her first dance as a young lady. They had practiced often enough when he had visited her home, so she felt perfectly at ease, while other young ladies were wondering whether they would tread on their partners' toes.

"Well, perhaps a little more weight wouldn't be amiss," she admitted, selecting another sweet after they had been seated. "Drew . . ."

"Oh, no," he said, lifting his hand to stop her. "Recognize that tone, and will not do anything to displease your father."

"How can you think that of me?" she asked innocently. "Besides, Father left for the country yesterday. He'll never know."

"Lord Carvey has a way of finding out things."

"I merely want some information from you," replied Elizabeth peevishly, impatient with his caution.

Drew looked at her suspiciously. "About?"

"About Helen's murder."

"No. Absolutely not. Was given orders not to say anything to disturb you."

"Hearing nothing at all disturbs me," she protested. "I am not, and never have been, a delicate piece of china. You, above everyone else, should know that. You have seen me through enough scrapes."

"But this is the worst," he said gravely.

"Yes, it is," she admitted. "But I will not be kept in the dark about what happened. I am going to learn all I can. I had hoped you would help me."

"But your father . . ."

"Is away for the time being as I have already informed you. And by the time he returns, I will have seen any number of people who could have spoken of it."

Drew observed the stubborn expression on Elizabeth's face and knew nothing could deter her. "Don't know anything other than what I've heard." Then he repeated the story that she already knew.

"Is there nothing else?"

Drew thought for a moment. "There are two men you might want to talk to when you're feeling more the thing."

"Do they know something?"

"Don't know. But they happened by the house at approximately the same time your father arrived. Followed him in, so I heard. Could have seen something more, but they've probably been questioned by the authorities already."

"Who are they?" Elizabeth asked eagerly.

"Robert Montgomery, Viscount Welford, and Jules Palmerton, Viscount Bromley. No one whose acquaintance you would normally seek out."

"I'll merely ask them a few questions," Elizabeth assured him. It wasn't much, but she at least had a starting point.

"Your aunt tells me you're going to join the Season."

"I've accepted an invitation to the Braxtons' ball Wednesday next. Will you be there?"

"Will make it a point to be," he promised. "Must save me the first dance."

"With pleasure," she replied, offering him another sweet.

It was odd attending a ball again. Elizabeth was a completely different person from the last time she had danced on the highly polished floor of a ballroom. Everything from her appearance to her view of the world had changed and, for a moment, Elizabeth felt as if she were looking through a stranger's eyes at the familiar scene.

"Wondered whether you were coming," said Drew, as he approached Elizabeth and Louisa.

"It has been a tiring day, which delayed me more than usual," said Elizabeth, unable to tell him she had nearly decided not to attend. She had considered the stares and speculation she would most probably attract, and her bravery had wavered. However, Aunt Louisa had discovered her indecision and had cajoled her into changing her mind.

"And she needed a little encouraging," added Louisa.

"No need. You look lovely this evening," Drew said.

"Thank you, but I'm more nervous than I was at my come-out."

Elizabeth was wearing a black gown with flounces, and a low-cut neckline that exposed more of her shoulders than she had been accustomed to in the past. She made a vastly different appearance than in the ill-fitting gowns she had been wearing since the beginning of her recovery.

Betsy had used all her skill to transform Elizabeth, and they both had been quite pleased with the results. There were startling changes in her, to be sure, but perhaps they would not draw as much comment as Elizabeth thought.

Immediately, she realized this was wishful thinking, for as soon as she crossed the threshold, her appearance caused a stir. She was extremely thankful to have Drew and Louisa by her side as she ran the gauntlet of friends, gossips, and the curiosity seekers. When Louisa felt it was safe, she joined her acquaintances, leaving Elizabeth with Drew.

"Would you rather sit out our dance?" asked Drew.

"That would be wonderful," sighed Elizabeth in relief. "I'm a little more nervous than I had thought I would be."

"To be expected," said Drew, guiding her toward the gilt chairs that had been placed at intervals around the wall.

"Would you like a cup of punch?"

"If you don't mind. My mouth is as dry as cotton," she admitted.

Drew had no sooner left her side than Thomas Manning, Lord Westbrook, appeared in front of her. "Lady Elizabeth, it is so good to have you join our company again."

"Thank you, my lord. I'm pleased to be here."

"Even with the changes, I could never mistake you for anyone else. You look more like your mother than ever with your hair the way it is now."

"My illness caused the change," explained Elizabeth.

"You can't imagine my relief to find you survived that unfortunate accident. I called several times while you were ill to see how you were progressing," he said, taking the seat next to hers.

"My aunt told me," Elizabeth replied. "She also mentioned numerous bouquets of flowers, too."

"I thought it might help."

"It did," she assured him, although she could remember none of the floral tributes which had arrived during her illness.

"Have you remembered anything about the day you were injured?" he inquired.

"Nothing yet, but the doctor still holds out hope that it may come back to me."

"Perhaps it would be better if it did not," he said. "I'm certain it's something you'd rather not relive."

"I would be happy to relive it if it revealed Helen's murderer," she responded.

"You are far too lovely to be thinking of such things. Ah, I see your young man returning," he said, rising. "I hope I may call on you and Lady Louisa now that you're well."

"Of course. You would be welcome any time."

"Thank you, my dear. I'm so happy you didn't suffer permanent damage from your accident." Murmuring goodbye, and making a small bow, he disappeared into the crowd.

"Was that Westbrook I saw talking to you?" asked Drew as he handed her a cup of suspicious-looking orange punch.

"Yes. Aunt Louisa said he was very faithful about inquiring as to the state of my health during my illness. He knew my mother when she first came out. He never married and has always taken a special interest in me."

Before Drew could comment, Elizabeth heard her name being called. She turned to see Lady Barrington approaching.

"My dear, dear Elizabeth," she cooed fondly. "How absolutely lovely to see you out and around again. I was beginning to think you had disappeared completely. You know, I called, but you were too ill to receive visitors."

"Thank you, ma'am," said Elizabeth, when she could get a word in.

"No need for thanks, my dear. You know how close dear Jane and I were when we were young girls. She would have wanted me to make sure you were well. It's too bad your mother didn't marry my brother, as we had planned. Then you would have been my niece, and Jane would have most likely still been alive. Cedric would have never permitted her to dabble with that foolish drawing that caused her death."

Elizabeth kept her tongue between her teeth. It would not do to be involved in a public argument on her first evening back in society.

"I'll never forgive your father for allowing her to suffer such a fate. If he had not done so, then Jane would be with us now, and William would not have put that woman in her place," she finished bitterly."

"I hardly think my father could have prevented my mother's death," replied Elizabeth, attempting to keep her voice even. "And I believe Helen was very good for my father."

"Well, it is only my opinion," sniffed Lady Barrington. "My, I'm thirsty. Carleton, bring me a cup of punch."

Elizabeth glanced at the blue- and gold-clad manservant standing a few paces away. After the death of her husband, Lady Barrington had begun the custom of keeping a servant constantly on call. But it had not been a maid. No, Lady Barrington liked to think herself an original, so she hired the most well-favored man she could find.

At first, the gossip was vicious; but as one well-set-up manservant succeeded another, many women cast envious eyes at Lady Barrington. It was said several married ladies had attempted to emulate Lady Barrington, but that their husbands forbade such an arrangement.

"Now, Elizabeth, I have just the thing to put some color into your cheeks. It is a special tisane that is to be drunk at bedtime. I drink it every evening and it does wonders. I will bring a supply by in the next few days, and you can begin drinking it at once."

"I thank you, but there's no need to go to any trouble," said Elizabeth.

The manservant returned, the punch cup looking very small in his large hands. Lady Barrington accepted the cup without acknowledging him in any way.

"It's no bother at all," Lady Barrington insisted. "I shall make a note to do it before the week is out. Now you must excuse me, my dear, I see Lady Fitzhugh across the room, and I must have a closer look at that hideous gown she's wearing." Handing her cup to Carleton, Lady Barrington drifted away through the crowd.

"Wouldn't want that to become a habit," commented Drew.

"She means no harm," replied Elizabeth. "She's merely made a habit of being eccentric. You don't see anyone else about to descend upon us, do you?"

"Not at the moment," said Drew, glancing around.

Elizabeth breathed a sigh of relief that the expressions of surprise, and sympathy, and the novelty of her appearance at the ball had been exclaimed upon and were over with for the present. She had survived the ordeal of returning to society after being involved in a scandalous affair. There would probably be more questions, but the worst was surely over.

There was a stir at the door, and Elizabeth nearly dropped her cup of punch when she saw Lord Roarke greeting his hostess. She had known she must face him at one time or another, but had hoped it would not be tonight. But he was here, and unless she immediately slipped out, sometime during the evening she would come face-to-face with him. The gossips would be terribly disappointed if they did not meet. A dozen glances were already bouncing from Roarke to Elizabeth, and whispers were being exchanged behind raised hands.

If that was to be the case, then she would determine when they would meet; it would at least give her a semblance of control over the situation. Assuring Drew she knew what she was doing, she handed him her cup, and began working her way around the room toward Roarke.

He had changed little since she had last seen him. Attired in black evening dress, with a large diamond sparkling in his cravat, to Elizabeth's way of thinking, Roarke was the most compelling man in the room. He did not have the even features of the classically handsome, but there was a strength about him that could not be denied. His thick black hair was combed away from his face, with a single errant lock falling over his forehead. A bit too long in the back, it curled over his starched white collar, and Elizabeth would wager any amount that there wasn't a woman in the room whose fingers didn't itch to feel the ebony strands. Albeit, she was not one of them, she assured herself.

Elizabeth's feelings toward Roarke had undergone a change since she had awakened from her illness. At first, she had refused to even consider that he had anything to do with Helen's death and her own injury. However, since then she had spent long hours contemplating Roarke's and Helen's association. She had never considered anything more intimate between them than admiration, but Elizabeth would be the first to admit she was inexperienced in affairs between men and women. From gossip, she knew that liaisons were common amongst the ton, but had never been close to anyone who had been involved in one.

Her father remained convinced that there was more between Roarke and Helen than mere friendship. Louisa had also warned her she would find that many others held the same opinion.

Elizabeth thought about the time that she, Helen, and Roarke had spent together, and began looking at Roarke's and Helen's friendship in a different light. Actions she had previously accepted as normal, now took on a different aspect, and she wondered whether she had been wrong about them all along. She was embarrassed to think she had been so childish about their association. No doubt they had both been amused at her acceptance of their acquaintance.

Not only was Elizabeth's altered thinking standing between them, but so was time. She had not seen Roarke for six months, and his influence on her had lessened considerably. She looked nothing like he remembered, and her girlish dreams had been left far behind. Even though she now entertained doubts about him, she could not help but wonder whether he would approve of the changes in her.

Elizabeth's courage faltered momentarily when she drew near to Roarke. Then she reminded herself that this was a man with whom she had spent hundreds of hours before her illness. They were in a room full of people, and she was perfectly safe.

Now that she saw him again, she wavered in her suspicion that he could have coldly murdered Helen. There was no proof of it, to be sure; but her father was not a man to make accusations lightly. She needed to hear from Roarke's own lips how he had come to be, not only in the same room, but in the same bed with Helen when they were found.

Straightening her shoulders, Elizabeth placed herself in a position in front of Roarke, but as he approached, he showed no sign of stopping to speak.

"Roarke?" Her voice sounded weak even in her own ears, but it was loud enough for him to hear.

He stopped, looking at her with a puzzled expression.

"Surely you have not forgotten me in six months," she said, forcing her cold lips into a semblance of a smile.

He did not burst out with an exclamation of surprise, nor did his mouth fall open, but it was a very near thing. Disbelief appeared briefly in his face, until it was erased with a smile that nearly melted her where she stood.

Three

"Elizabeth?" At her nod, he reached out and claimed both her hands. "Elizabeth, I can't believe it's you! I had heard you were improving, but I never thought to see you tonight. How are you?"

Roarke's apparent happiness at seeing her, and the touch of his hands, threw Elizabeth into confusion for a moment. She had forgotten the impact he had on her senses.

"I am well," she replied, in a controlled voice.

"You can't imagine my relief. I tried time and again to see you, but was refused."

"It would have done no good; I wouldn't have known you."

Elizabeth gave no indication she was aware the doctor had called him in, so Roarke did not mention it. Perhaps her family thought it better she not know he had seen her.

"You've changed a great deal." His eyes studied her intently, and she fought the inclination to blush like a schoolgirl.

"My illness affected my appearance," she said.

"But you are as lovely as always," he commented, raising her hand to his lips, glad that her eyes were not empty and staring as they had been the last time he had looked into them.

She had no answer to his compliment. His gaze was more intent than a gentleman who was merely engaging in a light flirtation. She did not know how to react to this new side of Roarke. They had been nothing more than friends before and, though she had hoped, he had never said anything to make her think otherwise.

She was determined not to allow his attention to distract her from her objective. "Roarke, I need to talk with you," she said abruptly.

"Of course, anytime you like," he agreed, still in possession of her hands.

Elizabeth was aware of the stares directed their way. "Now, if we can find a quiet corner."

Roarke considered her request for a moment. When she remained silent, without displaying even a hint of a smile, he nodded his head.

"Come with me. There's a small study just off the hall. We'll slip in there if it isn't already in use." He looked both ways when they reached the door, and pulled her quickly inside. "I don't think anyone saw us, so your reputation should remain intact."

Roarke observed Elizabeth in the light from the candles in the small room. The first shock of seeing her was wearing off, and he was able to examine her more closely. She looked far different from the image he carried with him. The last time he had seen her she had been lying in her bed, barely making a mound beneath the bedclothes that covered her. Her skeletal, blue-veined hands had remained unmoving, and though her eyes had been open, there had been no glimmer of recognition in them. The white lace cap on her head had made her appear even more fragile, and Roarke had feared he would never see her alive again.

"I would never have recognized you, had you not spoken," he said, his eyes never leaving her face.

Elizabeth felt uncomfortable under his close scrutiny. "I suppose I have changed quite a bit."

"There's no supposing about it." He smiled and, despite all she could do, her heart seemed to turn in her chest.

"Some people find the change too much for their liking," she ventured.

"Some people don't have the sense to come in out of the rain," he growled, assessing her appearance again. Before the incident, she had been a lovely young woman, with brown hair and a hint of childhood plumpness still showing in her face. Now he was confronted with an altogether different vision. Elizabeth's illness had stripped the baby fat from her bones. The weight she had regained since her illness had ended was distributed quite differently than before, and it contributed to curves which were enticingly noticeable. The black gown she wore sharply accentuated every one of those delectable curves, from its low round neckline to the heavily embroidered flounces that decorated the hem.

Even her face had changed dramatically. The loss of weight had uncovered high cheekbones which served to emphasize enormous blue eyes beneath the delicate arch of her brow. But most arresting was her hair; the thin light brown strands had grown back in thick short curls which framed her face, and revealed the graceful line of her neck. However, it was the color gleaming in the candlelight that caught his eye. It was a light silvery blond that shimmered with each move of her head.

"I remember Helen saying you were blond when you were a child."

"That's what my father says. I don't know whether I like the change or not," she admitted, watching for his reaction.

"Your appearance may be far different from when I last saw you, but you're still the same person you were," he said, hoping it was the right remark to make. "And you are as attractive as always."

"Thank you," she responded, disengaging her hands from his and taking a step away. She had thought she could remain calm, but she was in a turmoil seeing Roarke again after such a long separation. Even though she now admitted his story about Helen's death was flimsy at best, she discovered she had been unable to completely do away with her feelings for him. She must work harder at it, for it would not do to be in love with her stepmother's murderer.

"There is something I must ask you," she said, staring at her clasped hands as if they held a particular fascination for her.

"You've never sought my permission to ask a question before," he teased. When she did not respond, he became serious. "You may ask whatever you wish, Elizabeth."

"I have heard," she began, when suddenly her throat closed and she could not force a sound through it. After a moment she began again. "I have heard the story about what happened with . . . with . . ."

"With you and Helen and me," he said, completing her sentence.

Elizabeth nodded. "Yes," she whispered. "Now, I must hear it from you." She braved a glance at him. He leaned back against the desk that took up a great part of the small study. His hands grasping its edge in a white-knuckled grip were the only indication that her question was not easy for him either.

"This is not the place to go into it, Elizabeth."

"You said I could ask you anything."

"I had not thought you meant this."

"And what should we discuss? The weather? The latest on-dit? I think there is a little too much between us to follow the conventional conversation."

"Perhaps you're right," he admitted. "But you should leave what happened to those who are more able to handle it."

Elizabeth uttered a sound of disgust. "It has been left to others for the past six months, and what has been done? Nothing!" she answered, before he could respond.

"There are things you don't know," he began.

"Then tell me," she demanded. "Roarke, you have always spoken to me as an equal. Don't start treating me differently now, when it means so much."

"I'm not free to tell you everything. There were promises made."

"If you mean promises made to Helen, she's dead. What you are hiding might reveal her murderer."

"You don't believe your father then?" he asked, straightening away from the desk and taking a step toward her.

"I don't know what to believe, so I'm ruling out nothing. I know only what I remember, and what has been decided to be fit for my ears."

"What is it that you recall?" he asked, without attempting to hide his eagerness.

"Nothing that reveals what happened that day, if that is what you mean," she replied, backing away. "So you are safe."

"Then you *do* believe your father's accusations."

"I didn't say that. I only meant that I saw nothing more than you lying unconscious beside Helen. I shall never forget that image. Now you say I should pretend nothing has happened, and return to the ballroom to dance the night away."

"No. No, I'm not saying that at all," he said. He seemed so huge, looming over her in the dimly lit room, that she took a step back.

"Never say you're afraid of me?"

"Of course not," Elizabeth denied with a steady voice. "I'm simply anxious to hear your story, and upset that you won't answer me directly."

Roarke sighed. "If it will bring you any peace, I'll tell you. Though it would be better done at a different time and place." When she stubbornly held her silence, he began his story.

Roarke's version of what had happened on the day of Helen's death varied little from what she remembered, and from what her father had told her. However, she had come to know Roarke very well over the years of their acquaintance, and felt he wasn't telling her everything he knew.

"Could I see the note that Helen sent asking that you meet her?"

"I wish I had it. Then perhaps your father's suspicions could be put to rest, but it has disappeared."

They both fell silent, each busy with their own thoughts.

"How did you come to be in the room?" Roarke asked after a few moments.

"I don't remember. Dr. James says it isn't unusual to forget things. It may come back to me later, but for now I'm as puzzled as anyone."

Elizabeth had never been able to prevaricate well, and her ability hadn't improved with her illness. Roarke knew she wasn't telling him the truth, but he was in no position to press her at the moment.

"Are you sure you've told me everything?" she asked.

"Do you doubt my word, Elizabeth?" Roarke's anger flared. He had had his fill of questions and disbelief about Helen's death. He had done all he could to clear his name, yet it was apparent many still suspected him. Now, it seemed the one person he had counted on had turned against him.

"It isn't that I doubt you; I'm looking for the answer to this tragedy."

"Then you must look elsewhere, for I have told you all I know. And for future reference, if I *were* having an assignation with a woman, I would never be so ill-mannered as to go to bed with my boots on," he commented bitterly.

Elizabeth's face flamed at discussing such an intimate topic, but she was determined to see it through. "Perhaps you were seized by a fit of passion and did not have the patience for niceties, then passed out from too much liquor."

"And killed Helen while I was about it?" he suggested with a sneer. His words fell into a well of silence, and when he spoke again, his tone was that of a man worn to the bone. "I've grown accustomed to the gossip that has made the rounds, and to the stares and whispers, but I'm surprised you would listen. I had thought you a friend."

"I can be nothing to you until you tell me the truth of the matter," she whispered. "I can only surmise."

He turned abruptly and her small, sharp cry of regret was lost in the sound of the slamming door.

Elizabeth's encounter with Roarke the night before had not helped one whit. She sat at home the following morning wishing she were a gypsy and could look into a crystal ball to find the answers to her questions.

"I wonder," she murmured out loud, a speculative gleam in her eye. A possible solution to her dilemma crept uneasily into her mind. It would mean going against her father's wishes, but surely the end result would be worth it if she succeeded.

"Betsy," she called. "We are going shopping."

Louisa was in the hall when Elizabeth returned. "You've been to Bond Street," she said, eyeing the packages, happy that her niece was involved in normal pursuits again. "What have you bought?"

"Nothing of consequence," replied Elizabeth, climbing the stairs. "I'll be down to tea as soon as I remove my bonnet."

When Elizabeth reached her room, she unwrapped her purchases. The empty pages of a sketchbook beckoned her. She felt a flicker of anticipation, and realized that the joy of drawing had stayed with her through the years.

Elizabeth's mother had been a natural artist. She had encouraged Elizabeth to draw, and the two spent many happy hours together. But Lady Carvey's drawings had a disquieting element. Many of the things she drew were depictions of scenes from the past or future of which she had no prior knowledge. Elizabeth remembered her commenting that a power greater than hers guided her hand and she had no say in the matter.

One day, after a heavy spring rain, Lady Carvey drew a picture of a young girl caught in a swift flowing stream. She rushed out, and was drowned while saving Jeanette Gardiner, a four-year-old girl from the neighboring estate who had wandered away and fallen into the large flooded stream that ran between the two manor houses.

In her grief, Elizabeth had turned to her drawing. It somehow brought her closer to her mother. However, when Lord Carvey found her sketching, he had torn the paper from her hands, and forbade her to draw again. He had never been as harsh with her before or since, but he was determined not to lose his daughter as he had his wife.

Elizabeth had followed his orders until today. Now she must attempt to use the talent she remembered her mother recounting to her numerous times when she was only a child. It was as if Lady Carvey had known she would not live to see Elizabeth mature, and had wanted her to be aware of her legacy.

She had explained that a gift was passed down on the female side of Elizabeth's family. The women could see things, both past and present, that others could not. Sometimes the meaning was plain and meant exactly what was seen; but on other occasions it needed interpreting. The talent manifested itself in one of several ways: to some a scene would unfold before their very eyes, but Lady Carvey's visions had revealed themselves in her drawings.

Try as hard as she could, the young Elizabeth could discern nothing extraordinary in her simple drawings. When she voiced her concern, her mother gave her a hug and told her not to worry. All women, she insisted, who had the mark, also carried the gift within them.

Elizabeth crossed the room and looked into the mirror on her dressing table. She touched one finger to the small black beauty mark at the corner of her mouth. She hoped her mother's promise proved reliable, and that she could find the reason for Helen's death through her drawings. But Louisa was waiting in the drawing room, and Elizabeth had no time to linger. She cast another longing look at the sketchbook, then hurried downstairs to take tea with her aunt.

"You talked to Roarke last evening," stated Louisa, as she poured their tea.

Elizabeth accepted a cup, and sipped a little of the steaming brew before answering. It had been late when they returned home, and the two women had not discussed the evening. She supposed it had been wishful thinking that her meeting with Roarke would have gone unnoticed. She should have known Louisa would be keeping a close watch on her to insure she wasn't overdoing it on her first evening out.

"Yes," admitted Elizabeth, "there was no way to avoid him."

There were usually ways of eluding anyone if the desire was strong enough, thought Louisa, but she did not allow her skepticism to show. "What did he have to say?" she asked casually.

"Not much," replied Elizabeth shortly. When she realized Louisa would not be put off with such an ambiguous explanation, she related her meeting with Roarke.

"Do you believe he's innocent in the matter?" asked Louisa.

Elizabeth was surprised Louisa was instigating the conversation. It had been Lord Carvey's request that they not discuss Helen's death, and they had both honored his wish. But now that he was gone from the house, Louisa evidently felt they were free to talk about it.

"What are *your* feelings?" asked Elizabeth, avoiding her aunt's question.

Louisa set down her cup and clasped her hands together in the lap of her brown-striped gown. "I must admit that Roarke has never struck me as a man who would vent his anger on a woman. However, one can never know what a person may do in private."

"Do you think he and Helen were more than friends?" Elizabeth asked hesitantly.

"They were good friends, that I do know; but I never felt the awareness between them that one often does between people who are in love. However, I cannot say for sure. There are always exceptions to the rule."

Elizabeth shifted restlessly. She was learning nothing more than what she already knew.

"I do know that Lord Roarke was absolutely distraught about what happened to both you and Helen. After he recovered from his own injury, he attempted to call, but your father wouldn't allow him to step foot inside the house. I never said anything, but he stopped me in the bookstore one day, and begged me to tell him of your condition. I didn't have the heart to refuse, and when I related the magnitude of your illness, he was as pale as a ghost.

"Some might say his concern stemmed from thinking you would recover and implicate him in Helen's murder. But I didn't see a glimmer of fear in his eyes, only dismay at hearing about your condition."

Elizabeth was heartened by her aunt's disclosure. She prayed they were both right about Roarke's innocence; however, until there was proof, she was unable to banish the skepticism that her father had instilled in her over the past months.

"I don't know whether your father wanted you to know, but he allowed Roarke to visit you once while you were ill."

"No! I can't believe it; not with his feeling the way he does toward Roarke."

"Dr. James recommended it. He thought the sound of Roarke's voice might bring you back. Your father would have done anything to hear you speak again, so he agreed. However, William refused to be under the same roof with Roarke; so he left the house before Roarke arrived."

"What happened?"

"Roarke stayed with you until it was apparent you weren't

going to respond to him, then Dr. James asked him to leave. I thought for a moment he was going to refuse, but he finally released your hand and departed."

"He saw me looking as I did?" Elizabeth exclaimed, then was ashamed that her first thought had been a vain one. "He didn't say a word about it last night."

"Perhaps he was waiting until you mentioned it. He's very much aware of your father's feelings, and probably thought you might not have been told about it. No matter what anyone thinks of him, Roarke is still a gentleman. And I wouldn't worry about how you looked. Roarke treated you as he always had. He sat by your side and held your hand. He talked to you about people you knew, things you had done. He said he was still waiting to take you to the theater.

"Your father would be aghast, but my heart went out to him when he was forced to leave. I can't adequately describe the expression on his face, but it was full of helplessness and despair. I thought how hard it was on him if he were indeed innocent in the matter; to be accused of murdering Helen, then seeing you as you were."

"Father is convinced that Roarke is guilty," said Elizabeth.

"William will never admit it, but I believe he was jealous of Roarke. Roarke had known Helen longer, and even though she insisted they were no more than friends, I think William resented him. With the shock of Helen's death, it was all too easy for that resentment to turn into blame. Of course, the manner in which Roarke and Helen were found only added to his belief, as it would have with anyone."

"You seem to be saying that you believe Roarke is innocent."

"I am only saying a person shouldn't be judged guilty merely by how something looks. There should be proof, and in this case there is none. I have never argued about it with William. His pain is too great. And if Helen's death is never solved, then I will probably continue to keep silent on the subject. There would be no use in discussing it as long as his mind is made up."

"When Dr. James first told me of Helen's death, and Father blamed Roarke, my immediate reaction was to refuse to believe it of him," mused Elizabeth. "Since then, Father's conviction of

Roarke's guilt has made me doubt my own belief, and has brought a genuine question to my mind on whether he is innocent. I hadn't seen Roarke for so long, I had begun to picture him with horns and a pitchfork."

Louisa laughed. "He would be a handsome devil, wouldn't he?"

Elizabeth smiled. "Oh, Aunt Louisa! I'm so confused, I don't know what to think any longer. Roarke seemed so much like his old self, it's difficult to believe he's capable of murder. Yet there is no other explanation. No one else was seen in the room, or the halls, or even outside the house. He was drunk and lying in the same bed with Helen. I saw them," she whispered.

"What you say is true," agreed Louisa. "But if Roarke was unconscious or drunk, who struck you?"

"Father says my memory is mixed up and that Roarke hit me."

"It would be easier to believe that someone else entered the room after you. Perhaps someone who found the door open and thought to steal something. He could have seen what had happened and knocked you unconscious."

"But nothing was taken," reasoned Elizabeth. "If a thief had gone to all that trouble, why would he leave empty-handed?"

"Perhaps he heard your father and the Runner entering the house before he could take anything. He could have run out the back entrance without anyone being the wiser."

"You're right," said Elizabeth, her face brightening.

"Don't get your hopes up," advised Louisa. "I've already had this conversation with your father, and it didn't make him change his mind. He called it preposterous, and accused me of siding with the enemy. That was the last time I discussed it with him."

"Perhaps he's right," said Elizabeth, her sudden surge of hope-fulness gone.

"I've never known you to quibble," said Louisa. "You've always come to a conclusion and never wavered."

"Every other decision I've had to make pales in comparison to this one."

"You will do what you think is right. It will merely take you longer to decide what that is," judged Louisa.

Elizabeth did not know how she could decide with loyalties

pulling at her from every side. She needed to know more about what had happened; perhaps her drawings would bring her the much needed answers.

But Elizabeth was to be delayed in experimenting with her drawing. She had no sooner finished tea with her aunt, than Jeanette Gardiner called. Jeanette had been a close friend since Lady Carvey had pulled her from the icy stream that nearly claimed her life some fifteen years earlier. Three years younger than Elizabeth, she was making her come-out; and looked to Elizabeth for guidance, just as Elizabeth had looked to Helen.

During Elizabeth's recovery, Jeanette had visited as often as possible. She had spent hours reading aloud when Elizabeth was too weak to hold a book. She had related all the on-dits from a then sparsely populated London, and had brought small gifts to keep Elizabeth amused. Jeanette was one person upon whom Elizabeth could count to keep her confidences.

"You have certainly set London on its ear," said Jeanette, once she was seated.

"The Season must be sadly flat if I'm the topic of conversation," Elizabeth replied. "I can think of nothing I've done to deserve the honor."

"Merely your emergence after such a long illness would have been enough . . ."

"You make me sound like a bug," interrupted Elizabeth.

Jeanette giggled, then continued. "But your changed appearance astounded everyone. Then, just as the buzz was dying down over your looks, I heard Roarke arrived and the two of you disappeared, with Roarke stalking out the door looking like a thundercloud a short time later."

"It amazes me that anyone could have danced, or conversed, or even sipped punch, while attending to my movements during the evening."

"Surely, you knew to expect the attention," said Jeanette, her brown eyes sparkling with good humor.

"Of course, I did. But it is not nearly so comfortable being on the other end of speculation," Elizabeth grumbled. "Is that all that is being said?"

"It's all that I know. It seems no one was brave enough to chance getting close to the two of you to overhear your conversation. I daresay there were many who were disappointed you didn't slap his face, or at the very least give him the cut direct. The *ton* thrives on such scenes."

"Then I'm afraid they'll be disappointed if they hope to see me involved in something that vulgar. It has not been proven that Roarke is responsible for Helen's death."

"Elizabeth, you sound as if you're defending the man."

"Not defending, merely reserving judgment until I'm convinced Roarke is guilty. I will say our meeting was not all that amiable. But, after thinking about it, I cannot blame him for his response. No doubt, he has been the focus of a great deal of hostile speculation since Helen's death, and he has no way to combat it. Remaining calm in the face of such constant censure would weaken anyone's composure."

"What does Lord Carvey think of your actions?"

"He's in the country, and I hope he'll remain there until I'm convinced about Roarke one way or another."

"Do you mean you're going to see him again?"

"Not in the way you make it sound. I must talk to him if I am to discover the truth. I don't think he will be too eager to speak to me again; however, Roarke has always been a gentleman, and will surely not ignore me completely if I put myself in his way."

"You know that if the two of you are seen together again, the speculation will only increase," Jeanette pointed out.

"It cannot be helped. I will not let gossip keep me from finding out the truth about Helen's death. Now, let's speak of something more pleasant."

Despite her brave front for Jeanette's benefit, Elizabeth did not enjoy being the subject of gossip. However, she could do nothing else but disregard it, and hope some new scandal would soon offer itself for consumption. In the meantime, her fingers itched to hold her sketchbook.

As soon as Jeanette took her leave, Elizabeth returned to the privacy of her room, took up the sketchbook, and put a few tentative marks on the paper. It came far more easily than she had imagined, and her indecisiveness rapidly disappeared.

However, her first drawings gave her no help whatsoever in solving her problem. They were merely renderings of Helen when she was a child. Her large dark eyes and aristocratic nose were unmistakable. But Elizabeth did not expect miracles to happen. She had been away from drawing for too many years. It would take a little time to return to the art, and then perhaps to understand what she was seeing.

Elizabeth allowed her mind to roam, and her next drawing was of a ballroom. Louisa danced with a gentleman whose back was all that could be seen. Her aunt looked extremely happy and pleased with herself. Elizabeth wondered if Louisa had formed a tendre for someone while she had been ill.

Then she noticed that the other couple in the drawing was Jeanette and Drew. Good heaven! She didn't even know they knew one another. It seemed she had missed a great deal during the past months.

Elizabeth laid aside her drawing. She needed to do something more until she could rely upon her sketches to bring her answers. She searched her mind, and then remembered the two men who had been at the murder scene. Even though Drew doubted they could add anything new, Elizabeth decided to question them.

It required several days of searching to locate Viscount Welford and Viscount Bromley, but she finally came upon them one evening at a card party, and engaged them in conversation before they could take up a hand. The two young men were attempting to become Corinthians, yet falling far short of the mark as far as Elizabeth could see.

Welford's breeches and jacket were yellow, while Bromley had chosen puce in which to array his less than spectacular physique.

"I am Elizabeth Leighton," she said, introducing herself.

Their eyes widened slightly when she said her name.

"A pleasure," they replied, almost in unison.

"I wonder if I might ask you a few questions about what you saw last September?" The two men's faces immediately became wary, and Elizabeth wondered whether they had something to hide.

"I don't see how we can help you," said Bromley.

"But you don't even know what I intend to ask."

"Just so," said Welford. "Ask away, my lady."

"It's about the death of Lady Carvey," she began.

Bromley and Welford looked at one another with a smirk, as if sharing a great secret.

"Could you tell me what you saw that day?"

"We were merely passing by," said Bromley, "when we noticed Lord Carvey leaping out of his carriage without so much as waiting until the steps were let down."

"Then he rushed into the house," added Welford, "followed by a Bow Street Runner."

"We were intrigued and followed close behind," admitted Bromley, without a hint of embarrassment. "We arrived only a few seconds after Carvey, and were struck speechless by what we saw."

Their description of the scene inside the rented rooms was the same as Elizabeth had heard before. She questioned them further, but they had nothing to add. They had not noticed anyone leaving the building, nor had they passed anyone in the hall.

"It was no secret that Lady Carvey and Roarke were close. We concluded that Lady Carvey had attempted to break off with Roarke, and he was too foxed to accept her rejection," said Welford. "The smell of brandy was overpowering, and it was clear Roarke was completely castaway."

"He deserved to be punished even before he murdered Lady Carvey," declared Bromley, his chin thrust out aggressively.

"Why do you say that?" asked Elizabeth.

"Because we know from firsthand knowledge that he is a cheat at cards," answered Bromley.

"And a coward," added Welford. "We called him out after it was apparent he chiseled us in a game, but he refused. To this day, he has refused to give us satisfaction."

Elizabeth wondered whether they had both planned on dueling with Roarke at the same time. "So you feel he's guilty?"

"Absolutely," said Bromley, with fervor.

"Indubitably. And we were extremely happy to be able to view his downfall," said Welford with a great deal of satisfaction. "We're only disappointed that nothing's come of it yet."

"How did you come to be passing by at such an opportune time?" asked Elizabeth.

The two men looked at one another.

"Why, we were . . . er . . . ah . . ." stammered Bromley.

"We were meeting someone," said Welford quickly, "and were searching for the right house."

"You must excuse us," said Bromley.

"Yes, if we delay any longer, we won't find a free table," agreed Welford.

Seeing she could learn nothing more, Elizabeth thanked them for their time. They turned toward the card room looking a great deal relieved, and more than a little pleased with themselves.

Four

The next morning Elizabeth returned to her drawing. The first sketch was of her father, sitting at his desk in their country house. He looked sad, and she wished she could be there to keep him company. Next was Drew standing on her doorstep with the knocker raised, another bouquet of flowers in his hand. Glancing out the window, Elizabeth giggled, and checked her appearance in the mirror before dashing downstairs. She had just reached the drawing room when a knock sounded and Marston opened the front door.

"Show Viscount Stanford in," Elizabeth called from the doorway. "Oh, and bring the flowers into the drawing room once they are in a vase."

Drew appeared in the doorway, an astounded expression on his face. "Must be becoming predictable," he said, stepping over the threshold.

"Not at all," replied Elizabeth, smiling broadly. "Look at this." She produced the sketch that showed him at the door.

"Did you do this?"

"Of course. Are you surprised?"

"More than that. I thought Lord Carvcy would not let you near a sketchbook."

"Circumstances change."

"But not your father," said Drew.

"I will deal with my father when he returns. Now, will you look at my drawing?"

Drew gave her one last inquisitive glance, then took the sketchbook from her hand. "Amazing. But how did you know I would be here this morning?"

"Well, I knew it was morning from the slant of the shadows. And, look, there in the background." Elizabeth pointed to the house across the street, where a maid was polishing the knocker.

"What of it?" asked Drew.

"Lady Montclair's maid polishes the knocker every Wednesday morning without fail. It was something I observed while sitting by the window during my recovery. When I looked out a few minutes ago, I saw her coming through the door to begin the polishing, and knew you would arrive within a very short time."

"You are becoming altogether too capable for a young woman. Continue this path and you will undoubtedly never marry, for no gentleman wants a wife who will know his whereabouts and his activities without asking," he said in mock seriousness.

"Then I shall remain unmarried, and you shall be forced to escort me until we are both in our dotage."

"Shall be pleased to," he said.

"I found the viscounts Welford and Bromley last evening," she revealed, then went on to describe their encounter.

"Suggested you talk with them in case they might have noticed something no one else did. Evidently, they didn't. Wouldn't take their suppositions seriously," he advised.

"You didn't see their faces nor hear the viciousness of their remarks," said Elizabeth. "I think they would do anything to bring Roarke to his knees."

"There's bad blood between them and Roarke, no doubt about that," agreed Drew. "Story isn't exactly as they related it. Both of them lost a great deal of money gambling one evening at White's. Accused Roarke of cheating and called him out. Roarke refused to allow the fools to risk their lives. Instead, suggested they square off at Jackson's. Roarke took them on one right after the other and soundly whipped them both. They've held ill feelings against him since then. Said if he had faced them like a man, they would have won. Swore to get even with him no matter how long it took. Even if they had seen something which could help Roarke, doubt they would give up the information easily."

"If they hold such a grudge, do you think they could have been responsible for what happened to Helen?"

"Don't know."

"Surely a drubbing at Jackson's wouldn't be motive enough for murder," she added, after reflecting a moment longer.

"Can't tell. Might not be motive enough for most, but Welford and Bromley are sensitive that they not be held up to ridicule. The embarrassment of Roarke beating them at cards and in the ring might have been inducement enough for almost anything the two could come up with. It's possible they started out merely to embarrass Roarke, and the whole thing could have gotten out of hand."

"They certainly didn't hide their desire for revenge," Elizabeth murmured. She shuddered at the thought of a prank killing Helen.

It seemed that all of London was conspiring to keep Elizabeth from her drawings. After her success with predicting Drew's arrival, she was anxious to try again. But no sooner had Drew departed than Jeanette came to call.

"I heard a most interesting on-dit," confided Jeanette as she sat on a chair, spreading her skirts around her.

"And what is that?" asked Elizabeth, smiling at her friend's ability to know every bit of gossip that made the rounds.

Since Elizabeth had told Jeanette of her quest to find Helen's murder, the young woman had been clamoring to help. No doubt, Jeanette had been eavesdropping on every conversation she thought important, and very likely making a pest of herself by asking outrageous questions.

"I don't know if you want to hear it. It's about Lord Roarke."

"Why shouldn't I want to know what's being said?"

"Well, you *are* fond of him," ventured Jeanette.

"I was his friend before the incident," said Elizabeth. "I'm not certain what our relationship is at the moment, or even if we have one. Nevertheless, it does not mean I am blind to his faults."

"I have heard Roarke was acquainted with Lady Carvey before she came to London," revealed Jeanette. "I cannot swear it's true," she hastened to add, "and even then it might mean nothing at all."

"Thank you for telling me, Jeanette," said Elizabeth. If the on-dit were dependable, Elizabeth wondered whether there was enough between Roarke and Helen to cause an altercation abundantly serious to end in death. Elizabeth sighed; instead of becoming clearer, the situation was becoming increasingly obscure.

"Jeanette, I appreciate your help in this matter, but I must warn you to be extremely discreet in your inquiries."

"Do you think someone is watching?" asked Jeanette, excitement lighting her face.

"I don't know, but Helen could have been a threat to someone. If that person finds out we are delving into the matter, they might decide to silence us also." Elizabeth meant to frighten Jeanette, and it seemed she had fulfilled her ambitions.

"Surely you don't seriously believe we're in danger?" she asked in a whisper, her brown eyes appearing larger than usual in her small oval face.

"We very well could be. I think it would be better if you left the investigating to me. My mother wouldn't appreciate it if I were responsible for your injury, after she went to such trouble to save you," teased Elizabeth.

"I would never forgive myself if I deserted you in your hour of need," declared Jeanette, with all the drama that only an eighteen-year-old could express.

Elizabeth realized it would be no use attempting to dissuade her. "Then be careful, Jeanette. This is not a game," she warned. "Now, let's talk about something more pleasant. I heard you and Viscount Stanford spent quite a bit of time together the other evening."

A rosy blush appeared on Jeanette's face. "How did you know? You weren't even present."

Elizabeth thought of her drawing of Jeanette and Drew dancing together. She had been right again. "I'm not the only one who is the subject of on-dits," she teased, knowing that Jeanette would be pleased to have her name connected with Drew.

Jeanette was blushing furiously. "He is such a knowledgeable gentleman," Jeanette said, unable to meet Elizabeth's gaze.

"Yes, he is. I've known Drew since I was a young girl."

"Oh, I never thought. You must have feelings for him," said Jeanette.

"Not the kind you're thinking of," laughed Elizabeth. "Drew is more the brother I never had. Perhaps a bit more kind, for I understand a real brother often beleaguers his sister until she wishes him gone. Drew has been everything that is considerate to me since we first met. He and Helen guided me through my come-out, and he has always been my staunchest ally."

"I'm sorry. I didn't mean to remind you of Helen."

"Nonsense," replied Elizabeth. "I will not hide thoughts of Helen away as if she never existed in order to lessen my pain. She did nothing wrong to be banished from everyone's vocabulary. It's the cowardly monster who did this to her who should be punished, and I intend to do my best to see he's brought to justice."

"And if it is Lord Roarke?" asked Jeanette.

Elizabeth considered Jeanette's question, then sat a little straighter and squared her shoulders. "I pray that it isn't Roarke. But, if it is, he must pay for what he's done. However, I will not burden myself with that possibility until it's upon me."

"You are so brave," said Jeanette, an expression of admiration on her face.

Elizabeth poured a cup of tea for her friend, and handed it to her with a steady hand. If only Jeanette could see into her heart, she would not be so free with her compliments.

The next morning, Elizabeth sat on a bench in Hyde Park sketching. Betsy stood nearby flirting with a groom who had accompanied his master on an early morning ride. As if she had known he would be there, Elizabeth looked up and observed Roarke astride the giant black stallion he favored, only a short distance away. She remembered with amusement that when he first acquired the animal, she had thought of him as her white knight on a black horse. Now, her besmirched knight looked as if he would turn in the other direction rather than gallop to her rescue.

Roarke pulled the stallion to a halt and their eyes met. Since their initial meeting they had been unfailingly polite the few times they had encountered one another at various entertainments, but they had not indulged in private conversation again.

Elizabeth was haunted by Roarke's anger and the hurt that it covered. He had thought her a friend, and she had disappointed him. But surely he understood she could not turn her back on her father. Roarke had not been in love with her, nor had he offered for her, and he had never indicated his interest was anything more than friendship. He also knew what she had seen when she walked into those rented rooms that afternoon, and should realize how deeply shocked she had been. It was probably that, more than the blow to the head, that had caused her to remain silent for such a long period of time. Yes, Roarke had no reason to blame her for not believing in him; there was more than enough doubt to substantiate her reaction.

However, if she meant to find out everything she could, she could not completely sever her tie to Roarke. Whether he was innocent or guilty, he might be able to tell her something more about what had happened to her and Helen.

Roarke saw Elizabeth sitting on the bench in plenty of time to have avoided her, but he chose to face her no matter how painful it might prove to be. It was strange how he was drawn to her, despite her obvious suspicion that he was involved in Helen's death. He watched her at the events they both attended. He knew just how brightly her light blond hair gleamed beneath the chandeliers in the evenings; how the wind molded her gown to her softly curved figure during the day. She could too easily become an obsession with him, but he would not allow it. He would only be asking for more grief, falling in love with a woman who blamed him for the death of her stepmother.

But Roarke could not keep Elizabeth out of his mind. He had not felt this strongly about her before the incident, and wondered at his elevated interest now. It was more than the relief he felt knowing she had survived; more than that she had been Helen's closest friend. It was not even her new appearance that drew him. He had learned long ago to separate physical beauty from the true worth of a person.

He had thought about it long and hard, and finally decided it was Elizabeth's spirit that lured him. It had either changed during the six months she had been away from him, or she had kept it hidden, since there had been no reason for it to emerge until Helen's death. Either way, he admired her determination to solve the mystery behind her friend's death, even though he was her prime suspect. He was seeing a side of Elizabeth he had never seen before, and found he more than liked it.

But his concern and admiration for Elizabeth had not made a dent in her bearing toward him. She had let her feelings be known at their first meeting, and it was far different from what he had come to expect from her before the incident. He had no reason to think she had changed in the short time since their quarrel. Nevertheless, he found himself guiding his mount toward the bench where she sat, and stepping down when she invited him to do so. He wondered what was behind her unexpected overture.

"You've taken up your drawing again," he said, as if they had never exchanged the harsh words that still hung ominously between them. Roarke was aware of how the first Lady Carvey had died, and Lord Carvey's subsequent order that Elizabeth never draw again. "I'm happy to see your father has finally relented."

Elizabeth did not reveal that her father knew nothing of what she was doing; forthrightness had been removed from her vocabulary for the time being.

"You remember my mother's gift then?"

"Very well indeed."

"Do you also recall that Lord Ransley married a cousin of mine, Lady Claire Kingsley?"

"I attended their wedding as I remember."

"Did Ransley ever tell you how Claire had saved his life, and brought the ability to speak back to his daughter?" asked Elizabeth.

"He did," admitted Roarke.

"Then there should be no doubt in your mind that the gift is real."

"I must admit, I had been skeptical of your family's gift until then, but I couldn't dismiss what had happened. I'm convinced you are exactly what you say."

Their eyes met, and Elizabeth was mesmerized by his intent look. She should not be, she thought. She had been sure her mistrust of him would leave her totally immune to the attraction he held for her, but it seemed no matter how much she hardened her heart, he found a way to touch it.

"About the other evening," she began, before her courage gave way. He did not help her over her unexpected failure for words, but continued watching her intently, waiting for her to continue.

Apologies usually came hard for Elizabeth, and this was doubly so since she had doubts as to whether she should be making it. Nevertheless, she wished he would be gentleman enough to make the matter easier for her. However, if some members of society had treated him as poorly as she had heard, she could not blame him for his manner.

"Perhaps I didn't choose my words well," she continued. "My aim was merely to find out what had happened to Helen, not accuse you of murder."

The silence stretched to an almost unbearable point. Elizabeth finally looked up to find his gaze was still on her.

"Thank you," he said simply, taking her hand.

Feeling unexpectedly awkward by his nearness, Elizabeth's hold on her sketchbook loosened and it dropped to the ground. As Roarke leaned over to retrieve it, the breeze ruffled its pages until it fell open at the drawing of Helen as a young girl. Roarke's mouth tightened into a straight line, and a muscle ticked just above his jawline.

Elizabeth observed his discomfort at seeing the drawing, and considered it proof that he had something to hide.

"That was my first drawing," she commented. "Helen did not change much as she matured, did she?"

Roarke stared at her for a moment, then relaxed a bit. "No, she didn't," he agreed. "I had no trouble recognizing her."

Elizabeth accepted the sketchbook from his hand, turned to a fresh page, and began drawing as they talked. "Is it true you knew Helen before you came to London?" she persisted.

"I thought you no longer suspected me."

"I apologized for speaking in haste," Elizabeth clarified. "That doesn't mean I'm giving up on finding out what happened. I realized recently I knew very little about Helen's life before we met in London. When I heard your acquaintance was longer, I became curious."

"Who told you?" asked Roarke.

"I don't remember." Elizabeth was becoming better at prevarication. She sounded much more convincing when she uttered the false words. "It's something I heard recently. Neither you nor Helen ever mentioned knowing one another before she came to London, and I wondered whether it was true."

He did not rush to answer, and Elizabeth questioned whether he was formulating a story that would hide his previous relationship with Helen.

"If you don't wish to answer, I'm sure my drawings will soon answer every question I have." The image of Roarke's stallion had been taking shape beneath her fingers since they had been talking.

"Are you certain you've inherited your mother's talent?" he asked, as his stallion's ears began to take on the shape of a mule's ears.

"I am just a little out of practice," Elizabeth insisted, making the animal's ears smaller. "I have the mark of the gift," she insisted.

"Yes, I remember the mark. At first I thought you had brought back the old habit of wearing a patch, then I realized it was a natural mark." He reached out, taking her chin in a light grasp with his large hand, and turning it until she was looking at him. His eyes traveled over her face, seeming to memorize each of her features, until his gaze finally found the small dark mark near the corner of her lips. "A beauty mark," he murmured, tracing it with his finger.

Roarke's touch wiped everything from Elizabeth's mind, even that she should have immediately pulled away. He had never touched her like this; never gazed at her so intently. It took all her will to overcome the spell he had cast. Suddenly she regained her good sense and jerked away from his hand, forcing herself to concentrate on her drawing again. "It may take some time to see any real proof of my ability," she said, unable to keep a slight tremor out of her voice, "but my mother was certain I had it." Finishing the sketch in a few swift strokes, she held it up for his inspection.

The drawing showed Roarke's stallion racing down the park path, his reins flapping loose at his side. Roarke smiled and glanced over at his mount just as a small yapping dog rushed at the stallion, darting around his hooves and nipping at his fetlocks. The high-strung animal lunged backward, jerking the reins free from the loose knot that had secured him. Before Roarke could reach him, the stallion bolted down the path, avoiding several riders who attempted to intercept him. Casting a disgusted look at Elizabeth's drawing, Roarke stalked away without another word.

Elizabeth could not contain the smile that lifted the corners of her mouth. She would be willing to wager that Roarke wouldn't scoff at her drawings so easily in the future. Summoning Betsy, she closed her sketchbook and strolled down the path toward the entrance to the park.

Roarke had captured his stallion and was returning home when he encountered George Wendell. He had met Wendell and his sister, Sylvia, at a house party the year before. George had proved to be a pleasant companion, and they had continued their relationship upon returning to London for the Little Season the past September. The Wendells had been two of the few acquaintances who stood behind him during the scandal following Helen's death.

"Been doing some hard riding, I see," commented Wendell, looking at the black's sweat-dampened neck and withers.

"He's been doing some running, but not with me on board. You would think an animal this large wouldn't take fright at a dog barely larger than a teacup, but that's exactly what he did," grumbled Roarke. "Took most of the riders in the park to run him down for me. They thought it was great fun, but I didn't enjoy it a bit." At least, since I was warned in advance and didn't heed it, he thought to himself, remembering Elizabeth's drawing.

"I wanted to tell you before you heard it elsewhere, Sylvia and I plan on visiting Lady Elizabeth today."

"There's no reason you shouldn't," said Roarke.

"We didn't want you to think we were deserting you. It's awkward with the two of you at odds with one another."

"Oh, but we're doing the civilized thing," said Roarke with a smile. "In fact, I was with Elizabeth when my mount broke free and ran."

George's eyes widened. "You and Elizabeth talking?"

"Yes," Roarke confirmed. "I think her strategy is to get us back on speaking terms so she can question me about Helen."

"Good God! You don't mean it," exclaimed George.

"I'm afraid so. If I'm guilty, I imagine she hopes I may slip and say something revealing. If I'm innocent, she knows I'll never give up on searching for Helen's murderer, and probably expects I'll share my findings with her."

"I didn't know you were actively pursuing Helen's death," said George.

Roarke was still distracted by Elizabeth and spoke before he thought. "Elizabeth knows me too well; I'll never let it go, and it looks as if neither will she."

"I must go," George said abruptly. "Sylvia is waiting." He turned his horse sharply and, touching the animal with his spurs, galloped off down the path just a little too fast for safety, since the park was becoming crowded.

Not many men would be so considerate about meeting his sister, thought Roarke, watching George barely avoid another rider. Urging his own mount ahead, Roarke once again turned his thoughts to Elizabeth. Evidently she had inherited her mother's talents, and he worried it would lead her into trouble. If her drawings told her anything about the person who had murdered Helen, it would be just like Elizabeth to rush off without a thought for her own safety. Although they were speaking now, he was far from being in a position to insist she tell him if she discovered anything concerning Helen; but perhaps he knew someone who might be able to help.

Roarke had first met Andrew, Viscount Stanford, through his visits to Lord Carvey's home. They were slight acquaintances, seeing one another at the clubs, or on other social occasions. He knew that Stanford was a long-standing friend of Elizabeth's family. If he could raise enough concern in Stanford on Elizabeth's part, they might conspire to keep her safe. Armed with a plan, Roarke left the park to search for the viscount.

Elizabeth sat in her small sitting room later that afternoon staring at her sketchbook. Although she could boast of a few small successes, such as drawing Roarke's stallion that morning, she was annoyed by her lack of any real progress toward finding even the slightest clue about Helen's murder. Despite the confidence she displayed when confronting Roarke, she was not at all certain how long it would take to sharpen her talent to any worthwhile degree. In addition, it was only after she had returned home that she realized Roarke had never answered her question as to whether he and Helen had known one another before meeting in London. She was frustrated he had been able to avoid her inquiries so easily, and vowed to do better in the future.

It was a great relief when her thoughts were interrupted by a call from George Wendell and his sister, Sylvia. The Wendells were to have been members of the theater party on the evening of Helen's murder. Sylvia bore a resemblance to Helen, and Elizabeth found it more unsettling than she had thought it would be.

"We only arrived in town yesterday, and heard you were recovered," said Sylvia. "We came to call as soon as possible. We're so happy to see you well again."

"Yes, we certainly are," added George.

"But what has happened to you?" Sylvia asked, gazing at her in frank curiosity.

Elizabeth touched her curls self-consciously. "It was a result of the illness I suffered. Sometimes, when I sit in front of my mirror, I don't recognize myself. But I daresay I'll become accustomed to it eventually."

"It is very becoming," said George.

"You needn't flatter me."

"I always speak the truth, particularly to lovely ladies," George replied gallantly.

"It seems so odd that my life has changed so much since we last spoke," mused Elizabeth. "We were to go to the theater and have dinner that night. Were you left sitting very long?"

"Not at all," answered George. "We heard about the tragedy when we arrived at the theater. First, we rushed to your home and spoke briefly to your aunt Louisa. At that time, the doctor was still with you and she could tell us nothing."

"Then we called on Roarke," said Sylvia. "We were told he was abed and too groggy from the ordeal to see anyone. We didn't find out the particulars until the next day."

"And what was that?" asked Elizabeth, wondering what the gossip mill had served up.

"That you and Roarke had been found unconscious, and that Helen had been found dead in some rented rooms. There was an abundance of speculation on what you were all doing there," said George.

"I imagine there was," replied Elizabeth wryly.

"But we never believed any of it," vowed Sylvia.

"When we saw Roarke, he explained he could remember nothing of what happened to any of you, and we believed him," George said loyally. "Do you know any more?"

"I'm afraid I can add nothing to the story. It's such a mystery, I wonder whether it will ever be solved."

"Try not to worry about it," begged Sylvia. "You'll only make yourself sick again. George, we should be ashamed to make Elizabeth relive that horrible day. Let's talk about something else. I heard the most diverting on-dit just this morning about Lord Martinson."

After spending a pleasant half-hour exchanging bits of gossip, and extracting a promise from Elizabeth to join them for an excursion in the near future, the Wendells departed.

* * *

Elizabeth was alone in the drawing room when Louisa returned from an afternoon card party.

"Elizabeth! What are you doing?" said Louisa, looking over Elizabeth's shoulder as she sat sketching at the small rosewood desk in the corner of the room. "You know your father does not want you to draw."

"I've followed his instructions since my mother died," replied Elizabeth. "But I'm an adult now, and I refuse to be treated as a child any longer." There was a rebellious look to Elizabeth that seemed to be waiting for Louisa to challenge her decision.

"I happen to agree with you," said Louisa mildly. She was Elizabeth's aunt, not her mother. If William disagreed with his daughter's decision, let him take it up with her. It was not Louisa's place to do so. "Now, let me see what you've done."

"I have only just begun," said Elizabeth, sounding almost disappointed that Louisa hadn't argued with her.

"You're rapidly improving," judged Louisa, looking at the sketchbook.

"Yes, I do finally seem to be progressing," agreed Elizabeth, smiling at her success. "I've been drawing all manner of scenes, many I've never seen before. It's as if my hand has a mind of its own."

"You sound like your mother. She often said that very thing."

"Did she?" asked Elizabeth, tilting her head to one side inquiringly. "I thought I had remembered her saying something of the sort, but I wasn't sure. I suppose it's one of those things that stays with a child."

"I think it's very possible," replied Louisa. "Can I see what you've drawn?"

"Of course. There's one in particular I'd like to show you," said Elizabeth as she turned the pages of her sketchbook. "Here it is." She handed the book to Louisa, carefully watching her expression.

It was a strange drawing, thought Louisa, as she stared at the dark lines standing out in stark contrast against the white paper. Elizabeth had drawn two images of Helen in the same scene. One figure was in the foreground of the picture, and looked exactly like Helen. The second figure stood slightly behind the first, and the resemblance was not as marked.

"It is odd," agreed Louisa. "I don't suppose you know what it's meant to be?"

"I remember my mother telling me some drawings should be taken at face value, while others need interpreting. I assume this is one that means something more, but I'm puzzled over what exactly that might be." A frown creased her forehead as she studied the sketch again. "What if it means Helen was not what she seemed? That, indeed, there was more between her and Roarke, even after her marriage; thus the two faces of Helen?"

"Try not to dwell on it, my dear," soothed Louisa. "There is nothing to be done about it now."

"There is Helen's murderer still walking free," Elizabeth argued stubbornly.

"We do not know his identity, nor do we have enough evidence to prove him guilty."

"I must do what I can to help out in the matter."

"Elizabeth, this is not a game. If someone can murder one person, he will certainly not hesitate at the second if it means keeping himself free. You must leave this to others."

"I am annoyed beyond all reason at hearing that," complained Elizabeth. "My answer is the same. It has been left to others for six months, and nothing has come of it. To my knowledge, there is not even an active investigation going on."

"We don't always know what is happening with the authorities," reasoned Louisa.

Elizabeth gave an unladylike snort of derision. "And usually there is nothing. Even though Helen was Lady Carvey, the inquiry into her death is at an impasse. Father reminded me that Roarke's family is an influential one, and could bring a great deal of pressure to halt the proceedings."

"Have you decided that Roarke is guilty then?"

"No," replied Elizabeth exasperated. "But if he is the only suspect, and his name is as powerful as Father says, how avidly do you think the authorities will pursue him? And if he is innocent, and they don't continue the investigation, then they will never find the real murderer."

Louisa considered her niece's words, and concluded that it was possible they carried more than a hint of truth.

"Look at these," continued Elizabeth, turning the pages of her sketchbook until they revealed more drawings of Helen and Roarke. "Examine the backgrounds, and see whether you recognize the locations."

"I can't tell from these," said Louisa, looking at the first few drawings.

"Neither could I," agreed Elizabeth, "but inspect the others before you make a final judgment."

"It's Paris," said Louisa, after turning several pages.

"I believe so," concurred Elizabeth. "Now, consider these." She pointed out several more drawings which depicted Helen and Roarke on a ship approaching what was unmistakably the white cliffs of Dover on the coast of England.

Louisa did not comment, as Elizabeth slowly turned page after page. The drawing of Helen and Roarke at Bath was easily recognizable, as was the one in London. But there was a village and a house that was not familiar to either of the women. At the back of the house was a walled garden, with morning glories spilling over the wall in profusion.

"Do you have any idea where this is or what it means?" Louisa asked.

"No, but I'm going to do my best to find out," Elizabeth stated firmly. "I don't believe Roarke will ever willingly reveal Helen's past, so I must turn elsewhere. These drawings might be a key, but I don't understand them. I can't sit idly by until my grasp of them develops to the point where they will be of full use to me. Until then, I need help, and I've decided to hire a Bow Street Runner."

"Elizabeth, you mustn't! Your father would be scandalized."

"Why? He admitted he had hired a Runner himself. Even Nicole called on one last year, and you know how father dotes on her. If my father and my cousin can hire a Runner, I see no reason why I can't."

"It is much different for a man to be involved in these things," Louisa pointed out.

Elizabeth's face took on a stubborn look. "Nicole is not a man."

"But she was looking into a theft with her husband," objected Louisa.

"What does it matter? Nicole is also the Duchess of Weston, and if the Duke and Duchess of Weston can hire a Runner, surely Father cannot complain if I do so."

Louisa looked at her skeptically.

"And he may not even need to know," continued Elizabeth. "If everything works out well, we could have the answer to Helen's death before he returns to town."

"You should pray it works out that way, or else I'm afraid we'll both be banished to the country for the rest of our days," Louisa warned.

"Will you help me?" Elizabeth asked.

"I doubt there will be anything I can do, but if you need me, I'll do what I can," she promised.

"You are the best of all aunts," exclaimed Elizabeth, giving the older woman a swift hug.

"Don't speak too soon," warned Louisa. "There could be a great deal of trouble ahead of you yet."

Elizabeth prayed her aunt didn't also have a gift of prophecy.

Five

By the next afternoon, Elizabeth had arranged a meeting with a Bow Street Runner by the name of Warren. His punctuality and neatness of appearance were reassuring to Elizabeth, and she was more convinced than ever that she had made the right decision.

"Mr. Warren, my cousin, the Duchess of Weston, has spoken highly of you."

"She is a very special lady," replied the Runner. "I was honored to be of service to her."

"She told me you helped out on an extremely delicate matter in which she and the Duke were involved; that you exercised a great deal of discretion in an affair which could have become quite awkward."

"Her Grace is too kind," Warren said, modestly.

"Did you know she has an unusual talent?"

Warren studied her closely before answering. "His Grace explained about his wife after the matter was put to rest. He did it only because he had hired me to find her when she had been missing some years before. Not being able to locate her has been my one and only failure. He said he could not let me continue thinking it was my fault."

"You mean she used her talent to avoid you?"

"That is what His Grace conveyed to me."

"And did you believe him?"

"After seeing what happened with my own eyes, I had no other choice."

"Then would you believe I also have a gift, though not as well developed as my cousin's."

Warren's eyes widened. "You mean there is more than one?"

"I'm afraid so. It seems to run in the female side of the family."

"Heaven protect us!"

"Oh, no. We're not witches," Elizabeth reassured him. "We never use our gift to harm, only to help. I haven't used my second sight until now, and I find I need some assistance until I can develop it properly. That is why I called on you."

Warren was silent for a moment. "I suppose I'd rather be on your side than against you," he finally said.

"Thank you, Mr. Warren. You'll not regret it."

"I wonder," he replied, a wary smile lighting his thin face.

"Let me fill you in on the background," said Elizabeth, leaning toward him. She began to tell him everything she knew about what had happened on that day in September.

"That's a remarkable story," Warren said when she had finished. "Of course, I heard about the incident when it occurred, but it was hushed up quickly, and very little has been said since then. As I remember, the allegations against Lord Roarke went nowhere."

"That's true. I'm searching for a reason behind the murder. There's a possibility the motive might lie in either Helen's or Roarke's past, but for some reason Lord Roarke will not be candid with me about his and Lady Carvey's past relationship. I've heard they knew one another before she came to London. That is the first thing I need to know. But you must be extremely circumspect. No one should discover that you are searching into their pasts."

"I can meet your needs, my lady," he assured her. "As soon as I have the information, I'll report to you."

"Thank you, Mr. Warren. I believe our association will be a successful one."

Elizabeth sat for some time after Mr. Warren left, thinking of Roarke and their last meeting. After her apology, he had seemed to hold no ill feeling about their argument, and for that she was grateful. But it was even more apparent his demeanor toward her had changed since the previous September. His look and touch were entirely different from what she remembered, and there was an awareness between them that had not been there before. Elizabeth had not known it, but it was that exact awareness she had been yearning for Roarke to direct her way so many months ago. Now that he had, they were in a position where she could not respond to it as she wished.

A flush rose to Elizabeth's face as she remembered Roarke tracing the mark near the corner of her lips. The desire to press her lips to his fingers had been nearly overwhelming at the time, and she wondered anew at these unfamiliar feelings which were making themselves known. She had often imagined how Roarke's kiss would feel—she would not be human if she had not—but putting her lips against a man's fingers had never entered her mind until that moment in Hyde Park.

Roarke had held her spellbound with a look; had rendered her helpless with a touch. She did not want to consider how weak she might become if he kissed her. It was important that she retain enough objectivity to be able to judge the findings of her investigation. She found it humiliating that she harbored feelings for a man who was a suspect in Helen's murder. How could she even think of Roarke in that manner until he was cleared of suspicion? He had never made an overture toward her before her illness. Why, suddenly, was he acting as if he wanted more than friendship? Was he attempting to distract her from pursuing her inquiry?

Elizabeth sighed, and rose to go upstairs to ready herself for the evening's entertainment. If she could not understand her own heart, how could she hope to discover Helen's secrets?

"I should never have come this evening," said Elizabeth, as she and Louisa entered Lord and Lady Sherborne's ballroom.

"Are you not feeling well?" Louisa asked anxiously.

"I'm fine," Elizabeth reassured her. "It's merely that I'm already becoming tired of the same thing every evening." Her complaint was not exactly truthful. More to the point, she had just spied Roarke on the dance floor with a fragile-looking young woman, who stared up at him as if he were the only man walking the earth.

Even though Elizabeth had been ashamed at the feelings that swept over her each time she was near Roarke, she was equally chagrined by the jealousy she felt at seeing him with another woman. She lifted her chin stubbornly, and turned away from the dance floor. She would not allow herself to fall victim to such an unworthy emotion. She would stay at the ball, and have an enjoyable evening no matter how many women hung on Roarke's arm.

It wasn't long before her dance card was full, and she wondered whether she had taken on too large of a task as she found her toes being unmercifully punished by John Townsend's clumsy steps. Mr. Townsend was a witty conversationalist, but his dancing skills were woefully lacking. She felt a great deal of relief when the music came to an end, until she noticed Roarke approaching.

Roarke had been surreptitiously watching Elizabeth go from one man's arms to another. His resentment had grown until he no longer cared whether she welcomed his attentions. She looked different, to be sure, but the same heart lay beneath the black gown, the same mind functioned beneath the silver curls. Surely she could not have expunged every bit of feeling she had held for him.

"Am I fortunate enough to find you free for the next dance?" he asked when he reached her side.

"I'm sorry, it's already promised to Mr. Kimball."

Roarke glanced at the young man who was approaching. "Kimball is a good friend of mine, aren't you?" he said laying a hand on Kimball's shoulder. "I'm sure he'll relinquish his dance to me."

The young man flushed at the attention from Roarke. Despite the cloud hanging over his head, Roarke was still admired by the young blades in town.

"If Lady Elizabeth agrees, I have no objection," replied Kimball.

"I . . ." But she got no further.

"Thank you, Kimball. Join me for a glass of port the next time we're in White's," Roarke invited.

Elizabeth did not know whether to be amused or angered by Mr. Kimball's willing defection. Obviously, Roarke's attention meant more than a dance with her. There was much to be said for a mature gentleman who could appreciate the value of spending time with a lady, she observed wryly.

"You are now free," Roarke announced, with a satisfied air.

Elizabeth did not like his assumption that he could manage her life so easily. "Am I also free to refuse?" asked Elizabeth. "While you two gentlemen arranged things admirably between the two of you, my opinion was completely overlooked."

One dark eyebrow quirked quizzically, as Roarke studied her. "My apologies. Lady Elizabeth, would you honor me with the next dance?"

Suddenly, Elizabeth felt foolish. What was a dance anyway? And certainly Roarke was a marked improvement, both in dancing skills and conversation, over Mr. Kimball.

"I would be pleased to, my lord." Elizabeth took his arm, and they walked onto the floor just as the musicians began. She had waltzed with Roarke numerous times before, but as soon as he took her in his arms she knew this dance would be different. The very air between them changed as the touch of his hand burned through the thin material of her gown. He drew her closer and she followed willingly. His masculinity surrounded her, and she grew warmer than the activity of the dance warranted.

Their steps carried them around the room, and it was several moments before Roarke spoke. "It's been a long time since we've danced."

"More than six months," she said, looking everywhere but at Roarke. She did not want to be this close to him; she did not want to discuss their past relationship. And she certainly did not want to be captured by his gaze again.

"You are as graceful as you always were."

Elizabeth attempted to ignore the breath that tickled her ear as he leaned down to speak to her. His face was close enough that she could detect a light pleasant scent, probably from the shaving paste he had used earlier, and she suddenly wanted to stroke that freshly shaved cheek to see if it was as smooth as it looked. No, she scolded herself. She could not allow her emotions to gain the upper hand. There was too much left to do, and while Roarke might not be guilty of murder, Elizabeth was certain he knew more than he was telling. Until he was willing to be honest with her, she must fight her attraction to him.

"I can remember when we held conversations," she responded, pulling as far away from him as she could. "I can hear empty compliments from any of my dance partners."

"You never questioned my veracity before."

"I'm a different person now."

"Are you? I don't know whether or not I should be happy about that," he remarked, searching her face with his sharp glance.

"Your state of mind concerning my character is not of supreme importance to me," she snapped.

"Oh, Elizabeth, you wound me to the quick," he said, adjusting their positions until she was once again close to him.

Elizabeth blushed. She was usually not so sharp nor impolite, but her nerves were stretched to the limit with Roarke's nearness. She had warned him several times about the flummery he was spouting, but it didn't seem he had listened.

"You never felt the need to gammon me before," said Elizabeth. "Why do you find it necessary now?"

"I'm not giving you Spanish coin, my dear. I am merely expressing my thoughts. If I never told you that you dance exquisitely, then I should be horsewhipped for the oversight. You have always been an excellent dancer, Elizabeth. Perhaps I took it for granted; something I vow never to do again."

They danced silently for a few moments, and Elizabeth prayed the music would come to an end.

"Surely you don't mean to sulk for the rest of the dance," said Roarke.

"I never sulk."

"You never did before," he replied.

"And I am not doing so now," she said, concluding they sounded like two quarrelsome children.

"I believe what you said a moment ago; you are a different person. Your quiet demeanor hid more than I ever thought, for you are certainly not the same Elizabeth I once knew."

"And do you dislike this new one so much?" Elizabeth was anxious for his response, but afraid to hear it.

"Not at all. I'm looking forward to becoming acquainted with you again."

"Don't depend upon it, or you might be disappointed."

Roarke chose not to answer her sally, but exercised his much vaunted charm and smiled down at her. "You're looking lovely tonight," he said, switching subjects so abruptly that it took her a moment to respond.

There he went, flattering her again. Elizabeth decided not to be drawn into another useless argument about it. "I am looking the same as always."

Roarke studied the gown Elizabeth wore. It was black as were all her others, with a low neckline and tiny puffed sleeves. The hem of the skirt was heavily embellished with satin embroidery and jet beads. A modest plume of black feathers sprouted from several small black, crepe roses adorning her hair.

"Did you know that some call you the Black Rose?"

"Better than the Black Widow," she shot back.

Roarke smiled appreciatively. "It's good to see you still retain a sense of humor."

"I've always had a sense of humor, but you've never thought it necessary to comment upon it before."

Roarke sighed with exasperation. "Elizabeth, can you not simply accept a compliment, even if you don't believe it's sincere?"

"About as easily as you can tell me the truth about Helen."

His lips tightened into a firm line. "So we're back to that."

"You make it sound so unimportant," charged Elizabeth. "We're talking about Helen, and you act as if it's a subject of supreme indifference that should be swept under the rug."

Roarke guided her to the edge of the dance floor and led her through a French door onto the terrace. The cool night air washed over her bare arms, making her shiver slightly.

He swung her around to face him; his grip on her upper arms too tight to be comfortable. "Don't ever accuse me of not caring about Helen," he ordered, his voice filled with repressed anger. "There are things you don't know about the two of us, but disinterest isn't one of them. I will say this to you once: I didn't kill Helen. I don't know what happened in that room, but the one thing you may be sure of is that I never harmed her." He stared down at her, waiting for her response.

"You're hurting my arms," said Elizabeth in a dispassionate tone.

"Damn!" exclaimed Roarke, loosening his hold. "I didn't mean to hurt you." He rubbed her arms lightly, as if his touch could take away the sting.

She took a step away and turned toward the door. "We should be getting back."

"Elizabeth."

She hesitated, uncertain whether to ignore him and continue on her way, or give him her full attention. Deciding to compromise, she looked over her shoulder at him. His features were thrown partly into shadows on the dimly lit terrace, and he appeared far more menacing than he had only moments before.

"Use your gift; prove that I'm a murderer."

"I'm trying," she whispered. She could not see his reaction, but could imagine the frozen features of his face. He did not speak for several moments, and Elizabeth was held captive by the ominous silence.

"We are not through with this, Elizabeth," was all he said, but it was enough.

She turned and walked away, his warning ringing in her ears.

Roarke stayed on the terrace long after Elizabeth had disappeared through the doors and melted into the throng of people in the crowded room. What was wrong with him? Everything he said to Elizabeth seemed to indicate he was guilty in the matter of Helen's murder. It was true he was not telling Elizabeth everything he knew, but he had made a promise to Helen and he meant to keep it. He should not need to prove himself to Elizabeth; she should know him well enough to trust him. Roarke returned to the ball, convinced he was acting as any honorable man would.

Roarke had not seen Viscount Stanford since he vowed to enlist his help in keeping Elizabeth safe. He left the Sherbornes' house, ordering his carriage to take him to White's. Stanford could usually be found there late in the evening.

When he arrived he saw he had been right in his assumption. Viscount Stanford was seated before a low burning fire, with a bottle of brandy on a table at his elbow. After the men exchanged greetings, the viscount invited Roarke to join him.

"Have some brandy," said Drew, indicating the bottle.

"No, thank you," replied Roarke, holding up his hand. "I overindulged on brandy when I was but a young cub, and haven't been able to abide it since." Roarke called for port, then settled back in his chair.

"I know you're a close friend of Elizabeth's," said Roarke, once he had a glass in his hand. "I wondered whether you could help me protect her."

"From what?" asked Drew, appearing only slightly interested.

Roarke was relieved that Drew was at least willing to listen. "From herself. Are you aware that Elizabeth is pursuing her drawing again?"

"She told me," admitted Drew.

"Then I'm certain you're aware of the talent the females in her family inherit."

Drew nodded, and took another sip of brandy.

The viscount wasn't going to make this easy, thought Roarke. "I've seen some of Elizabeth's drawings, and I'm afraid they could lead her into trouble."

"How so?" asked Drew.

"If she draws a suspect, or anything else that indicates who murdered Helen, I think she might run off without asking for help. If her drawings prove true, she would not be capable of standing up to such a monster."

Drew didn't answer, and for the moment Roarke was the mind reader. "You're probably thinking I could be the killer. I swear to you, I didn't harm Helen, nor Elizabeth. I would just as soon raise my hands to my mother."

Drew observed him for a few moments. Roarke met his gaze without flinching. "Been friends with Elizabeth since she was a young girl. Wouldn't turn against her now."

"I'm not asking you to betray her friendship. I merely want to ensure she'll be around for you to continue it."

Drew took another sip of brandy and stared into the flames for a few moments. "Can't promise anything, but am willing to listen."

Roarke breathed a sigh of relief. "Elizabeth trusts you. She might show you the drawings or tell you about them before she decides to take action. You would be in a position to watch over her, or to let me know so I may do so."

"Elizabeth is stubborn," said Drew. "I doubt whether she would even listen to me, if she had her mind made up on a particular action. Could offer to join her, and if I'm fortunate, she might allow me to do that."

"She probably confides in her aunt," said Roarke. "Perhaps you could ask Lady Louisa to let you know if Elizabeth plans anything outrageous. She might be happy to have someone to call on."

"Possibly," admitted Drew. "Don't like to go behind Elizabeth's back though, but will talk to Louisa the next time I call. See what I can work out. While I don't want to cross Elizabeth, am concerned for her well-being."

The two men talked a while longer, and while Drew would not promise anything, Roarke believed he would be more watchful of Elizabeth in the future. It was early morning before Roarke returned home and stretched out on the large mahogany bed that generations of his ancestors had used. His thoughts were still fully occupied by Elizabeth.

He had watched as other men were drawn to her since her return to society. It wasn't merely the change in her appearance that attracted them—there were many lovely ladies in the *ton*—but a change of heart. Elizabeth was on a mission, and it was reflected in her every move. Her intentness and vitality lured men to her side, and Roarke found he did not like it at all. It wasn't until the sky began to lighten that he was able to fall into a restless sleep.

"I see you couldn't avoid Roarke again tonight," said Louisa wryly, as they were returning home that evening.

"He insisted I dance with him. He even bribed that dandy Kimball with a glass of port."

"I thought you liked Mr. Kimball."

"I did until he gave over so easily to Roarke. A glass of port! Surely I am worth more than that."

Louisa could not help but laugh. "It seems you're more angry at the price than the loss of a dance with Mr. Kimball."

"Perhaps so," grumbled Elizabeth. "There is no doubt that Roarke is by far the lightest on his feet, while Kimball is heaviest on mine. And he is far more entertaining when he puts his mind to it."

"Then he must have wanted to dance with you quite badly to endure Kimball for the length of even one glass of port."

"I hadn't thought of it in that light," admitted Elizabeth.

"I'm certain you didn't waste your time talking about the latest on-dit. Did you learn anything more from him?"

He still refuses to speak about Helen's past. He also swears he didn't harm her."

"And what do you think?"

"I want to believe him," said Elizabeth, with a sigh that was audible in the coach, even as they rumbled over the cobblestones. "But how can I trust *him* if he will not trust *me* enough to confide in me?"

"With a man such as Roarke, trust and honor are bound together. If he truly made a commitment to Helen, he'll carry through on that vow no matter what the cost."

"Even if it means I will think him guilty of murder?"

"He may deeply regret it, but he will keep his word. Don't you know many people have already lost confidence in him? People whom he thought were his friends now give him the cut direct. He may not show it outwardly, but he is not as untouched by it as he seems to be. Losing you might hurt him more than all the others combined, but he will nonetheless continue."

"I don't know what to do," murmured Elizabeth.

"You will do exactly as you have been doing, for you are the same as Roarke: you can do nothing else. Heaven help us if your objectives are ever at odds."

"They are now."

"If you believe Roarke is innocent, then your objectives are the same," responded Louisa. "Both of you want to know who killed Helen. It's merely the method each of you are using to reach your goal that's different. Life would be easier if the two of you could agree to work together."

"Roarke will not even give me a hint of what he's holding back. I can't imagine his ever cooperating with me."

"No, I suppose it's too much to ask," replied Louisa. "I hope you're not planning on doing anything foolish to prove to Roarke that you don't need his help."

"Unless Mr. Warren or my drawings tell me something, I'm fresh out of ideas," admitted Elizabeth.

"Thank heaven for that," said Louisa.

Elizabeth was still smarting from Roarke's treatment when Lady Barrington paid her promised call. She sailed into the sitting room with her latest manservant trailing behind, carrying the tisane she had promised Elizabeth.

"James," she commanded, holding out her hand for the container. The servant handed her the container, then positioned himself by the door. "Here, my dear. This will do you more good than any doctor."

"Thank you, my lady," replied Elizabeth, her nose twitching from the scent of the herb mix in the tisane. Marston lingered in the door, observing Lady Barrington and her servant with undisguised interest. "Would you take this to the kitchen, Marston, and bring a tea tray?"

"Oh, don't worry with tea for me, my dear. As I recall, your father has a very good cellar, and I would like a taste of his very special brandy."

Elizabeth nodded at Marston and he left the room, holding the tisane at arm's length.

"I always say brandy is the only civilized drink," continued Lady Barrington, taking a seat and settling her skirt around her. "At least, that's what your father asserted years ago. I suppose he influenced me a great deal. Did I ever tell you that William and I went about together occasionally when I first came out?"

Elizabeth could not imagine her father with Lady Barrington, but she supposed they were both very different people then. "No, you didn't."

"I developed a tendre toward him very quickly," Lady Barrington admitted. "But after he met your mother, he never gave me a second look. Oh, I held no grudge, for Jane became a very good friend. As I mentioned the other evening, we often planned she would marry my brother, Cedric, and then we would be real sisters. But it was soon apparent she was as taken by William as he was with her. Cedric and I stepped aside, and it wasn't long before your father offered for her and she accepted."

Marston entered with the tray, and Elizabeth poured the brandy and tea. Lady Barrington did not believe in sipping the excellent brandy, and soon refilled her glass.

"What happened to Cedric?" asked Elizabeth, unaware that Lady Barrington had a brother.

"Oh, he's spent his life traveling. He comes home occasionally, but doesn't stay long until he's off again. I always thought it was because he lost Jane."

"Did you get to know Helen?" asked Elizabeth.

"I hope you won't take it amiss, my dear, but I never wanted to become acquainted. Oh, we said all the polite things when we met, but I always resented anyone taking my dear Jane's place. Unless it would have been me, of course." Lady Barrington tittered, and emptied her glass again.

"We are so close, I know you will understand when I say I attempted to gain your father's interest after the mourning for my late husband was over. But once again, I was too late. He was already involved with Helen to the point where he could see no one else. So I have lost him twice," she said, serving herself from the brandy decanter.

Elizabeth did not know how much longer she could tolerate Lady Barrington's thoughtless remarks. She was certain the woman's version of her relationship with Lord Carvey was highly influenced by the brandy she consumed at such a rapid rate.

"My father was very happy with Helen," Elizabeth said quietly.

"Oh, I'm quite sure he was," agreed Lady Barrington, waving her glass. "She was a lovely young woman that any man his age would have been proud to marry. But one must wonder what she did to amuse herself when he wasn't around."

"Lady Barrington!"

"Oh, don't fly into the boughs merely because I speak plainly. She went into that house as if she had been there a dozen times before."

"How do you know?" asked Elizabeth.

"What?"

"I asked how you know what she looked like when she arrived at the rooms that day," repeated Elizabeth.

"Why I . . . I happened to be driving by and saw her."

Elizabeth decided that she would be just as forthcoming as Lady Barrington if the woman prized that trait. "Most of those houses are rented rooms. Who would you be calling on there?"

"I . . . it was . . ." Lady Barrington emptied her glass and set it down with a sharp crack. "I'm afraid you must excuse me, my dear. I didn't know the time had passed so quickly. I have an appointment to ride in Hyde Park this afternoon and must go home to change."

Before Elizabeth could say anything, Lady Barrington was at the door. "Come, James," she said not even looking in the man's direction. "I will call on you when I can stay longer, my dear."

Elizabeth sat in the silence of the room feeling as if she had been caught up in a whirlwind. She couldn't believe Lady Barrington had the nerve to say much of what she did. She wished Louisa had been at home, for the two women were of an age where her aunt could have effectively administered a set-down to Lady Barrington. If Elizabeth had tried, the insufferable woman no doubt would have only patted her on the head and told her to behave.

And what was Lady Barrington doing near the rented rooms on the very same day that Helen was murdered? Elizabeth had spoken the truth; she could think of no reason for the woman to have been there. Add her presence to that of viscounts Welford and Bromley, and there was a curious collection of people near that particular house that day. Instead of becoming clearer, the matter was becoming more muddled by the minute.

Several days later, Mr. Warren called to report his activities.

"Lady Carvey had been in London approximately a year before you met her," began Warren. "I have heard she lived in Bath prior to arriving in town, but I could not definitely substantiate the claim. Lord Roarke and the then Miss Northrup were seen in one another's company quite often, and acted as if they were old acquaintances. It was not particularly remarked upon, for Lord Roarke traveled extensively and it was well within reason that they had met on one of his trips."

Elizabeth felt a sense of achievement that her drawings were correct.

"Lord Roarke's attention assured Miss Northrup's success, and it wasn't long before she had a throng of admirers," Warren continued. "However, her association with Lord Roarke never seemed to be more than friendship. Or, if it was, they were discreet. As you well know, even after Miss Northrup married Lord Carvey, she continued her acquaintance with Lord Roarke."

"Yes, I'm well aware of it." Elizabeth mulled over what he had told her. "Did you find out anything about the day Lady Carvey died?"

"Only rumors, my lady. Society is divided on Lord Roarke's guilt or innocence in the matter, and the gossip cannot be relied upon. I could look further into Lady Carvey's background, if you wish. I might find something there that could explain what happened to her."

"Yes, that's a good idea. Perhaps someone in Bath had a reason to want to hurt her. Before you go though, I want to show you my drawings. They might help you in your search."

Elizabeth displayed the sketches of Helen and Roarke in Paris and in Bath for Mr. Warren. Then she turned to the drawings of the village and the house she had been unable to recognize. Warren studied them closely before he left. He would depart for Bath the first thing in the morning in hopes of finding the thread to unraveling Helen's past.

Roarke had not been able to completely rid his mind of Elizabeth since their confrontation at the ball. His thoughts centered on either taking her in his arms, or turning her over his knee; there was nothing in between. Life would be far simpler if she would stay out of the mystery surrounding Helen's death.

As for her drawings, they were becoming alarmingly true to the facts. The gift that Elizabeth inherited might be a blessing to some, but in this case it was definitely working against him. Several of her drawings already revealed more than he liked, and it was only Elizabeth's inability to interpret them that had saved him. He wondered how long it would be before she would sketch something so explicit that she would understand without benefit of explanation.

However, it was the very spirit that drove Elizabeth, and brought her so close to uncovering his and Helen's secret, that attracted him most. He had always known she was loyal, but her tenaciousness surprised him. He admired that trait, be the person man or woman.

The physical attraction he felt had been a surprise. He would be the first to admit he had not felt this way toward her before the accident. She had been a pleasant, undemanding companion, who always deferred to Helen, fading into the background whenever her friend was near. Roarke now realized that this had been a conscious action on her part. While Helen had been a special friend to Roarke, she had always insisted upon being the center of attention, and no one had challenged her to this right.

However, Helen's death had been Elizabeth's awakening. Perhaps the change in her appearance had made her feel she was a different person, for now her dress as well as her demeanor had changed. The black she wore set her apart in every room she entered. Her gowns were far more daring in cut than they had previously been, and her silvery curls were a perfect foil for her new image. The gentlemen flocked to her side, and Roarke had experienced a few pangs of indignation that they would treat her with so much familiarity.

He was beginning to wish he had the right to send them on their way, but while the ghost of Helen stood between them, that could never be. Even if the real murderer was found, he wondered whether Elizabeth could think of him in terms of a suitor. He was certain her father would not welcome him into the family, and Elizabeth was particularly devoted to Lord Carvey.

She was such a stubborn woman, thought Roarke. He had not liked it at all when Elizabeth had walked away from him at the ball. He had warned her they were not finished, and meant every word. He might not be able to call on Elizabeth at home, but he would find her this evening and they would continue their discussion. He could be just as stubborn as she was when he chose to do so.

That evening, there was a certain decisiveness in Roarke's manner as he made his way through the crush of people toward Elizabeth that declared he would not be easily put off again.

Drew had escorted Elizabeth, Louisa, and Jeanette to the ball, but for the moment Elizabeth was standing alone. How could she have allowed this to happen? she fumed. She had known that Roarke was there; had seen him dancing with several young ladies after her party had first arrived. Their eyes had met earlier in the evening, but as he began to approach, Elizabeth had turned her back on him. No matter whether he was honor-bound by a promise, she planned on holding him at arm's length until he revealed what he knew about Helen's death.

Elizabeth had been uncommonly careful about keeping the expanse of the ballroom between them for the entire evening and evading his glance whenever it seemed he might meet her eye. But now, because of one unguarded moment, she had been caught without the safe barrier of either Drew, Louisa, or Jeanette to put between her and Roarke.

Elizabeth squared her shoulders, took a deep breath, and arranged her features into an expressionless demeanor as Roarke drew near. She would not allow any sign of weakness to betray her.

"Elizabeth," Roarke greeted her in a silky voice. "We have missed one another all evening, so I decided to take advantage of this small lull in the dancing to present myself, and inquire after your health."

Elizabeth's features remained frozen in place. "My health is very well, my lord."

"So formal, Elizabeth? One would never know that once we were so close."

Elizabeth knew he said it only to tease her, yet she could not help but rise to the bait. "You know very well that we were never as close as you insinuate," she hissed, as the frustration of the last three years rushed to the surface. "I was a convenience, that is all. Someone you could safely take about without fear I would make any demands on you."

Roarke took her arm and led her toward a window embrasure that provided a bit of privacy and a breath of fresh air. Unwilling to make a spectacle of herself by struggling, she grudgingly accompanied him.

Placing himself between Elizabeth and the room, Roarke glared down at her. "Don't ever think that you meant so little to me. I may not have paid you the attention I should have at times, but you seemed such a levelheaded person, I didn't think I needed to constantly indulge in flummery with you."

Elizabeth had not realized she had so strongly resented Roarke's treatment of her while Helen was alive, but evidently she had buried it deep inside and ignored it until the shock of Helen's death had brought her true feelings to the surface. She met his gaze without flinching and fought the unreasonable anger that filled her, but she was not entirely successful. "I meant what

I said the last time we met. I didn't need flattery then, sir, and I certainly don't need it now. Especially from you!"

"And just what does that mean?" asked Roarke, his eyes narrowing.

"It means that the only reason I spent so much time in your company was to keep the rumors away from Helen. She was particularly insistent that I be with her whenever you were to be one of the party. I now know why," she spat out.

Roarke's face paled as the significance of her words struck him. "Please accept my apologies, my lady. It seems more has changed than your appearance. I had falsely assumed you held a small belief of my innocence. I shall not force my attentions on you any longer." With a small, sharp bow he was gone, making his way rapidly across the floor until he disappeared altogether.

Elizabeth stayed in the embrasure applying her silk and ivory fan to cool her overheated face. She had wanted to be rid of him, hadn't she? Then why did she feel so empty? So desolate? Nothing had changed in her life, except Roarke was no longer in it. He had forced the confrontation. She would have been willing to leave well enough alone until her investigation was complete, and either his innocence or guilt had been proven. But he had not allowed it. The scene was entirely his fault, but he had made her feel the villain.

Six

The next afternoon Warren returned from his trip to Bath. Elizabeth had remained home all day questioning her remarks to Roarke the night before. She regretted their argument, but he had provoked her beyond all reason, and she had struck back with the most hurtful comment she could think of at the moment. It had been unfair of her, but it was far too late to recall the words. So it was with a great deal of relief that she welcomed Warren; perhaps he would be able to divert her mind from last evening's argument.

"Were you able to learn anything, Mr. Warren?" she asked, eager to hear any news he might have.

"Some, my lady. I found it's true that Lady Carvey had been in Bath before coming to London. While there, she let it be known she had recently come from the continent, where she had lived with an elderly aunt until her demise. Lord Roarke arrived a few days later, and they greeted one another as old friends. Lady Carvey, the then Miss Northrup, was readily accepted into every level of Bath society because of her acquaintance with the earl," he reported.

So it was just as her drawings had shown, thought Elizabeth. Helen and Roarke had known one another before she had come to London; even before they had arrived at Bath. And, with growing confidence in her talent, Elizabeth would wager the remainder of her sketches proved accurate. Their relationship had extended past the English Channel to Paris. Elizabeth wondered how they came to know one another and exactly what they meant to one another.

"There is one discrepancy," said Warren.

Elizabeth pulled her thoughts back to the present. "And what is that, Mr. Warren?"

"I traced Lady Carvey's route from Bath to the coast. Between embarking at Dover and before reaching Bath, she disappeared for several weeks. She left a posting inn one morning, and I couldn't find a sign of her until she appeared at Bath a fortnight later."

"But where could she have gone?"

"I searched as far as I could, but none of the inns remembered her. Of course, she could have stayed at a private home. If so, it would be nearly impossible to locate."

"And she could have been with Lord Roarke," said Elizabeth in a dull voice.

"Yes, my lady, that's entirely possible. I could attempt to track his movements after he returned to England," he suggested. "But you should realize I might discover something you'd rather not know."

"I already know more than I like," she replied. "But you're right. Lady Carvey's disappearance might hold the answer to her death. Can you leave right away? I want this over and done with before my father returns. If he learns of my inquiries, he'll insist I end them, and I'll never be able to rest until I discover everything I can."

"I'll leave immediately, my lady."

"Good. Let me know as soon as you return."

"Drew seemed very attentive last night," commented Elizabeth as she inspected a bit of ribbon in one of the Bond Street shops the next morning. She glanced at Jeanette and was pleased to see a flush on the young girl's cheeks.

"We danced, and he brought me a cup of punch," Jeanette admitted. "But I wouldn't consider it more that just a thoughtful gesture."

"Drew is every inch the gentleman," admitted Elizabeth, "but he does not usually spend so much time in a young lady's company as he does with you."

"You know him quite well, don't you?"

"Yes, I do. We are the best of friends."

"Do you think . . . ? Is it true he has a tendre for someone else? I know I shouldn't ask such personal questions, but I would like to know."

"Drew has harbored feelings for a sister of one of his friends. However, that hasn't worked out as he had hoped, and nothing may ever come of it. He's not the kind to languish, so his interest in you is perfectly normal. I'm unaware of any commitments he has made to a woman."

"I'm so glad. When I heard he was interested in someone else, my heart just fell," Jeanette admitted, placing her hand over the offending organ. "Do you think there's a chance he finds me attractive?"

"Drew is always straightforward. If he's spending time with you, it's because he wants to be there. Don't question your appeal. Simply accept his company and enjoy yourself. That is what your come-out is all about."

"You're right. I will do exactly as you recommend," she said, lifting her chin firmly. "Now, do you think Viscount Stanford would admire this?" Jeanette held up a turban in a brilliant shade of purple, with an enormous feather plume attached to the side.

"It is exactly the thing if you never want to see Drew again," pronounced Elizabeth solemnly.

Jeanette giggled, and put the turban aside. "But what of you and Lord Roarke?" she asked.

"There's nothing between Roarke and me except the need to find out what happened to Helen."

"But you make the most handsome couple. Surely there could be more to it than that if you find him innocent."

"I cannot think that far ahead," said Elizabeth. "Roarke and I are on very poor terms at the moment. He's hiding something from me, and I can't forgive him for his silence. Instead of helping, he spends his time flattering me as if I were a green girl. He doesn't understand it will take more than a few sweet words to distract me from my purpose."

"Lord Roarke doesn't seem to be the kind of man who would accept a woman putting herself in danger."

"There's no doubt he's overly protective," complained Elizabeth. "But I am not his to protect. Besides, I cannot help thinking his concern is merely another way to keep me from my investigation, and I won't allow that."

"I would not dare cross Lord Roarke," said Jeanette.

"That is what he would like to hear from me, but he never will," vowed Elizabeth. "I intend to keep searching until I find the answers to why Helen was killed, and who did it."

"Perhaps you're being too harsh with him; perhaps he's innocent and is merely concerned for your safety after all."

"I don't want to talk about it anymore," grumbled Elizabeth. "Or else I might buy that purple turban to frighten him away."

Nothing more serious than the shade of ribbons was discussed during the rest of their shopping trip, nor during their visit to Gunter's.

Elizabeth was still thinking of their conversation about Roarke the next morning. While there was a possibility he was more than an innocent victim, nothing substantial had yet been proven. And if he knew more than he said, he had no obligation to reveal it to her. After all, he probably suspected she was holding back information. She now regretted her harsh words. She had allowed emotion to enter where logic should have prevailed. Elizabeth would contrive to meet Roarke again, and attempt to keep them on speaking terms until her investigation was completed.

It was still early, so Elizabeth gathered up her sketchbook, called Betsy, and went to Hyde Park again. Roarke rode every morning, and she hoped to be in time to encounter him. Taking her place on the same bench she had occupied on their last meeting, she watched the path for Roarke. Once again, Betsy found a young man to distract her, leaving Elizabeth to her thoughts. She was so totally immersed in her musing that she nearly missed Roarke. He had spied her sitting on the bench and had drawn his stallion to a halt, ready to take a path leading away from her.

Elizabeth looked up, raising a hand to catch his attention. Roarke hesitated, then cautiously approached, remaining on his mount.

"Won't you sit with me awhile?" Elizabeth asked, her heart suddenly pounding. She did not know what she would do if he refused.

"It was my distinct impression the other evening that you wanted nothing more to do with someone with such an unsavory reputation as I have acquired, my lady."

"Perhaps I overreacted," Elizabeth confessed, looking at him from under her lashes, wondering whether he would accept such a weak explanation.

Roarke remained silent, staring at her quizzically.

When it was apparent he was not going to speak, Elizabeth took a deep breath. "All right. I did overreact. I was angry, but surely you cannot hold that against me."

"Why not?" he asked abruptly.

"Because I have learned nothing of what happened to Helen, and it's driving me to behave in ways I would never consider in the normal course of events," she answered sharply.

"I know nothing either," he replied swiftly. "Although I do not expect you to believe me."

"I don't know what to believe," she confessed. "One moment I was enjoying a sunny September day, and the next morning I awaken to sleet pounding against the windowpanes, and to receive the news that my best friend and stepmother was dead. No one has yet offered a convincing explanation. I am merely patted on the head and told to forget all about it, to go about my business as usual. Well, I can't forget it, nor can I continue my life until I find out what happened!" She blinked rapidly; she would not shed a tear in front of him. She would not have him think her so weak.

Roarke swung down from his mount and approached the bench. He hesitated a moment, then took a seat beside her. "You hide it so well, I sometimes forget what you have been through. Losing four months out of your life, then finding out what had happened would be a great shock to anyone. No matter what others may tell you, Elizabeth, you are a strong woman, and you will come through this affair stronger than ever. I admire you for that, even though you do not welcome my regard."

Elizabeth remained near tears. How she would have cherished his words if they had been spoken while Helen was still alive. She could have accepted them at face value then, and held them close to her heart. But the situation was altogether different now: Helen was dead, and Roarke acted as if he had something to hide.

Elizabeth regained her composure and reached for her sketch-book. "I have some drawings. I wonder if you would look at them?"

Roarke gave her a curious glance, but accepted the sketchbook and studied the drawings that Elizabeth had made of him with Helen. He remained silent, his face expressionless, as he turned the pages. "It seems your talent is improving," he said, handing the book back to her.

"Is it? Are these drawings true?" Elizabeth held her breath waiting for him to reply.

"If I denied it, would you believe me?" he asked, watching her with a mocking smile on his face. "I thought not," he said, when she remained silent.

"I suppose it will do no harm to tell you. Perhaps it will even help ease your mind a bit," Roarke continued. "It's true that Helen and I knew one another before she came to London for the Season. In fact, we had met in Paris some time before."

"Why didn't either of you say anything?"

"I suppose because it didn't seem important that anyone else know. I had been at the Congress of Vienna, and stopped in Paris for a few days. I met Helen, and we were friends from the start. Her aunt had recently died, and even though she had been expecting it, she was still quite sad. I decided to create a diversion for her so she wouldn't give in to her grief. We spent some enjoyable days taking in the sights. Then, when it was time to leave, we took the same ship home. Upon reaching England, we both went our separate ways."

"But that wasn't all," said Elizabeth, thinking of her drawings.

"No, it wasn't. We met again, quite by accident, in Bath. Helen was amusing company, so we saw one another there. I introduced her around so she wouldn't be lonely once I left. After a fortnight,

THE HEADSTRONG HEART 99

I traveled on to my estate to conduct some business which had been waiting since my trip to the continent."

"What about the drawings of the village and the house? I didn't recognize them and couldn't place their location."

"Helen and I spent several days at Dover when we landed. We went for a drive one afternoon and explored a small village. It was nothing more than a destination to entertain us in an area sadly lacking in diversions. I'm not certain, but the drawings could be of that village. You're the one with the gift of second sight; you should be able to tell *me* where they are," he said smiling.

Elizabeth was so grateful he was teasing her again that she took no umbrage at his remark. "I don't think my gift is so well developed yet that I could make such a prediction."

"Don't worry, you're making great strides. You'll soon be as proficient as any of your ancestors."

Elizabeth hoped he was right. She was torn between believing him and questioning him further. If she could rely upon her talent, she would have no need to risk his anger again. Until she heard from Mr. Warren, Elizabeth decided to accept what Roarke said without inquiring further.

"Have your drawings revealed anything else?"

"There is one," said Elizabeth, thinking of the two images of Helen. She began turning the pages in her sketchbook. Perhaps Roarke would have an explanation for the puzzling drawing. She turned a page and the drawing of Helen as a young girl appeared. A vision flashed in her mind, and she immediately turned to a new page in the sketchbook. Her fingers flew as she quickly sketched another drawing of the young Helen. Only this time Helen was dressed differently, and was playing in a garden. Elizabeth was distracted by a small noise from Roarke. She glanced at him and found him staring transfixed at the drawing.

"What is it?" she asked.

"I've just remembered an appointment. I hope you'll pardon my abrupt departure, but I'm already late."

"Of course," she murmured, but he was already on his horse riding away.

Elizabeth did not believe Roarke's excuse. She studied the drawing she had just completed, but found nothing alarming about it. What could have caused Roarke to react as he had?

Elizabeth's brow wrinkled as she stared again at the girl in the garden. Then she saw something familiar: a morning glory climbed the garden wall, spilling over in a profusion of blooms. The garden in which the young Helen played, looked the same as the one which had shown up in her drawings of Roarke and Helen. But what did it mean?

The answer came in a flash. The drawing had to have come from Roarke's thoughts. The girl was wearing a different dress than in the other sketch, so it had to mean he had seen her. Possibly the house was Helen's home, and they had visited after they had reached London. If so, Roarke could have seen a childhood portrait of Helen, and could have been thinking of it strongly enough that she had received the vision. Or perhaps Roarke had known Helen longer than he admitted; perhaps he had known her since childhood.

No matter what, he would have been startled to see his thoughts immediately appear on paper before him. It would be rather disconcerting, thought Elizabeth, to find that someone could see into your mind. But if her surmises were correct, why couldn't Roarke tell her about a visit to Helen's home? What could be so secretive in such an innocent act? And if he had known Helen since childhood, why would he hide it?

Elizabeth's thoughts were in a spin. She was certain she had discovered something, but didn't know what it all meant. Drat her second sight! It wasn't such a gift if it only told her half of what she needed to know. And to top off the whole morning, Roarke had been in such a rush to escape, she hadn't had the opportunity to show him the picture of the two Helens.

The next morning, one of Elizabeth's worries was solved. She received a letter from her father explaining he must stay at the estate a little longer, unless she would like him to return. Elizabeth was relieved to have additional time to continue her investigation. She sat down and quickly wrote Lord Carvey that she was doing very well indeed, and that he must stay as long as he deemed it necessary.

She had just finished the letter when George and Sylvia Wendell were announced.

"Have you received an invitation to Lord and Lady Marston's card party?" Sylvia asked, as soon as they were seated.

"Yes, it came this morning."

"You must come with us then. Their parties are always so enjoyable."

"Please do," added George.

"I would be delighted," replied Elizabeth.

"And your dear father, how is he?" inquired Sylvia.

"He's in the country at the moment, and I'm hoping that will do him some good. Although he has lost some weight since Helen's death, and does not sleep as well as he might, I don't think his health has been seriously affected. However, I worry that he dwells on Helen. I know it hasn't been long enough for him to forget, and I don't expect him to; but he's ordered Helen's room to be left as it was the last time she was in it. I fear he's setting up a shrine to her, and might grow even more despondent as time passes."

"How sad," said Sylvia. "As soon as his mourning is over, we must urge him to come out with us. In the meantime, perhaps we could visit when he returns and attempt to restore his spirit."

"I'm certain he would delight in seeing you," replied Elizabeth.

"We must go," said George. "We have other calls to pay this morning. We shall call for you a little after ten for the Marstons' card party."

"I'll be ready," Elizabeth said, walking with them to the drawing room door.

The house seemed far too quiet after the Wendells left. Louisa was out for the day, so Elizabeth called Betsy and went out to indulge in a few hours of needless shopping.

* * *

Lord Chesterfield had invited Louisa and Elizabeth to join him at the theater that evening. The earl was a widower, and had been an admirer of Louisa's for several years now. But as far as Elizabeth knew, Louisa had never given him a sign she was interested in deepening their relationship. Elizabeth realized it was Lord Chesterfield who had been dancing with Louisa in the drawing she had done earlier, and she hoped her aunt would not decide too late that she and the earl would suit.

After they were seated in their box at the Royal Opera House, Elizabeth glanced at the occupants of the other boxes. She nodded at several acquaintances, and then her gaze fell on Roarke. He was with the woman who had been gazing up at him so adoringly at the Sherbornes' ball. His head was bent near hers, and the two were oblivious of the others around them as they conversed. At that moment, Roarke looked up and stared directly at Elizabeth. His glance lingered only a moment, for the woman by his side once again claimed his attention.

Elizabeth focused her gaze on the stage. It was none of her business how, or with whom, Roarke chose to spend his time. If he found such a short, curved version of a woman attractive, it meant nothing to Elizabeth except that she had been totally oblivious to his appalling lack of taste.

Elizabeth's eyes remained fixed on the stage during the remainder of the evening; yet she did not join in the conversation afterwards for she could remember nothing at all about the play.

Elizabeth was still taking extraordinary care not to think about Roarke the next morning, when the Bow Street Runner was shown into her sitting room.

"Mr. Warren, I'm so happy you returned today. I am in dire need of distraction and news."

"I may be able to offer you a little of each, my lady." At her indication, he seated himself across from her and gave his report.

"I have learned that Lord Roarke and Lady Carvey were on the continent at the same time, and that they returned to England on the same ship."

"I know," replied Elizabeth, and hastened to tell him Roarke had identified the drawings, and explained what was behind them.

"So, he isn't attempting to hide their acquaintance any longer?"

"I don't know whether he would have admitted it without seeing the pictures, but I think the drawings shocked him into it. He is also aware of my family's reputation for accuracy with our second sight." Elizabeth almost giggled at Warren's raised eyebrows. "Don't tell me you continue to doubt it, Mr. Warren?"

"Not after my experience with your cousin, my lady. But you must admit, it does take some getting used to."

"I've no doubt it does," agreed Elizabeth. "Now, did you find out any more while you were away?"

"One thing that is very interesting. Lord Roarke disappeared during the same time as Lady Carvey. It's true they left Dover separately, but then I lost both their trails shortly thereafter. I could find no trace of either of them until a fortnight later. That's when Lady Carvey showed up in Bath, and Lord Roarke appeared at his country home. He stayed a sennight, then traveled onto Bath, where he once again met up with Lady Carvey."

Circumstances were mounting that Roarke and Helen were more than close friends, and Elizabeth's heart dropped. She had been hoping she could prove Roarke innocent, but now it seemed she was solidifying the case against him.

"While I was showing Lord Roarke my drawings of Paris and Bath, he saw some of my other sketches," said Elizabeth. "When he observed the drawing of Lady Carvey as a young girl, I received a strong vision. I immediately put it to paper, and it was another drawing of Lady Carvey that was nearly the same, except she was dressed differently. I could also tell that she was in the garden of the house I had drawn earlier. Roarke watched as I drew it and reacted quite strangely; he left immediately."

"Perhaps it was the shock of seeing his thoughts on paper," suggested Warren.

"I considered that," replied Elizabeth. "I even thought that perhaps he and Lady Carvey had visited her childhood home, and he had seen a portrait of her as a young girl. Or that they had known one another as children." She looked at Warren, hoping he would agree with her.

"I could do no more than guess," he said, shrugging his shoulders. "I kept an eye out for the house in every village I came to, but I saw nothing like it."

"I don't know what to do next," sighed Elizabeth.

"If I may make a suggestion, my lady?"

"Please do."

"I've been observing Lord Roarke's schedule. It seems that once a week he leaves town for the day. The first time it happened, the streets were particularly crowded, and I lost him. I put another runner on him while I was away, and it appears to be a habit with him to disappear once a week."

"You don't know where he goes?"

"I haven't attempted to follow him yet. I wanted to see whether you desired me to do so."

Elizabeth thought for a moment, wondering whether she had the right to pry into Roarke's private life so thoroughly. Her answer was simple: she needed to find out all she could in order to solve Helen's death. If Roarke would only be forthright with her, all this subterfuge would be unnecessary, and his private life could remain his own. Since he had chosen to tell her only what was forced from him, she could do nothing else than to continue her investigation into his movements until she proved him either innocent or guilty.

"Follow him," she said quickly, before she could change her mind.

"I'll keep him under strict observation, my lady. You may be sure I won't lose him again," Warren vowed.

"You'll report to me straight away?"

"As soon as I return," he promised.

Elizabeth attempted to keep her mind occupied after the Bow Street Runner left. It could be days until she heard from him again, and she could not just sit waiting. When George and Sylvia

Wendell called that afternoon, Elizabeth welcomed them effusively.

"We've called to see if you are free to join us for a ride in Hyde Park," said Sylvia, after the initial greetings were over.

"Of course I am. Let me get my bonnet and gloves. I'm afraid I can't match that lovely confection you're wearing though," said Elizabeth, glancing enviously at the cerulean blue satin bonnet lined with white and decorated with an ostrich plume. "Oh, but there is a smudge on it. Come upstairs with me and Betsy will clean it."

Sylvia appeared in some confusion. "There's no need," she objected. "My maid will handle it when I reach home. I'm sure it won't be noticed until then."

"Nonsense," replied Elizabeth. "Betsy can do it in a trice. Now come along."

George and Sylvia exchanged a worried glance before Sylvia followed Elizabeth through the door and up the stairs. Once they were upstairs, Betsy took Sylvia's bonnet and examined it closely.

"This will only take a moment," she said, leaving the room.

By the time Elizabeth donned her bonnet, pelisse, and gloves, Betsy had returned with Sylvia's bonnet.

"There it is, miss. As good as new."

"Thank you, Betsy," said Sylvia, as she stood in front of the mirror arranging the bonnet on her dark curls. "We should go now. George doesn't like the cattle to stand too long."

It was perfect weather and all the *ton* was out to see and be seen. Carriages were often forced to a standstill as occupants paused to greet friends.

"How are your inquiries going?" asked George in one of the conversational lulls.

Elizabeth knew he could only mean one thing, but she wondered how he had found out she was investigating Helen's death. "What inquiries?"

"I'm sorry," said George. "Perhaps I shouldn't have mentioned it, but Roarke didn't tell me it was confidential. He said the two of you were looking into the . . . er . . . incident that occurred last September."

George looked extremely uncomfortable. Perhaps he realized too late that a lovely day in the park was not the place to discuss death. Elizabeth took pity on him.

"There's nothing secret about what either of us are doing," she said, stretching the truth a bit. "It's merely something one doesn't announce to the public."

"I've often wondered what part of England Helen came from," commented Sylvia. "I knew some Northrups when I was a child."

"I only know she said she was from York, but never mentioned anything more," said Elizabeth.

"Perhaps that is something you and Roarke can discover," added George.

"Perhaps," said Elizabeth, then changed the subject.

It was odd that George and Sylvia were taking such an interest in her investigation into Helen's death, thought Elizabeth, as she climbed the stairs to her room after leaving the Wendells. It seemed they should be attempting to take her mind from it rather than asking questions that would bring it to her attention again. But some people were fascinated with the darker aspects of life, and perhaps the Wendells were part of that group.

She entered her room, where Betsy was waiting to assist her in changing clothes.

"Would you have believed it, my lady?" asked Betsy, helping her out of her pelisse.

Elizabeth had no idea what her maid meant. "Would I have believed what, Betsy?"

"That Miss Wendell colors her hair," she divulged with relish.

"How, for the love of heaven, would you know that?"

"Why the smudge on her bonnet, my lady. There was more on the inside of the bonnet. I've seen enough in my time to know hair dye when I see it. When you first put it on, it rubs off easier. I wonder if she has gray hair and is trying to hide it? I had an aunt who turned off gray when she was only a girl. It runs in some families, so they say."

"I don't know, Betsy. But I hope you'll keep what you've learned to yourself. It's not for us to reveal such a thing to anyone else. It would probably embarrass Miss Wendell, and I wouldn't want that to happen."

"Of course not, my lady. I won't say a word to nobody else."

Elizabeth puzzled over why Sylvia thought it necessary to dye her hair. But it could be as Betsy mentioned; that her hair was turning gray at an inordinately early age. Elizabeth shrugged. No matter, it was none of her business. She would do as she advised Betsy and keep it to herself.

Seven

Elizabeth was being torn apart by her warring emotions. On the one hand, she was forced to doubt Roarke's innocence in Helen's murder. Her father, the one person she could trust above all others, believed Roarke to be guilty. And if she looked at the evidence dispassionately, it plainly proved that Roarke had been alone with Helen and had the best opportunity to bring about her death.

On the other hand, Elizabeth's heart told her that the man she had known for the past few years was incapable of carrying out such a cruel act. At the same time, she must consider that her belief in Roarke might be wishful thinking, fueled by her previous tendre for him. Previous? It was time for her to at least admit to herself that she still yearned for him. How she would resolve this conflict, she did not know.

In the meantime, she must still see Roarke at various entertainments. Her heart twisted painfully in her chest when she saw him with other women, and there were many who ignored the ugly rumors swirling around about Helen's death to have a chance at catching the interest of a handsome, wealthy, and titled gentleman, such as Roarke.

Lately, it seemed Roarke had made it a point to approach her at every opportunity. She wondered at his motivation. Was he truly interested in her, or was he merely keeping an eye on her, hoping to ascertain what she was learning about Helen? If the mystery was solved, and Roarke was proven innocent, would he disappear from her life? Dare she fan the small flame of hope burning in her heart that Roarke pursued her for herself alone?

It was still morning, and already Elizabeth's mind was numb from considering her problems. She called for Betsy and began dressing. A walk to the bookstore would clear her mind and a novel would allow her to lose herself in someone else's life for a short time.

Elizabeth had selected her books and was on her way out of the store when she saw Roarke enter with Lady Anne Wardell. It was no secret Lady Anne was intent upon finding a husband before the Season was out. She had been on the marriage mart for several years, and her father was determined she would not embarrass him by remaining single any longer.

Elizabeth darted between two shelves to avoid being seen, but wasn't at all certain that Roarke hadn't caught sight of her. She was feigning interest in a volume she had plucked at random from the shelves when he found her.

"I thought I had seen you, but you moved so quickly, I was left wondering."

"Well, as you can see, here I am," she said brightly and inanely, hating herself for responding like some green girl right out of the schoolroom.

"It seems you've found something to keep you occupied," he observed, nodding at her books.

"I'm rereading Jane Austen. I admire her work."

"Will you be reading Miss Austen this evening?" he asked, a teasing light in his eyes.

"No," she answered stiffly, not volunteering any additional information.

"Perhaps I shall see you later then," he said, again giving her an opportunity to reveal her destination that evening.

"I'm certain you'll be far too involved with Lady Anne to concern yourself with me." As soon as the words were out of her mouth, Elizabeth wished she could recall them.

"I'm positive I could manage to dance at least one dance or, at the very least, to engage in a few minutes of polite conversation."

He was bamming her and she knew it, but she could not help but respond. "I wouldn't want to take you away from Lady Anne for even a short time. In fact, I feel guilty keeping you from her side now." Elizabeth moved to step past him, but he blocked her.

"Please don't be conscious-stricken. I'm convinced Lady Anne isn't suffering at all. There's always some gentleman or another who is happy to keep her company."

"Then all the more reason for you to get back to her," said Elizabeth, wondering how mere words could hurt so much.

"I would much rather be here with you," he said, all teasing gone from his voice. His dark eyes bore into hers, holding her prisoner by their intentness. "Don't you know that by now, Elizabeth? Has your father completely poisoned you against me?"

"My father has said nothing that isn't the truth," she shot back, her temper flaring.

"Your father is only a man like me, prone to make a mistake now and then."

Elizabeth remained stubbornly silent.

"The truth can be viewed from many sides," he continued. "I don't want to fight with you, Elizabeth. I'm weary of fighting."

Elizabeth's anger quickly died. Roarke did sound tired. If he were innocent, she thought, what a misery his life must have been since last September. He had been forced to carry a shield between himself and the rest of society to protect himself from the stares and slurs cast at him.

"I don't wish to argue either," she agreed, "but it is becoming a natural occurrence whenever we meet."

"At one time we got along together quite well, didn't we?" he asked.

Elizabeth smiled, remembering their better times. "Very well indeed," she agreed.

"I want it to be that way again," he said, reaching out to brush his finger down the side of her cheek.

Roarke's touch set Elizabeth's skin on fire. Her back was against the bookshelves and she could not move away; but then, she found she had no desire to do so. Her eyes drifted closed as his finger traced the outline of her lips. She forgot the people a few feet away, and thought only of his touch.

"Elizabeth," he murmured. "Open your eyes."

Her lids felt so heavy she wondered whether she could do as

he requested, but after several attempts her eyes slowly opened. He was so close he filled her entire vision.

"I want to kiss you, Elizabeth." His finger still rested against her lips.

This time she did not fight the urge. She kissed him, reaching out with the tip of her tongue to taste him. She heard his indrawn breath, then watched as his face took on a fierce expression of desire. She had never been this close to raw passion before, and it fascinated her.

Loud voices from the other side of the shelf broke the spell between them.

"This won't do," said Roarke, drawing away from her. "We're fortunate you chose a particularly dull section of books when you hid from me."

"I wasn't hiding," protested Elizabeth, still dazed from their encounter.

Roarke let her objection pass without comment. "Will you tell me where you will be this evening?"

"I . . . I don't remember," she stammered out.

Roarke stepped even farther away, his expression guarded. "As you wish," he said stiffly, turning away.

"No, wait . . ." she protested, but he was already gone. Elizabeth had genuinely forgotten what event she was attending that evening. Roarke's touch had wiped every thought from her mind except a desire to remain with him forever. What must he think of her now?

It was difficult for Roarke to smile and make conversation with Lady Anne during the time it took to reach her home. He had met her outside the bookstore and before he knew it had agreed to take her home after she made her selections. Roarke had known from the first time they met that Lady Anne was pursuing him, but he didn't feel threatened, for he had learned not to be caught in a compromising situation with any young lady.

When he first saw Elizabeth in the bookstore, he thought if it had not been for Lady Anne, he could have escorted Elizabeth home. However, after his encounter with Elizabeth, he was glad to have an attractive woman waiting for him. That Elizabeth would not reveal her plans merely to avoid him hurt Roarke more than any other cut he had received. It would be difficult, but he would do as he had done with the others. He would continue as if nothing had happened, and the devil take them all!

Elizabeth had no heart for going out that evening. The only thing that drove her was the possibility of seeing Roarke and explaining the events which had occurred in the bookstore that afternoon. She paid particular attention to her appearance that evening, wearing a new gown she had received just the day before. When Elizabeth reached the soiree, she took up a place near the door where she could observe everyone who entered. She waited patiently until the receiving line had dispersed, but Roarke did not put in an appearance.

"Do you remember any of the other invitations we received for this evening?" she asked Louisa.

"Some. Why do you ask?"

"I'm restless tonight. I'd like to attend a few others," Elizabeth replied.

"Why ever would you want to do that?" asked Louisa. "It's unseasonably cool this evening to be traipsing about from house to house."

"I see Drew is here. If you don't feel up to it, I'll ask him to escort me."

Louisa studied her closely. "There's more to it than being restless, isn't there? What are you up to, Elizabeth?"

Elizabeth blushed beneath her regard, and awareness lit Louisa's eyes. "It's Roarke, isn't it? He isn't here, and you're going to attempt to find him. Good Lord, Elizabeth! Don't you have more pride than to be running after the man accused of killing your stepmother?"

"You don't understand," said Elizabeth, attempting to explain. "We had a misunderstanding this afternoon."

We'd Like to Invite You to Subscribe to Zebra's Regency Romance Book Club and Give You a Gift of 4 Free Books as Your Introduction! (Worth $19.96!)

If you're a Regency lover, imagine the joy of getting **4 FREE Zebra Regency Romances** and then the chance to have the lovely stories delivered to your home each month at the lowest prices available! Well, that's our offer to you and here's how you benefit by becoming a Zebra Home Subscription Service subscriber:

- **4 FREE Introductory Regency Romances are delivered to your doorst**
- **4 BRAND NEW Regencies are then delivered each month (usually befor they're available in bookstores)**
- **Subscribers save almost $4.00 every month**
- **Home delivery is always FREE**
- **You also receive a FREE monthly newsletter, *Zebra/ Pinnacle Roman News* which features author profiles, contests, subscriber benefits, bo previews and more**
- **No risks or obligations...in other words you can cancel whenever you wish with no questions asked**

Join the thousands of readers who enjoy the savings and convenience offered to Regency Romance subscribers. After your initial introductory shipment, you receive 4 brand-new Zebra Regency Romances each month to examine for 10 days. Then, if you decide to keep the books, you'll pay the preferred subscriber's price of just $4.00 per title. That's only $16.00 for all 4 books and there's never an extra charge for shipping and handling.

It's a no-lose proposition, so return the FREE BOOK CERTIFICATE today!

Say Yes to 4 Free Books!
Complete and return the order card to receive this $19.96 value, ABSOLUTELY FREE!

(If the certificate is missing below, write to:)
Zebra Home Subscription Service, Inc.,
120 Brighton Road, P.O. Box 5214, Clifton, New Jersey 07015-5214
or call TOLL-FREE 1-888-345-BOOK

FREE BOOK CERTIFICATE

YES! Please rush me 4 Zebra Regency Romances without cost or obligation. I understand that each month thereafter I will be able to preview 4 brand-new Regency Romances FREE for 10 days. Then, if I should decide to keep them, I will pay the money-saving preferred subscriber's price of just $16.00 for all 4...that's a savings of almost $4 off the publisher's price with no additional charge for shipping and handling. I may return any shipment within 10 days and owe nothing, and I may cancel this subscription at any time. My 4 FREE books will be mine to keep in any case.

Name _____

Address _____ Apt. _____

City _____ State ____ Zip ____

Telephone (___) _____

Signature _____ RG0499
(If under 18, parent or guardian must sign.)

We'd Like to Invite You to Subscribe to Zebra's Regency Romance Book Club and Give You a Gift of 4 Free Books as Your Introduction! (Worth $19.96!)

If you're a Regency lover, imagine the joy of getting **4 FREE Zebra Regency Romances** and then the chance to have the lovely stories delivered to your home each month at the lowest prices available! Well, that's our offer to you and here's how you benefit by becoming a Zebra Home Subscription Service subscriber:

- **4 FREE Introductory Regency Romances are delivered to your doorst**
- **4 BRAND NEW Regencies are then delivered each month (usually befor they're available in bookstores)**
- **Subscribers save almost $4.00 every month**
- **Home delivery is always FREE**
- **You also receive a FREE monthly newsletter, *Zebra/ Pinnacle Roman News* which features author profiles, contests, subscriber benefits, bo previews and more**
- No risks or obligations...in other words you can cancel whenever you wish with no questions asked

Join the thousands of readers who enjoy the savings and convenience offered to Regency Romance subscribers. After your initial introductory shipment, you receive 4 brand-new Zebra Regency Romances each month to examine for 10 days. Then, if you decide to keep the books, you'll pay the preferred subscriber's price of just $4.00 per title. That's only $16.00 for all 4 books and there's never an extra charge for shipping and handling.

It's a no-lose proposition, so return the FREE BOOK CERTIFICATE today!

Say Yes to 4 Free Books!
Complete and return the order card to receive this $19.96 value, ABSOLUTELY FREE!

(If the certificate is missing below, write to:)
Zebra Home Subscription Service, Inc.,
120 Brighton Road, P.O. Box 5214, Clifton, New Jersey 07015-5214
or call TOLL-FREE 1-888-345-BOOK

FREE BOOK CERTIFICATE

YES! Please rush me 4 Zebra Regency Romances without cost or obligation. I understand that each month thereafter I will be able to preview 4 brand-new Regency Romances FREE for 10 days. Then, if I should decide to keep them, I will pay the money-saving preferred subscriber's price of just $16.00 for all 4...that's a savings of almost $4 off the publisher's price with no additional charge for shipping and handling. I may return any shipment within 10 days and owe nothing, and I may cancel this subscription at any time. My 4 FREE books will be mine to keep in any case.

Name _____

Address_____ Apt. _____

City _____ State_____ Zip _____

Telephone ( )_____

Signature _____ RG0499
(If under 18, parent or guardian must sign.)

Terms and prices subject to change. Orders subject to acceptance by Zebra Home Subscription Service, Inc.

ZEBRA HOME SUBSCRIPTION SERVICE, INC.

120 BRIGHTON ROAD

P.O. BOX 5214

CLIFTON, NEW JERSEY 07015-5214

AFFIX
STAMP
HERE

"Your father does not acknowledge the man exists; you should not even be speaking to him long enough to allow for a misunderstanding. I've gone along with you because of your illness and the shock of Helen's death, but I cannot approve of you searching out Roarke at public events."

"But you've indicated you don't believe he's guilty," said Elizabeth.

"That's a long way from endorsing him as a companion suitable for you. I cannot believe that whatever has caused this start is important enough to put your reputation at risk."

"I would only be responding to invitations we had received," reasoned Elizabeth.

"I don't think you need bother," replied Louisa, nodding toward the door.

Elizabeth turned, and saw Roarke, along with George and Sylvia, entering the room.

"I warn you, Elizabeth, don't make a fool of yourself. I can tolerate most anything but that." Louisa stalked away, leaving Elizabeth standing alone, wondering how best to approach Roarke.

Roarke was immediately aware of Elizabeth when he stepped through the door. She did not turn away when she saw him, but stood staring in his direction. She could look all she wanted as far as he was concerned. He would not conveniently keep out of her sight, nor would he beg her to dance with him again.

"Oh, look," cried Sylvia. "There's Elizabeth. Shall we join her?"

"I don't think . . ." began Roarke.

"You must come with us," said Sylvia. "I refuse to abandon you." Taking his arm, she pulled him along until they reached Elizabeth.

"Sylvia, George, how good to see you," she said. "Roarke, did you find what you wanted at the bookstore this afternoon?"

"I thought I had, but I was mistaken," he said, barely keeping the bitterness out of his voice.

"You should have let me select a volume for you. Sometimes a different perspective helps," replied Elizabeth, holding his gaze.

Roarke wondered what game she was playing now. He would see how far she was willing to go. "Perhaps you would join me on a stroll around the room and enlighten me on what is au courant in literature. If you will excuse us," he said to the Wendells, as he held out his arm to Elizabeth.

Elizabeth placed her hand on his arm with barely a tremble. She dared not look in her aunt's direction, but accompanied Roarke through the crowd toward the refreshment room. "Would you care for something to drink?" he asked.

"Perhaps a cup of punch would be welcome," she agreed.

As soon as she had cup in hand, she wasted no time in getting to the reason for her forwardness. "Roarke, I want to explain something."

"I believe the subject was books," he replied smoothly.

"You know that isn't the issue here."

"After the ups and downs of our encounters, I have absolutely no idea what is or is not the issue. One moment you are cold as the driven snow, the next you seem more . . . ," he paused, his gaze going for a moment to her lips. "More amiable."

"I realize my actions haven't been consistent, but you must understand how confused I am. My loyalty to my father pulls me one way, while—"

"While what?" he asked, his tone a little gentler than before. "While I pull you another?"

"Perhaps," she said, all of a sudden reluctant to express her feelings. "There's something you must understand about today."

"I think I understood perfectly well. You did not want to tell me where you would be in order to avoid my presence. Well, it seems your ploy didn't work, for here we are despite all you did."

"That wasn't what I meant," she said quickly, eager to explain. "When you asked where I would be this evening, and I said I didn't know, I was telling the truth. At the time, I couldn't think. I was so . . . so . . ." She stammered to a stop, then tried again. "You were so close that I—" Overwhelmed by the inability to express herself without appearing the fool, Elizabeth gave up the attempt.

Understanding, and a great deal of relief, washed over Roarke. He looked around the refreshment room. They were virtually alone at this time of the evening, and the few people who were partaking of refreshments were paying them no heed. "Do you want to try it again and see if you are still so. . . . ?" he asked, a devilish smile on his face.

"Don't you dare," she hissed, stepping back. "Louisa has already rung a peal over my head because of my determination to find you this evening and explain. I will not suffer through it again."

"Louisa is nowhere around," Roarke replied lazily, following Elizabeth as she moved backward until she came up against the wall.

"Roarke, please," she begged.

He took pity on her and stepped back. "Lady Elizabeth, shall we consider this afternoon an unfortunate misunderstanding and seal our bargain with a dance?"

"I would like that above all things," she replied gratefully.

Elizabeth was still living on the memories of her dance with Roarke the next day when Mr. Warren called. She had nearly completely succumbed to Roarke's charm, and prayed that a miracle would clear his name. She was heartened by the smile on the Bow Street Runner's face.

"You have good news?"

Warren was unable to hide his pleasure at his achievement. "I was successful in my venture," he said.

Elizabeth had an irrational urge to refuse to hear what Mr. Warren had to say, and to call off the search entirely. She did not want to know about Roarke, particularly if it concerned Helen. Quickly, she pulled her scattered senses together. She had begun the inquiry into Helen's death, and she could not abandon it.

"You know where Roarke has been disappearing to all this time?" she asked, still feeling as if she were betraying him.

"I do, and I think you'll find it interesting," claimed Warren. "He's been visiting a house near a small village, a few hours outside of London. The same village and the identical house that is depicted in your drawings," he announced with an air of satisfaction.

Elizabeth abruptly sat down in the nearest chair.

"Are you all right, my lady?" asked Warren, thinking he should have broken the news in a more gentle manner.

"Yes," she assured him, as her thoughts raced, choosing and discarding reasons for Roarke's actions. "I was merely surprised at your news. Were you able to observe anything else?"

"I wasn't close enough to see who opened the door, but Lord Roarke stayed several hours, and I assume had luncheon while he was there. He left early enough to reach town before nightfall. It's a small village and I didn't want to arouse suspicion, but I went into the local inn for a bite to eat. I was able to learn that a widow and her child lived in the house."

Elizabeth could not believe what she was hearing. Was it possible that Roarke had a mistress and a child tucked away in a house outside of London? Could he and Helen have truly been no more than friends? Or did it merely mean that Roarke kept a mistress in addition to Helen? Elizabeth knew a little about men's proclivities toward keeping a mistress, but she was outraged that Roarke, the man she had long admired, would do such a thing. All the good will she had felt the evening before dissipated in the harsh reality of Mr. Warren's disclosures.

Anger hardened both her heart and her voice. "I want you to continue watching Lord Roarke," she said. "When he goes to the cottage again, *I* will follow him this time."

"My lady, I don't think it would be wise for you to do so."

"Perhaps not; perhaps nothing I am doing is wise, but I am nevertheless going to see it through. When he leaves town, you will contact me. If you don't wish to accompany me, I shall go by myself."

"I couldn't allow you to do that," said Warren. He did not approve of what she was doing, but could not let her go alone. "Besides, I know the way, and there will be no need to follow closely behind."

* * *

"I can't believe it," said Jeanette, an accompanying expression of disbelief on her face.

Elizabeth had needed to share what she had learned with someone else. After Louisa's reaction the night before, she could not expect a sympathetic ear from her, so she had turned to Jeanette. She knew that her friend would never break the confidences she entrusted to her.

"I'm afraid it's true," replied Elizabeth. "There's no reason Mr. Warren would play false with me. But I'm going to see for myself the next time Roarke visits the house."

"Won't that be dangerous?" Jeanette asked.

"No matter what he's done, I can't accept that Roarke would hurt me."

"Someone hit you, and killed Helen. Your father believes it was Lord Roarke," pointed out Jeanette.

"You might feel better to know that Mr. Warren insisted on going with me. I shall be perfectly safe," Elizabeth assured her friend.

"Would you allow me to come along?"

"Oh, Jeanette. Thank you, but your parents would never forgive me if I put you in any kind of danger."

"You just told me you would be safe."

"And I will, but what if something else happens? A carriage accident, for instance. How could I explain that? Your offer means a great deal to me, but I must do this alone."

"Will you tell me what happened?"

"As soon as I return," Elizabeth promised.

A few days later, the butler brought Elizabeth a note. After she lifted the letter from the silver tray and read it, she felt a slight pang of doubt as to whether she was doing the right thing. Then she rose from the chair and straightened her shoulders, bolstering her courage by repeating to herself that what she did was all for Helen.

She climbed the stairs a little more slowly than normal. "Betsy," she called, as she entered her room. "Bring my bonnet and gloves; we are going out."

"Shopping?" asked the maid, always ready to look at all the merchandise the shops had to offer.

"No, we are going on a short trip; a place just outside of town. And, Betsy, when we return, you will forget everything you see or hear. You will even forget we ever went. Do you understand?"

Betsy was overwhelmed by being involved in such a secret event. "Oh, yes, my lady," she replied, her eyes wide with excitement. "I swear I'll never mention it to a soul."

"I've written a note to Aunt Louisa explaining our absence. Please take it to her room so she will get it as soon as she returns. I don't want her raising an alarm if we are gone overly long."

Betsy took the paper and hurried out of the room. She was back in an instant, helping Elizabeth to ready herself for the journey.

Mr. Warren was waiting in the hall when Elizabeth and Betsy descended the stairs. "I have a carriage waiting. I thought it better if we used one that would not be easily recognized."

"Thank you, Mr. Warren. I hadn't considered that."

Elizabeth settled herself on one seat, while Mr. Warren and Betsy sat across from her. She barely contained a smile when she saw Betsy glancing surreptitiously at the Runner, and wondered whether Warren was as oblivious to her abigail as he seemed. If she was any judge, Betsy would find a way to draw his attention before their journey was over.

"I've given orders to the driver," Warren said. "He knows our destination, and will let me know if we approach another carriage. Although it isn't likely, we wouldn't want to pass Lord Roarke on the road."

Conversation was minimal as the coach rolled through London. Then the traffic lessened as they took a road leading east out of the city. They were far enough behind Lord Roarke that they never encountered so much as the dust of his passing.

* * *

The village was small, but pleasant. The largest building by far was the inn which served as a temporary sanctuary for visitors and was bustling with activity when they pulled into the yard. Their arrival was nothing to be commented upon, since a fully laden coach was discharging its passengers for a quick meal at the inn.

Elizabeth and Warren left Betsy to enjoy a cup of tea, while they ostensibly went out for a short walk. Warren guided Elizabeth toward a house at the end of the village. Elizabeth immediately recognized it as the one in her drawing. They continued past the property, when suddenly Elizabeth came to a stop. The garden wall was visible, and vining over it were the morning glories that were also in her drawings. Perhaps she was mistaken about a mistress. This could be Helen's home, and Roarke could be visiting what family she had left. For once, Elizabeth prayed she was wrong with her first assumptions.

"Do you want to go back to the inn?" asked Warren.

"No. We'll wait until Lord Roarke departs. We might catch a glimpse of who is occupying the house."

"Perhaps we should withdraw a bit, so he won't see us when he leaves," suggested Warren.

Elizabeth agreed, but when Roarke left the house some time later, it was apparent that they had not needed to take the extra precautions in concealing themselves. When the earl stepped through the door there was a smile on his face, and his hair was slightly disheveled. He made his way to his carriage and climbed inside without sparing so much as a glance for the world about him.

Elizabeth released a sigh she did not realize she was holding. Roarke had not looked as if he had just paid a call to an aged relative of Helen's; he looked as if he had spent several hours in a completely pleasurable pursuit.

"What would you like to do now?" asked Warren.

Elizabeth found she was unable to rationally consider her next step. "I don't know," she replied. "Perhaps we had better return to town for the present."

Relief washed over Warren as he escorted her back to the inn.

* * *

As usual, Roarke had enjoyed his visit to the house he kept outside London but, during the drive back to town, his thoughts were consumed by Elizabeth. When he had first seen her after her illness, her appearance had astonished him. She had been the total antithesis of the woman he had last seen lying so still and pale. She had regained her health, and looked a great deal different from the Elizabeth he remembered. If it had not been for her blue eyes, he might not have believed she was the girl he once knew. That is until she spoke, then he recognized the gentleness of her voice. But even that was different, for they had exchanged fiery words on several occasions now. Roarke smiled. He liked Elizabeth all the more for standing up to him, however much he disliked what she had implied. Yes, Lady Elizabeth Leighton was lovely, a diamond of the first water, and he was convinced no matter how she responded to him, there was a part of her that still suspected him of murder.

Oh, she had not come right out and said it, but it was apparent from her questions she was convinced he knew more than he was telling about Helen's death. And it was true, he did know more about Helen, but not about why she had died. Roarke had made promises to Helen, which he was honor-bond to keep, and for a moment—while thinking of Elizabeth—he begrudged being bound by that vow. If he could explain, perhaps Elizabeth would believe in his innocence, and consider him in a more favorable light.

He did not like arguing with Elizabeth; he would much rather be enjoying more pleasurable pursuits with the lady. But each time he thought the time was right, she would bring out those damnable drawings of hers and demand an explanation. Her family might consider their talent a gift, but he was beginning to question it.

Then there was the matter of her reading his mind. Could she really see what he was thinking? He had accepted the truth of her gift, just as he had accepted her mother's and her cousin's. But now that he was the object of her talent, he did not know whether he liked it or not. The new drawing that she referred to as the young Helen had appeared beneath her fingers in the exact detail that he had thought of a moment earlier. The likeness was extraordinary, and made him wonder what else she could pull from his mind and put to paper. Roarke shrugged his shoulders and shifted uncomfortably on the leather seat. He was not at all pleased with the thought. A man could think any number of things that were unfit for a lady's ears, or mind, or whatever part of Elizabeth it was that assimilated his thoughts.

Then she had seen him with Lady Anne Wardell the other evening at the theater. He had been irritated with Elizabeth when he had accepted the invitation to join the party, and had regretted it almost immediately. Although Lady Anne was an appealing young lady with large dark eyes and a voluptuous body, she did not hold the allure for Roarke that Elizabeth did.

Yesterday had been a day of emotional highs and lows. Their meeting at the bookstore had left him yearning to leave England forever, and be rid of this damnable curse that seemed to hang over him. But last night, when Elizabeth attempted to explain why she had been unable to tell him where she would be, made up for the anguish he had suffered that day. They had danced again and she fit in his arms as if she had been created for that very thing. For the first time since Helen's death, he had been content.

There had been enough pain in all their lives. He wanted Elizabeth's goodwill again. He was surprised to find it meant more to him than he had thought possible. As Roarke entered the outskirts of London, he hoped someday soon things might be right with them again.

Elizabeth was silent on the way home. The tender moments she and Roarke had shared were now sullied beyond repair by what she had seen in the village. Perhaps it was better not to know what was going on, she reasoned, as she remembered Roarke leaving the house in the country. The expression on his face left no doubt to even the most casual observer that he had greatly enjoyed his visit. She did not need to use her imagination to any great extent to conclude what might have taken place while he was inside. Her face burned at the thought.

If what she had discovered became common knowledge, it would be surmised that Helen had found out about Roarke's other lover and had fought with him until, in a fit of rage, he had smothered her. At the time, Elizabeth could think of nothing to dispute the theory.

Elizabeth was pleased she was engaged to attend a musical with the Wendells that evening; it left her little time to agonize over Roarke. She dressed quickly and met Drew in the drawing room. He had agreed to join Elizabeth and the Wendells to even up the numbers.

"I'm happy you could come with us this evening," said Elizabeth, wondering whether he held any feelings toward Sylvia. She could understand it if he did, for Sylvia was a diverting companion, but she could not help but think of Jeanette having her heart broken if it were true.

"More than pleased to be seen with two lovely ladies," replied Drew.

"You are always the flatterer," she said, tapping him on the arm with her fan. "The Wendells should be here anytime now. Would you like something to drink?"

"I'll wait until they arrive."

"It sounds as if that has just occurred," said Elizabeth, turning toward the door as Marston showed the Wendells into the room.

"Elizabeth, I must prevail upon your kindness," said Sylvia. "I tore my gown getting out of the carriage. If I could have the privacy of a room for a moment, I'll repair it."

"I'll have Betsy show you upstairs. She will fix it in a trice."

"Thank you so much." A few moments later, Sylvia followed Betsy from the room.

"Shall we have something to drink while we wait?" asked Elizabeth, signaling the butler to bring a tray of refreshments to the drawing room.

Drew and George were engaged in a conversation about hunting, when Elizabeth excused herself to check on Sylvia. She ascended the stairs and turned down the hall toward her suite of rooms, when she noticed a light beneath Helen's door. A chill ran down her spine, raising bumps on her arm. As far as she knew, no one was ever in the rooms except the maids when they were cleaning.

She cautiously eased open the door and peeped inside. A gasp of shock escaped from between her lips, and she felt light-headed, as Helen turned toward her in the dim candlelight. The apparition moved toward her; Elizabeth's breath shortened, then turned into a nervous laugh when she recognized Sylvia.

The paleness of her face must have been apparent, for Sylvia reached out to her.

"Are you all right?" she asked solicitously.

"I'm fine now. Your similarity to Helen merely startled me, particularly since no one comes into her room any longer."

"I'm sorry. I never thought about it," said Sylvia. "I shouldn't have intruded, I know, but the door was ajar, and when I saw this lovely Aubusson carpet, I had to view it at a closer range. I'm looking for a new carpet for my bedroom, and this is exactly what I want."

"Helen had excellent taste," commented Elizabeth, as she closed the door.

"I hope I haven't disturbed you," said Sylvia, apologizing again. "George is always complaining that I should think before I act."

"There was no harm done," said Elizabeth. "If you like, I'll give you the direction of the merchant where Helen selected the carpet."

"I would appreciate that above all things," replied Sylvia. "I suppose we should hurry downstairs, George is not good at waiting."

"I wouldn't worry. He and Drew are absorbed in outdoing one another with hunting stories."

Smiling, the women retraced their steps to join the men and soon left for the evening's entertainment.

Eight

The musical was ready to begin when Elizabeth's party arrived. They quickly located seats near the back, but not before Elizabeth saw Jeanette turn her head to observe them as they entered. She hoped the young woman would not be too disappointed to see Drew and Sylvia together.

At the first break in the music, Elizabeth made her way toward Jeanette.

"You look lovely in that gown," she said, upon greeting Jeanette. The young woman wore a pink confection which was a perfect foil for her coloring.

"It doesn't seem to be doing much good," complained Jeanette. "Viscount Stanford is here with Sylvia Wendell, not me."

"He merely came along to make up the numbers," Elizabeth assured her. "Really as a favor to me. I certainly don't consider myself as being with George, and I'm sure Drew doesn't believe he has an obligation to Sylvia."

"Do you think so?"

"I know so," confirmed Elizabeth. "You must come and speak to him. Let him see you in that gown."

"I will, but first tell me whether you've learned anything more. Have you been to the house that Lord Roarke visited yet?"

Elizabeth did not want to talk about it so soon, but she had promised Jeanette. "We followed him today. It was just as Mr. Warren said. Roarke spent several hours inside, and when he came out, he was too distracted to even notice us."

"I'm so sorry. I had been hoping it was all a mistake," commiserated Jeanette.

"If only it had been."

"What will you do now?" asked Jeanette.

"I don't know. I need to think on it before I make a decision. But that isn't something I can do tonight, so come with me and we'll hunt Drew down and make him notice you."

"I couldn't," demurred Jeanette.

"Well, I can," said Elizabeth, taking a firm hold on her arm and guiding her across the room to where Drew was standing.

The evening had not turned out to be a disaster after all, thought Elizabeth as she returned home some hours later. If only this business with Roarke wasn't hanging over her head, she would have thoroughly enjoyed herself. But, nevertheless, the music had been better than usual, and Drew's company always kept her on an even keel.

Jeanette had joined them for the last of the performances, and Elizabeth had arranged matters so she was seated by Drew. He had been attentive to the young woman for the remainder of the evening, and if the expression on Jeanette's face meant anything, she would have happy dreams this evening. If only Elizabeth's dreams could be half as sweet.

"I didn't expect to see you up so early," commented Louisa, as Elizabeth joined her at the breakfast table the next morning. Louisa had remained piqued by her niece's behavior toward Roarke, but she cared for her too much to carry the argument any farther.

"I could stay abed no longer," said Elizabeth, picking up a plate.

Louisa watched while Elizabeth chose buttered eggs, ham, and a muffin from the sideboard. It was doubtful her niece was becoming ill again if she intended to eat such a hearty breakfast. "Is anything specific bothering you?" she asked.

Elizabeth took a seat before speaking. While Louisa was an unusually tolerant person, she might not react well to Elizabeth following Roarke to his mistress's house. However, keeping it a secret from Louisa would be even worse. Making up her mind to confess, Elizabeth hesitated, attempting to choose the right way to begin.

"There's something you should know."

"I don't like the sound of this," said Louisa warily, laying down her fork and knife, and giving Elizabeth her full attention.

"You will probably like it less by the time I finish," warned Elizabeth.

Louisa took a sip of tea to fortify herself. "Then get it over with," she demanded.

"First, I need to tell you what the Runner found out about Roarke and Helen." Elizabeth quickly explained that Mr. Warren's findings supported what she had drawn.

"That Helen and Roarke knew one another before coming to London is not surprising," said Louisa. "Your drawings confirm that much."

"But there was a village and a house we couldn't identify, if you will remember."

"I remember it well. There were morning glories trailing over the wall."

"Blue morning glories," clarified Elizabeth, while buttering her muffin.

"How do you know that?" questioned Louisa. "Your drawing wasn't in colors."

"Mr. Warren's investigation has located the village and the house," revealed Elizabeth.

"What! And you have kept me hanging; tell me," urged Louisa.

Elizabeth swallowed a bit of muffin. "You're always advising me to eat first and talk later," she teased.

"Now is not the time to begin following my recommendations. Put down that muffin and tell me what you've discovered," she demanded.

Elizabeth told her aunt about the Runner following Roarke and what he had found out at the village inn.

"You mean Roarke is keeping a mistress and a child near London?" Louisa's face showed complete surprise at Elizabeth's revelation. "I cannot believe it. Of course, many men have mistresses tucked away, but I cannot believe Roarke would be so careless as to have an illegitimate child," protested Louisa.

"It's true, for I have seen it myself," confessed Elizabeth.

"What? How in the name of heaven could you have seen it?"

Elizabeth remained silent.

"Oh, no, Elizabeth. Tell me it isn't so. You didn't call on her, did you?"

"No, I only followed him to the village. Mr. Warren and Betsy accompanied me, so it was very proper."

"How can following a man to his mistress's home be proper? You are fortunate no one saw you, or you would never be welcome in any drawing room in London."

"You make too much of it, Aunt."

"And your illness must have made you forget the strictures of society."

"No one will learn of it," Elizabeth reassured her.

"With Betsy along? That girl knows every bit of gossip making the rounds. Do you think she will keep this to herself?"

"She knows if she does not she will be looking for a new position without a reference," replied Elizabeth.

"We shall see," said Louisa skeptically. Though she did not approve of what Elizabeth had done, she could not suppress her curiosity. "Just what did you observe on your spying excursion?"

"Not much," Elizabeth admitted. "I saw the house, of course, but Roarke had already gone inside. We waited until he departed, and I must say that he looked very pleased with himself upon his departure."

"And well he should be, I would think," shot back Louisa. "I do not even want to consider what your father will do if he ever finds out about this escapade."

"Then what I am going to do next would upset him beyond all bearing," said Elizabeth, determined to get everything out in the open at one time.

"What are you planning now?" asked Louisa cautiously.

"I am going to meet the woman who lives in the house," announced Elizabeth.

Elizabeth expected a dressing down from her aunt, but she

was to be disappointed, for Louisa only looked at her long and hard before speaking.

"You are going to ruin yourself," she predicted. "Beyond that, I cannot say. If either your father or Roarke finds out about what you're planning, I pity you."

"I will be exceedingly careful. She will never even know my real name," explained Elizabeth.

"Don't do this," begged Louisa.

"Don't you see I must? I will never be able to rest until I know what happened to Helen, and this is all a part of it; I know it is. If I'm ruined while finding out the truth, then that's the chance I must take."

Louisa placed her napkin beside her plate and rose. "I can see there's no use talking to you."

"Don't be angry, Aunt Louisa," pleaded Elizabeth.

"I don't know what to be," Louisa confessed, "but I cannot be happy." Without another word she turned and left the room.

Elizabeth sat at the table, deep in thought, while the food on her plate became cold and unappetizing. She reviewed everything she knew and questioned what she was planning. Her answer was still the same: she must continue on her course. Leaving the breakfast room, she collected her drawing materials and made her way to the small sitting room, which afforded her the most privacy.

Roarke had avoided the crush of society's entertainments in favor of his club for the past few evenings. Since their last meeting, he had been preoccupied thinking of Elizabeth. In his vulnerable state, he was leery of her; wondering whether she would draw an image from his thoughts as she had done once before. He smiled, recalling how he had spent his time practicing keeping his mind blank so he could safely see Elizabeth again. It was far harder to accomplish than he had at first thought. It was boring to consider nothing at all; stray thoughts kept popping up when he least expected them. Most of them were of Elizabeth, and it would never do to allow her access to them.

However, he had grown weary of male companionship. Men, for the most part, were dreary creatures. Dressing in black or equally dull colors, conversing about politics and horses, and content to sit hour after hour at the green baize table losing and winning until their pockets were to let and their heads clouded with liquor.

Roarke enjoyed the different hues of the ladies' gowns, the variety of their tone of voice and, of course, their willingness to listen to him no matter what the subject. Whether they were empty-headed chatterboxes or the bluest blue-stocking, he was unfailingly polite to them all. Which—until Helen's murder—had made him a favorite among the ladies.

He missed being able to walk into a room and be welcome in any group he chose. But he would not accept being frozen out. He was the Earl of Roarke, heir apparent to the Duke of Granville, an old and honorable family which had a reputation for tenacity. He would prove that he had nothing to do with Helen's death, no matter how long it took.

His thoughts had consumed him, and his carriage came to a halt sooner than he expected. Richard Melbourne, Lord Rathersby, had stood by Roarke during the entire affair of Helen's death, and Roarke looked forward to seeing his friend again tonight. Lord and Lady Rathersby were still in the receiving line when Roarke arrived, and both greeted him warmly.

"I'll find you as soon as I'm free," said Rathersby.

Roarke nodded and moved into the ballroom. He wondered at his ability to locate Elizabeth so quickly. She should have been lost amidst all the men's black evening clothes, but his eyes were immediately drawn to her. He took back every thought he had about black being a dull color. Elizabeth made it seem altogether different. Ignoring the tradition of black bombazine or crape, she chose the richest of material, which shimmered beneath the chandeliers. Her gowns seemed to invite a man to touch, ignite a need to feel that opulence beneath his fingers, to caress an arm or a shoulder or a back as the softness flowed beneath his hand.

Roarke smiled wryly. He wondered whether he would be welcome to follow his inclination, then hoped his practice blocking his thoughts proved successful when Elizabeth was near. Her modesty would never allow her to draw what he was thinking; but if she had no control over her visions, she would certainly be shocked at what her hand put to paper.

Elizabeth knew Roarke was in the room before she ever saw him. Perhaps it was part of her evolving gift, but whatever it was she was happy to he warned of his presence. He did not approach her, and she wondered whether he was attempting to avoid any risk of scandal or whether he merely had no desire to speak with her.

Jeanette was standing by her side, and had also noticed Roarke enter the room. "Do you mean to ignore him all evening?" she asked curiously.

"I don't know. Since we've been speaking, he might think it odd if I don't at least acknowledge him. But I don't know whether I can carry on a casual conversation with him after what I have learned."

"Perhaps letting nature take its course would be the best," suggested Jeanette. "If fate should bring you together, then I'm certain both of you will act reasonably. If it does not, then you will have been saved the worry of what to do."

Elizabeth laughed. "Jeanette, sometimes I think you are the wisest person on earth."

Jeanette blushed at her compliment. "I only wish Drew were here," she said, changing the subject.

"He was promised to dinner with a friend of his, but he will be here later. Don't despair. I'm certain you'll be dancing with him before long."

"Do you really think so?" asked Jeanette, her cheeks pink and her eyes bright.

"I would place a wager on it. I will repeat your advice: let nature takes it course."

"I think it is about to," whispered Jeanette, looking over Elizabeth's shoulder.

"Oh, is Drew already here?" Elizabeth asked, turning in the direction of Jeanette's gaze.

"No, but Lord Roarke is," said Jeanette from behind her.

* * *

Even though Elizabeth and Roarke had straightened out their misunderstanding the last time they met, they had shared only the one dance. It was then Roarke decided he should beware of Elizabeth until he could keep his thoughts to himself. Now, he faced the possibility that Elizabeth might have interpreted his absence as a lack of desire for her company. Roarke was determined to disperse that notion before it became a problem.

"Miss Gardiner," Roarke said, bowing to Jeanette. "And Lady Elizabeth." He took her hand and raised it to his lips.

Elizabeth was held speechless while he bowed over her hand. The last time she had seen Roarke, he was leaving the house in the village. An icicle had formed in the center of her chest as she observed the satisfied smile on his face. She would not allow him to see the pain he had unknowingly brought to her life, nor could she permit him to know she was aware of his closely guarded secret.

Elizabeth summoned up her brightest smile. "Lord Roarke, I'm surprised to see you."

"And why is that, my lady?"

"We've been bereft of your company for several days and thought perhaps you were out of town."

"I had some business to attend to, but I'm flattered you missed me," he replied, smiling as the color rose in her cheeks. His charm would win her over yet.

Elizabeth's anger made her cheeks burn. How could he come straight from his mistress, and think she would welcome his flummery? It was too bad she couldn't tell him exactly what she thought of his honor, but she must wait until the time was right.

"I've come to see whether you have the next dance free."

Elizabeth could think of no reason to refuse him without ruining the rapport they had built the last time they had met. "I . . ."

"There is no Mr. Kimball lurking around to claim you, is there? I would deplore spending another evening with such a callow youth; but if it means a dance with you, I would willingly sacrifice it."

"No, there is no one," Elizabeth admitted, realizing she had no choice but to dance with the womanizer.

Roarke was not one to let chance pass him by. "Good, the music is ready to begin. Please excuse us," he said to Jeanette, as he swept Elizabeth onto the highly polished wood floor.

Roarke took Elizabeth into his arms, and thought holding her felt as good as he remembered. Which was astonishing, considering things seldom measured up to his dreams. The material beneath his hand on her slim waist was as seductive as he had imagined. Her scent wrapped itself around him and, as much as he tried, he could not completely control his thoughts. It was good she was not carrying her sketchbook.

Elizabeth felt the heat of his thoughts. Her fingers itched with the urge to draw, and she rubbed them against his jacket. She wanted to rush from the room and put whatever was struggling to escape on paper, but she would surely be marked a madwoman if she followed her inclination and left Roarke standing on the floor.

Roarke felt her fingers moving on his shoulder and wondered whether it was an attempt at a small caress or merely nervousness. They had not spoken since they had begun dancing. She was staring over his shoulder, not lifting her eyes to his. Her lips were pressed firmly together, as if she were completing an unwelcome task, and her expression was as bland as milk toast.

"Our silences were once companionable," Roarke remarked, determined to force her into speech.

She looked at him; studying him closely as if an answer would be written somewhere on his countenance. "There was nothing standing between us then," she replied, thinking of the woman and child hidden away outside of London.

To be fair, she had to admit that many of the men she talked and danced with probably had mistresses tucked away somewhere, and that did not diminish her enjoyment of their company. She did not judge them, and it in no way affected her thoughts of them. Perhaps that was wrong, but society accepted it; and she was not brave enough to begin a one-woman campaign against it.

Now, faced with Roarke's mistress and child, the power of her reaction surprised even herself. It was far stronger than when she first learned that Roarke and Helen might have been more than friends.

She needed to know more about the woman and child, then she could confront Roarke with a reason for a deadly argument with Helen. People had died for far less.

Until then, she would be as congenial as possible to Roarke. She did not want to arouse his suspicions until she had all the proof she needed.

Roarke had begun speaking again, and Elizabeth forced herself to attend to his words.

"You've made it clear you have doubts about me," he said, deciding to be blunt, "but I thought we were on much better footing the last time we met."

"We were," agreed Elizabeth.

"Then what happened between now and then to bring us to this point?"

"There's nothing wrong, my lord. I'm merely blue-deviled today. Dr. James says it isn't unusual to feel this way after an illness such as mine."

"I'm sorry you've had to experience such a difficult time. I wish there was some way I could make it right."

"But there isn't," Elizabeth replied in a practical voice. "Time will help, or so I'm told."

"In the meantime, I will do my best to help replace those memories with something more pleasant." He smiled, and she marveled at his brazen behavior.

"At least our conversation is thwarting the gossip-mongers who are watching us."

Elizabeth did not look around the room, but she knew he was right. There were probably many eyes avidly watching them, waiting to grab on the slightest change in their expression. "It is gossip enough that I am even dancing with you," she admitted, with a small smile.

"That's much better," he replied, happy to see a bit of her spirit returning. "Just why do you dance with me when it's so obvious everyone disapproves?"

"My father's away, and Louisa will not lock me in my room as he surely would."

Roarke threw his head back and laughed out loud, which garnered a few raised eyebrows. He ignored them and continued to smile down at Elizabeth, greatly amused.

"You do not need to do it up too brown," she complained.

"I am sincerely diverted," replied Roarke. "Not many ladies would be quite so forthcoming." Then his amusement died. "I am fully aware of what your father thinks of me, but it's unjustified, and someday I intend to prove it."

"Why didn't you tell me you had visited me when I was ill?" Elizabeth asked suddenly.

The question took him by surprise. "Because I didn't know whether your family had told you," he confessed. "I thought you would mention it if they had. Until then I decided to keep it to myself."

"Louisa told me about it a few days ago. I wish they hadn't allowed anyone to see me in that condition."

Roarke nearly stopped dancing, then resumed the tempo of his steps. "Elizabeth, you were ill. It is common knowledge that people are not at their best when they are in poor health. I didn't expect you to be dressed to the nines. I will admit that the seriousness of your illness disconcerted me. I was greatly worried about you, but I was never repelled by your appearance."

Roarke seemed a little less guarded, and Elizabeth decided to attempt to gain more information from him. "You say you want to prove your innocence, but you are keeping something from me."

"I'm telling you everything I can at the moment," he said, praying her drawings had revealed nothing about him.

Elizabeth thought again of the woman and child who waited for him each week, and doubted whether he would ever confess their existence to her. She wanted to draw away from him, but the dance floor was too crowded, and he was holding her too tightly. She felt the heat of his thoughts again, the accompanying itch in her fingers, and decided she must escape his arms before she did something foolish.

"It's unbearable stuffy in here," she complained.

"Follow me," he said, guiding her toward the edge of the dance floor. "I know just the place." He led her through the door and out into the hallway. Turning left he made his way to a medium-sized picture gallery.

"How did you know this was here?" asked Elizabeth.

"Rathersby's a good friend of mine. I've visited here often. Since you've taken up your drawing again, I thought you might be interested."

"There are some wonderful paintings here."

"A good collection," he agreed. "The family have been collecting for years. This is small in comparison to the gallery at his country estate. We must see it one day."

"I would enjoy that above all things," said Elizabeth, forgetting for a moment to whom she was speaking.

"Is your drawing progressing?" he asked casually.

"Yes, I'm quite pleased with the results I'm getting. They've proven amazingly accurate; but there is one I've yet to interpret." She explained the drawing of the two Helens as best she could.

Roarke was truly baffled by her description. "Perhaps if I could see it, I might be better able to guess its meaning."

"I'm sure I'll see you in the park again," Elizabeth said. "I'll show it to you then."

Roarke felt her slipping away and could not let her go so easily. "What is wrong, Elizabeth? We haven't been as close as we were before your illness, but there's something more tonight. Tell me so I can make it right. We don't need any further misunderstanding between us."

"I don't believe it's a misunderstanding at all," replied Elizabeth before thinking about what she might reveal.

"You've heard something more about Helen's death, haven't you?"

"No, not about her death," Elizabeth answered with a defiant look.

"Then about me," he said. She did not speak, but the color rose fast and furious to her face. "What is it?" His voice was soft and gentle, laced with a great deal of sadness.

"I can't speak of it now," she said.

"Can't or won't?"

"Perhaps both," she answered honestly.

He drew close to her. "Elizabeth, why can't you trust me?"

She was in his arms before she knew it, and his lips claimed hers with a certainty that left no room for doubt that he expected her surrender. All speculations of murder, and mistresses, were swept from her mind, as she clung to his broad shoulders. Once again, his thoughts burned into her mind, and her fingers itched with the desire to draw what was being communicated to them. Deprived of that occupation, they laced themselves around Roarke's neck and buried themselves in the black hair that curled over his collar.

This is what had seduced both Helen and Roarke's mistress, thought Elizabeth, as he drew her even closer. But it did not matter, for she couldn't gather enough resentment to overcome the sweet hot warmth that enfolded her.

Roarke's lips left hers, trailing kisses to her ear, where his husky voice murmured words she would remember later with burning cheeks. Then, suddenly, her gown had slipped lower, and her breath left her body as he placed the first kiss on her bare shoulder.

A small sound escaped Elizabeth. Roarke did not know whether it was fear or desire, but he could not stop pressing his lips to the soft silkiness of her skin. She made no move to push him away, but clung to him, her slender body pressed tightly to his. The pulse in her throat beat wildly, and he placed a tender kiss on it before returning to claim her lips.

A weakness spread through Elizabeth, but Roarke held her tight enough to keep her from sinking to the polished floor of the gallery. His lips were more demanding the second time he kissed her. His hands molded her to the hard length of his body until they were as one in the shadows of the room. All thought of anything else but the two of them was fast disappearing from Elizabeth's mind; there was no one left in her world but Roarke, no one she wanted but Roarke. A strangled sound of need came from her as she attempted to press closer. In answer, Roarke's hand moved to her hips, pulling her tighter.

The urge to continue what they had begun was strong, but Roarke was forced to his senses by the realization that a picture gallery in his friend's home was no place to be making love, particularly to Elizabeth. They were fortunate no one had chanced upon them before now.

Roarke raised his lips from Elizabeth's, placing small kisses on her mouth and face, allowing their passion to cool slowly. Finally, her trembling stopped and her breathing returned to normal once again, but she still stayed within the shelter of his arms, her head resting on his broad shoulder.

When he spoke, his voice was husky with desire. "I won't apologize, even though I should." His breath stirred the curls near her ear, and she shivered slightly.

"You would spoil my image of you if you did," she replied, a smile in her voice.

"And that is?"

"You are a pirate at heart. You take whatever you want."

"That isn't completely true. I've wanted to kiss you like that for some time now, and have restrained myself admirably."

Elizabeth felt a flash of joy at his words, but good sense quickly reasserted itself. She had to wonder whether he had said the same thing to Helen and to the woman who occupied the house outside of London. Too much had happened for her to accept what he said at face value.

"I wish you had continued your restraint."

Elizabeth's comment hit him with the force of a cold spring rain. "You responded to me passionately," he declared roughly. "Don't try to convince me you didn't enjoy it as much as I did. I'm not a young, inexperienced cub."

"I would never accuse you of being that," she shot back.

"Don't attempt to change the subject," he warned, tightening his arms about her. "I won't allow you to fool yourself as well as me. You enjoyed our kiss, and if we had been private, there might have been more."

"If you hadn't taken me by surprise, there wouldn't have been a kiss."

"Elizabeth," he chided, gently tipping her chin up with his finger. "You should never prevaricate, particularly with me." His lips brushed hers as he spoke. "Tell me you don't like this. Move away, I won't stop you." His lips covered her possessively, but his hands did not touch her. She stood a moment until he deepened the kiss, then she moved against him, pressing close. Roarke's arms enclosed her again. When he raised his head a gleam of satisfaction showed in his eyes.

Elizabeth's confusion was apparent, but Roarke did not tease her about it. He was charmed that she was experiencing desire for the first time in his arms and found herself wanting more.

"You do not play fairly," she complained.

"I am not playing at all."

"You are too experienced. I would probably respond the same way to any gentleman."

"If you believe that, then you're even more inexperienced than I thought."

"I'm not going to argue with something so trivial—"

"Trivial!" he burst out in disbelief.

"I'm going to completely forget about it. I hope you do, too. Now, I must get back. I'm sure Aunt Louisa is wondering where I've disappeared to."

"Then you should straighten your gown," he bit out between gritted teeth. "I'm certain you don't want to display your charms to the entire *ton*."

Elizabeth adjusted the bodice of her gown, feeling exceedingly awkward with Roarke watching. They did not exchange another word as she turned and left the gallery.

Nine

Elizabeth did not go home to a night of restful sleep. She paced her room, and thought of what had happened with Roarke. As she reminisced, she picked up her sketchbook and drew the thoughts that had plagued her since he had first taken her in his arms. The scenes that formed on the paper took her breath away, and made her turn hot with embarrassment even though no one else was in the room with her. Elizabeth doubted she would ever be able to look at Roarke again after drawing these pictures.

As the first light of day appeared, Elizabeth faced the truth. Roarke had been right; she had enjoyed his kiss. And if he hadn't stopped, they might have ended up engaging in the activities her drawings portrayed.

Her own father thought him guilty of killing Helen; he kept a mistress and child, yet she could not deny the desire that rose in her each time she thought of their kiss. What kind of a person was she?

The question still hounded her as she went downstairs later in the day. She had missed breakfast and lunch, and craved a cup of tea. Asking Marston to have a tea tray sent in, she went into the drawing room, to find Louisa already there.

"I wondered whether you were going to sleep the day away," Louisa commented. "You must have worn yourself out dancing, to stay abed so late."

"It was quite tiring," agreed Elizabeth.

"You are a little pale; perhaps you should rest this evening."

"I am feeling a bit fatigued."

"Then it's an early dinner and bed for you. Your father would never forgive me if I allowed you to become ill again. Betsy can brew a pot of chamomile tea for you to drink, and you should get a good night's rest."

Elizabeth doubted whether chamomile tea would rid her of what was keeping her from sleep, but she had no time to voice her doubts before Marston appeared in the doorway.

"Viscount Stanford," announced the butler, as Drew entered the room.

"Drew, how good to see you," said Louisa, smiling as he bowed over her hand. "I don't want to appear rude, but you will excuse me I'm sure. I have an engagement this afternoon, and have only just enough time to arrive without being late. I'll tell Marston to make certain there's more than tea on the tray when it arrives. I'll be back before dinner," she said to Elizabeth, before disappearing through the door.

"I missed you last evening," said Elizabeth, once Drew had taken a chair.

"Got there late. Saw you from across the room, but you were gone before I could make my way to you."

"It became too hot and crowded," she said, rubbing her hands over the sketchbook laying on her lap.

"Saw Jeanette," she explained."

Without appearing to realize it, Elizabeth began drawing.

"Said you were dancing with Roarke and then she lost sight of you."

"We were viewing the Rathersbys' gallery," replied Elizabeth.

Drew's eyebrows rose a fraction. "Was it crowded there as well?"

"No. Roarke is a good friend of the family, and knew the location of the gallery. We were the only ones there."

"Thinking a man's guilty of murder, then going off to a deserted gallery with him?"

"Drew! What are you suggesting?"

"Nothing, except you're taking a lot of chances with a man you don't trust."

"The only way I can find out about Roarke is to get to know him as he is now. If that puts me in danger then it's little enough to find out if he's guilty of harming Helen." Elizabeth's conscience gave her a tweak. She had not been thinking of Helen at all last night when Roarke was kissing her.

Her hand stopped moving, and she looked down at her drawing. Drew was in the middle of the page, with Jeanette on one side of him, and Alura Courtney on the other. Alura was the sister-in-law of Elizabeth's cousin, Claire Kingsley. Drew was a close friend of the family and had held a tendre for Alura even before she left the schoolroom.

"What do you make of this?" Elizabeth asked, handing the sketchbook to him.

A frown settled on his face as he studied the drawing.

"Do you care for each of them equally?"

"Don't know. Haven't seen Alura for months. She's on a trip with Ransley and Claire."

"I thought she cared for you," said Elizabeth.

"She treats me like a big brother," complained Drew. "And I won't grovel."

"Jeanette certainly doesn't think of you as a brother."

"I know," he replied, his features softening. "Don't intend to raise her hopes, but can't seem to stay away from her."

"And when Alura comes back?" prodded Elizabeth.

"Don't know. She could be betrothed by then."

"Or she could be ready to settle down with you."

Drew looked at the sketch again, the worry lines growing deeper on his face.

Elizabeth removed the sketchbook from his fingers and tore the sheet from the book. "Think about it," she advised, handing the sketch to him.

"Refreshments, just when we need them most," she said, as Marston entered the room followed by a footman carrying a tray. "Perhaps we'll both have something stronger than tea."

Elizabeth's encounter with Roarke forced her to admit she needed to decide on his guilt or innocence as quickly as possible. She spent the next several days concentrating on her drawings while waiting to see whether Mr. Warren could find out anything further about Roarke's relationship with Helen. Focusing her attention on the day of the murder, she repeatedly drew the scenes leading up to her injury, hoping to jog her memory.

During one of her drawing sessions, she looked down to see that she had drawn herself coming through a door. She did not remember drawing it, but there it was. In the sketch, Elizabeth's hand was clutched to her breast, while she stared wide-eyed at something out of view. But what captured Elizabeth's attention in the sketch was the dark shadow behind the partially opened door behind her. It was no more than a hazy figure, with no clear features, but it was there nevertheless. Excitement filled Elizabeth. Roarke could not have been lying in bed with Helen and hiding behind the door at the same time. There *had* been another person in the room that day, and she was drawing closer to finding out just who that was.

Caution tempered her elation when she thought of what her father had said. He had suggested that perhaps her memory was not what it should be after her long illness. That perhaps she had overheard a discussion and her mind had absorbed it. When she awakened, she had taken what she had heard as her own memory. If that were the case, then the figure behind the door might be Roarke, or possibly he had an accomplice. But for what reason? That was the question that lay beneath all of Elizabeth's inquiries.

If Roarke had arranged to meet Helen, and if they had been lovers and were quarreling, why would he have murdered her? Many affairs were terminated without harm to either party. Even if Helen had discovered Roarke had another mistress tucked away in a village outside of town, Elizabeth found it hard to accept that he would think it necessary to silence Helen forever. After all, Helen was the one who was married and would suffer the most from their affair being revealed. Despite her speculation, Elizabeth still had found no proof that would exonerate Roarke. The next morning Elizabeth sent a message to Mr. Warren, asking him to call that afternoon.

* * *

"Have you discovered anything new?" she asked, as soon as Warren arrived. "Not yet, my lady, but I'm continuing to search."

"I would like your escort again, Mr. Warren," she said.

"And what would be our destination?" he inquired amicably.

"I would like to go back to the house we visited last week. This time on a day other than the one on which Lord Roarke visits." she requested politely.

"You would be risking a great deal by returning, my lady. If we visit too often it is bound to attract notice, particularly in such a small village."

"We need draw little notice, Mr. Warren. I merely intend to pay a short visit to the occupants of the house."

Mr. Warren did not attempt to hide his surprise. "You realize you're running the risk of Lord Roarke's finding out you were there?"

"I think I can hide the true intent of my visit. It will be so innocuous he will probably never hear of it, and if he does, he will never suspect it of being any more than it appears."

"I don't suppose there is anything I can say to dissuade you?"

Elizabeth smiled at him. She was becoming quite fond of Mr. Warren, and would miss him when this was all over. "Nothing at all. Keep an eye on Roarke. We will make our trip on the day after he visits. That should ensure we will not meet him."

Roarke had thought of little else but Elizabeth since the night he had held her in his arms and kissed her. He had been amused when she attempted to refuse to admit she had enjoyed the kiss, and even vigorously participated in it. But his pleasure in the event had quickly ebbed as he realized Elizabeth would continue to reject him until he was cleared of Helen's death. No one would ever know the hurt and humiliation he suffered when people he considered his friends turned away from him. He had never thought Elizabeth would be one of them.

He slammed his hand down on his desk in frustration. He had men working on Helen's background, attempting to find out where she came from before he met her in Paris, but they had been unable to trace her. Roarke needed to locate her home. The man she was running from might still be living there; and Roarke wanted to have a nice, long conversation with him. He would hire more men if necessary, but the mystery of Helen's past must be solved.

In the meantime, if Elizabeth thought he was going to meekly step aside and permit another man to come between them, she was wrong. He would not allow her to forget the feelings that simmered between them. He would remind her of them each time they met, and he would arrange to make that happen very often indeed.

Elizabeth was silent as Betsy helped her into her gown. She did not look forward to the evening's entertainment. She knew with a certainty that Roarke would be there and that he would insist she dance with him. He would probably also arrange, in that effortless manner of his, to spend some private time alone with her, making her well aware of the attraction she felt toward him.

To be fair, she could not place the blame entirely on Roarke. If she were firmly opposed to being with him, she could call on Drew to help her avoid his attentions. What bothered her most was being caught between what she was expected to do and what her heart told her. She could not resolve the warring factions within her, and found herself both dreading and looking forward to seeing Roarke.

When Elizabeth reached the ball that evening, she was still unnaturally subdued. She felt a heaviness of spirit hovering over the evening, and if Louisa hadn't urged her forward, she would have returned to the coach and the safety of home.

The ball was a crush, and the deeper she moved into the ballroom, the more difficult it became for her to breathe. Louisa accepted an invitation to dance from Lord Chesterfield, leaving Elizabeth alone. Both Drew and Jeanette were to be here this evening, but she could see neither of them in the seething mass of people around her.

"Lady Elizabeth," said a voice from behind her. When she turned, she encountered Viscount Welford and his friend, Viscount Bromley. Her eyes were nearly blinded by their sartorial splendor. Welford wore a jacket of pistachio with a waistcoat heavily embroidered with yellow flowers and green vines. His cravat was tied so high and tight that he could barely move his head or bend his neck.

Bromley's jacket was a violent bluish purple color, over a striped waistcoat. His cravat rivaled Welford's in style, causing his shirt points to threaten his cheeks each time he attempted to turn his head.

"You are looking well this evening," said Bromley.

Elizabeth was in no mood to listen to sly innuendos concerning Helen and Roarke from the two men. "Thank you." Her reply was polite, but cool, meant to discourage them from lingering.

Bromley looked down his nose and over his cravat at her. "Have you discovered anything more about Lady Carvey's tragic demise?"

Elizabeth had not noticed the last time they had spoken just how small and evil-looking Viscount Bromley's eyes were. She was not about to divulge anything of interest to the viscount. "Nothing of consequence," she replied shortly.

Welford stared at her, a peculiar expression on his face. "I don't believe the lady is happy to see us," he said to Bromley. "She has gotten all that we know from us, and we are no longer of any use."

"It isn't that at all," protested Elizabeth, embarrassed to be caught.

"Oh, I think it is," insisted Welford.

Elizabeth could see the anger rising in him. She did not need to be involved in a public scene with two such men over Helen's death.

"Or perhaps Roarke has turned her up sweet, and she no longer thinks him guilty," suggested Bromley.

"Is that it, my lady? Have you fallen victim to Roarke's charm?" asked Welford. "If you have, you could very well end up as Lady Carvey did."

The threat in his words chilled Elizabeth, and she wondered again at the depth of their hatred for Roarke.

"Elizabeth, I've been looking all over for you," said Jeanette, approaching the small group.

"And you have found me," replied Elizabeth, relieved that the girl had unknowingly extricated her from a potentially embarrassing situation.

"Forgive us," she said to the viscounts Bromley and Welford. "We have a matter of importance to discuss." She hurried Jeanette away from the two men before they could even offer a stiff bow.

"What is it that we have to consider?" whispered Jeanette to Elizabeth as they pushed their way through the crowd.

Elizabeth breathed a little easier now that she was away from the two men. "Nothing, unless you have come across some news."

Jeanette looked puzzled. "Then, why . . . ?"

"I had to get away from Bromley and Welford," Elizabeth explained in a low voice.

"Oh. Oh, I see," said Jeanette, her face lighting with excitement. "You told me they were at the rooms when Helen was discovered. Do you suspect they had something to do with it?"

"I'm not certain," said Elizabeth. "I do know they are very uncomfortable men to be around. They are worse than gossipy women, for they are full of malice, and I don't intend to abet them in anyway."

"Look, there is Drew," said Jeanette, her interest in Bromley and Welford immediately disappearing. "But he is talking to the Wendells." Her face fell as she watched Drew take Sylvia's hand.

"He is merely greeting her," said Elizabeth. "I don't think his interest lies there."

Jeanette's small oval face was a study of sadness. "I wish I could believe that."

"You will be far happier if you do," advised Elizabeth. "Drew is every inch the gentleman, and he would never slight any lady."

"Oh my," murmured Jeanette, but her warning was too late for Elizabeth to escape.

"Elizabeth, my dear," said Lady Barrington, tapping her on

THE HEADSTRONG HEART

147

the shoulder with her fan. "I'm so glad to see you this evening.
I wanted to apologize for anything untoward I said when I called
on you."

"There's no need."

"I'm certain there is," insisted Lady Barrington. "You see I
had a terrible case of the megrims and had taken a sip or two of
brandy before I called to chase it away. I'm afraid my tongue
was looser than it should have been. Ofttimes I do run on more
than I should."

"There was no harm done, my lady. I had already put it from
my mind."

"You are too kind, my dear. When you need more of the tisane,
let me know." Lady Barrington cut a swath through the crowd,
her blue- and gold-clad servant following in her footsteps.

Elizabeth was becoming more agitated the longer she spent
in the room. The darkness still hung over her and she longed to
be safe at home. However, they were approaching Drew and the
Wendells and it would cause talk if she were to bolt from the
ballroom.

When Elizabeth and Jeanette joined the group, Drew immediately asked Jeanette to dance, and the two disappeared into the
throng to take their places for the next set.

"Have you found out anything new from your inquiries about
Lady Carvey?" asked George.

"George, that is not at all the thing to discuss here," chastised
Sylvia.

"Sorry," said George. "Just hate to see such a crime go un-
punished."

"There's no harm done," Elizabeth assured him, wondering
how many times she was destined to repeat those same words
tonight. She was not about to tell anyone what she was doing. It
was a terrible thing to say, but she could trust no one at the
moment, and was determined to keep whatever she learned to
herself. She would not allow Helen's life to become an on-dit for
society's amusement. "I've found nothing more, and doubt
whether I ever shall."

"Perhaps it's better if you leave it to the authorities," said
George. "They've handled this sort of thing before."

Elizabeth did not repeat her argument that the authorities had done nothing so far. "I only hope that someday someone pays for what happened to Helen," she replied. Suddenly the darkness grew more intense, clouding her vision. Her fingers tightened on the ivory sticks in her fan, and the desire to draw became incredibly strong.

"Elizabeth, are you well?" asked Sylvia anxiously. "You look exceedingly pale all of a sudden. George, fetch a cup of punch."

"No, that isn't necessary," objected Elizabeth. "It's merely a little stuffy; a bit of fresh air will do the trick. Please, excuse me."

"I'll go with you," offered Sylvia.

"No, I'll be absolutely fine," Elizabeth said adamantly. She offered the Wendells a smile and began making her way through the crowd toward the door. The darkness followed her, closing in until it began to smother her, then pulling far enough away for her to recover her senses. If she could only escape the room, she felt she would be rid of the shadow.

"Elizabeth, how good to see you."

Lord Westbrook was standing in front of her, but this was one time she could not afford to be gracious to the man. "I'm afraid I can't stop, my lord. I have promised the next dance." She moved away from him as quickly as the press of people would allow. She would make it up to him the next time they met. The darkness had become crushing, and she knew she must reach the door soon.

"Elizabeth, what is wrong?" She would know Roarke's voice anywhere, but it wasn't welcome at the moment.

"Nothing," she replied shortly, beginning to tire of repeating herself. She turned and discovered Roarke with Lady Anne once again clinging to his arm. An unladylike burst of anger flashed through her when she saw the woman. She quickly extinguished it and, after a brief nod, turned her attention to Roarke.

He was watching her closely, a concerned expression on his face. "I'm merely attempting to leave and am having a difficult time making my way to the door," she explained. The darkness surrounded her, pushing at her shoulders, her back, her arms.

Her fingers itched dreadfully and she rubbed them together, attempting to overcome the urge to draw.

Elizabeth noticed Lady Anne staring at her hands. "New gloves," she explained succinctly. "They're bothering me something dreadful."

"Perhaps it's your illness that has made you so sensitive," said Lady Anne, her comment harmless, but her eyes burning with something very close to jealousy.

"That could be so," said Elizabeth, willing to agree to anything if it meant a quick escape. "I'll bid you a good evening." The blackness barely made room for her as she turned once more toward the door.

"I'll escort you," said Roarke, murmuring an excuse and freeing himself from Lady Anne's clutch.

"There's no need," objected Elizabeth. But she was too late, Roarke was already beside her, taking her arm and offering her his strength.

The darkness followed her out of the ballroom, through the hall and outside into the night air.

"Let me ride home with you," said Roarke, helping her into the carriage.

"No, I don't want to take you away from Lady Anne."

"Lady Anne doesn't matter now," he said, watching her closely.

All thoughts of Roarke's mistress had been wiped from Elizabeth's mind by the threatening blackness. She spared the woman not one thought as she wondered how a few short words could make her so happy. "I need only to rest," she assured him. "I've been overdoing it of late."

"If you're certain . . ."

"I am. Now go back to the ball and enjoy yourself." They were the hardest words she had yet to utter, and she was miserable again as Roarke closed the carriage door.

It was some minutes later when she realized that the heavy darkness that had hung about her all evening had gone. She could breathe much easier and, while she still felt the urge to draw, her fingers were not itching as badly as they had been earlier at the ball. Elizabeth was anxious to reach her room and take up her sketchbook.

Elizabeth saw only Marston and Betsy when she reached home. Betsy remarked that her aunt had returned earlier that evening, escorted by Lord Chesterfield. As soon as the maid left the room, Elizabeth gathered her drawing materials and sat near the candle on the table in front of the fireplace.

Elizabeth was almost afraid to begin. So strong had the urge been to draw while she was under the influence of the darkness, she was certain no good could come of it. She put a few tentative marks on the paper. Then her eyes closed and her hand began moving faster and surer until the pristine paper bore no likeness to when she began.

Finally, Elizabeth's hand stilled, and slowly her eyes opened. She blinked several times, looking at her surroundings as if she had never seen them before. If Louisa had been in the room, she would have surely called for Dr. James. But Elizabeth was alone and able to readjust in her own time.

It took several minutes before Elizabeth made a move to look at what she had drawn. She had never been affected so acutely by her gift before, and feared it boded no good. She lowered her eyes to the sketchbook. It took her a moment to take in what she saw, but when she did, her breath caught in her throat and her heart beat as if it would burst through the fine fabric of her nightgown.

Elizabeth breathed deeply until she felt calm enough to study the drawing at length. After all, it was nothing but paper, and could not harm her. She looked again, and it was as she remembered it. The darkness she had felt surrounding her during the evening had been real. The picture she had drawn was of the ballroom, and the darkness hung over it just as heavily as it had when Elizabeth had been there. But the darkness was in the form of a figure. The same figure that Elizabeth had drawn behind the door in the room where Helen had been killed.

It had to mean the killer had been in the room that evening.

He had been near her; his presence threatening enough that it had precipitated her visions, and caused her physical distress.

Elizabeth's thoughts were in a spin. There had been scores of people in the ballroom; how could she hope to know which had been the dark figure behind the door? Elizabeth's head ached and her eyes were dry and scratchy. It was very early morning, and she could not come up with an answer. Hiding the sketchbook in a drawer, she crawled into her bed, searching for a few hours of oblivion.

The next day did not bring Elizabeth any closer to an answer to her question. She kept her drawing private. She did not want others speculating until she was convinced she could go no further with her own conjecture. She did not like to think anyone at the ball capable of murder. The viscounts Bromley and Welford were two for whom she held no fond feelings, but she would not wish them ill if they were innocent of the fact. Then there was Lady Anne. Although she admitted she would like to see the last of the woman, it had nothing to do with Helen's murder, and everything to do with how she clung to Roarke.

She put off Louisa's concern by saying she was merely tired from a late night. That afternoon she received a message from Mr. Warren; Roarke had made his trip out of town that day. They could make their journey the next morning if she wished. Elizabeth answered in the affirmative, and stayed in that evening to rest up for the trip.

Louisa had an engagement with Lord Chesterfield to go to Richmond the next day, so it wasn't at all difficult for Elizabeth to avoid her aunt.

Elizabeth, Mr. Warren, and Betsy arrived at the village just before luncheon. Again, they left their carriage at the inn. After ordering refreshments for Betsy and seeing her safely settled at the inn, Elizabeth and the Runner strolled down the road toward the house. Leaving Mr. Warren in the same place they had waited before, Elizabeth knocked at the door. For a moment she was speechless, when a gray-haired woman opened the door.

"I hope you'll excuse me," she said politely. "I'm Lady Russell, and I'm traveling up to town."

"Good afternoon, my lady," said the woman, giving a small curtsey. "I am Mrs. Marybourn."

"I stopped at the inn for luncheon, "Elizabeth continued, "and took a walk to relieve the tedium of sitting so long. I noticed the morning glories on your wall and couldn't resist." While the expression on the woman's face was pleasant, it registered puzzlement.

"I'm an avid gardener," Elizabeth explained quickly, "and I wondered whether you would allow me to view the rest of your garden?"

"I'm sure it isn't much compared to what you're accustomed to," said the woman, a little flustered by Elizabeth's request.

"It isn't always the size of a garden that makes it admirable," replied Elizabeth. "I can tell by the wealth of blossoms on the morning glory that it's well cared for."

"Well, I do dote on it," admitted Mrs. Marybourn.

"I thought so," said Elizabeth smiling.

"If you would like to see it, please come through." Mrs. Marybourn opened the door, inviting Elizabeth to enter. She led her down a hallway running through the middle of the house to the back door. Although Elizabeth looked as carefully as she could, she could see no one else in any of the rooms.

Her bafflement grew. Mrs. Marybourn was definitely not Roarke's mistress. Perhaps she was the housekeeper, and his chere amie was away at the moment. Drat! What if Elizabeth had missed her, and this had been all for nothing. But as Elizabeth stepped from the cool dimness of the house, into the sunlit garden, she was to be proven wrong. She blinked for a moment in the sunlight, thinking her eyes were deceiving her. But when she looked again, the features of the figure standing before her were the same. She had come face-to-face with the subject of one of her drawings. The young girl, whom Elizabeth had mistakenly identified as Helen in her drawings, was standing before her, looking at her from Helen's eyes, smiling Helen's smile.

* * *

A shock traveled through Elizabeth, rendering her immobile.

"You have startled our guest," Mrs. Marybourn scolded the girl, "just appearing without warning."

"The sun merely struck me in the eyes," objected Elizabeth. "I could never be frightened by such a lovely child as your daughter."

Mrs. Marybourn laughed. "Oh, I'm flattered, but I'm far too old to have a child this age. Mine are all grown, and married, with children of their own. Say hello to Lady Russell, Alexandra."

"Good morning, ma'am," the girl said, making a curtsey to Elizabeth.

"Good morning to you," replied Elizabeth, still unsettled by seeing a miniature of Helen standing before her.

"Now, run along and play. Lady Russell is here to view the garden," said Mrs. Marybourn, before Elizabeth could say anymore to the child.

"She is such a good child," said Mrs. Marybourn, watching the girl skip down the garden path. "She suffered the loss of her mother not long ago, yet hasn't given me the slightest bit of trouble."

"How sad," remarked Elizabeth. "Was it an accident?"

"I really shouldn't be talking about it," said Mrs. Marybourn. "Let me show you around the garden, Lady Russell. There is a bed of roses in which you might be interested."

Elizabeth attempted to display the proper amount of interest as Mrs. Marybourn led her on a tour of the small garden, but her thoughts were absorbed by the child that could be no other than Helen's daughter.

She thanked Mrs. Marybourn and promised to send her several cuttings from her garden. She hoped the woman would not feel compelled to tell her employer about Lady Russell's visit. If Roarke heard of it and failed to find a Lady Russell in London's society, he might become suspicious.

On the way back to town, Elizabeth was extremely quiet. She

was aware Betsy and Mr. Warren were conversing, but paid no attention to what they were saying. She felt betrayed by both Helen and Roarke. They had carried on an affair and had a child together, hiding it from everyone, and continuing their lives as if they were no more than friends.

Doubts that had lingered in her mind about Roarke's innocence seemed more substantial because of her discovery. If he could deceive her about something so important as a child, he surely had the capacity to mislead her about anything.

She did not know what to do with the information she had obtained. Revealing to her father that Helen had a child would do no good at present. Elizabeth did not know what his reaction would be, but there was no need to cause him more pain than he was already suffering. She needed time to consider the situation, and to find out Roarke's intention toward Alexandra. No matter what he decided, Elizabeth was determined her stepsister would be part of her life.

Then her thoughts took her where she did not want to go. Perhaps her father had found out about Helen's affair and her child? Had his tale about the boy bringing him a message to go to the rented rooms been a trumped-up story? If so, it could point to him having a hand in luring Roarke and Helen to the rooms. Or had Roarke tired of a woman who would not let him go? One with an illegitimate child to hold over his head? Elizabeth leaned her head back against the leather squabs of the seat, attempting to will away the beginnings of a headache forming behind her eyes. But no matter how she tried, she could not escape the fact that she was in the unenviable position of doubting the two men who were the most important in her life.

Ten

Elizabeth had to talk to someone about what she had learned. When she returned home she found Louisa in the small sitting room and took the chair across from her.

"You have something serious on your mind, don't you?" asked Louisa.

"I do," admitted Elizabeth. "I carried out my plan to visit the house that Roarke visits."

"I never expected you to do differently," said Louisa, her manner a bit stiff. "Did you find what you expected?"

"I found a woman and a child, but that was the end of the similarities to what I anticipated."

"Whatever do you mean?" asked Louisa.

"I found a woman far too old to be anything but an employee to Roarke, and a child who looked remarkably like Helen."

"Are you saying Helen had a child?" asked Louisa, astonished at the news.

"Evidently. The likeness is remarkable. Alexandra is the girl I've been drawing, not Helen. I must have been reading Roarke's thoughts about her. I could tell he was shocked the first time I showed them to him, but I didn't know why. I was such a fool," she said, her face growing, warm with embarrassment. "I gave him the perfect excuse by saying the drawing was Helen as a young girl; he didn't even need to exert himself to explain the picture.

"But the next time, I must have received the image from his mind when he thought of it," she mused. Elizabeth smiled wryly. "It was no wonder he left as quickly as possible; he was probably afraid of what I would find out next." The smile turned into an outright laugh. "I imagine Lord Roarke is attempting to be extremely careful of his thoughts when we meet." But he had not been completely successful, considered Elizabeth, remembering the drawings she had done after the Rathersbys' ball.

"It might not be so amusing," warned her aunt.

"You mean you think Roarke would attempt to harm me because I can draw his thoughts?"

"Perhaps."

"It would be a terrible coincidence if both Helen and I were to die under mysterious circumstances," replied Elizabeth, "particularly if Roarke were involved in any way. And if he is guilty and decides I know too much, he would be forced to do away with Mr. Warren, Jeanette, and you. No, I think I'm perfectly safe with Lord Roarke for the moment."

"What do you mean to do?" questioned Louisa.

"I don't know. Perhaps I'll do some drawings of what I've seen and simply ask Roarke about them."

"And if he denies any knowledge of the child?"

"He cannot. I have seen him enter the cottage with my own eyes."

"If I thought it would do any good, I would tell you to stop this dangerous scheme. If your father finds out I did nothing to intervene, he will likely throw me out of the house, and he would be right to do so."

"Aunt Louisa, Father knows from experience you could not deter me once I have made up my mind. And I promise not to confront Roarke in a private place, nor to place myself in a position where anyone else will have an opportunity to harm me."

"I wish you would leave it until your father returns," begged Louisa again.

"I can't," said Elizabeth sadly. "It must be done before he comes back to town, so he will not be involved. I must find out what happened to Helen or none of us shall ever have any peace in our lifetimes. And you must remember, I was also struck down. What if the person who did this thinks I may remember something more? If I don't find out his name, he could finish the job anywhere, anytime, and no one would be the wiser. No. For myself, and for Helen, I must continue."

"Then let me come with you."

"I don't think Roarke would be forthcoming with you there," replied Elizabeth. "But if it will make you feel better, I'll talk to him within your sight."

"That's better than waiting here at home. When are you going to approach him?"

"As soon as I can arrange a chance meeting," said Elizabeth, giving her aunt an assuring smile.

Elizabeth's and Roarke's chance encounter occurred at the Duchess of Claiborne's Venetian Breakfast. It had not been as difficult as Elizabeth had imagined. She had merely spoken to the various individuals who were entertaining and had put their thoughts to paper. It wasn't until she had conversed with the duchess that Roarke had shown up in her sketch. Once again, Lady Anne was by his side. Elizabeth had torn the paper into tiny shreds, all the while wondering what Roarke saw in the woman. If Lady Anne appealed to him, he could spend all the time he desired in her company, thought Elizabeth, but first she meant to have some time alone with him to ask her questions.

"It's a lovely afternoon," said Louisa, as they strolled the grounds of the Claibornes' home just outside of London.

"Where is Roarke?" grumbled Elizabeth. "He should be here."

"Perhaps you're wrong," suggested Louisa. "If I remember correctly, the gift is not always accurate."

"Not this time," replied Elizabeth with conviction. "I know he will be here. I just wish he would hurry. I'm anxious to hear his explanation for my drawings."

"Don't push too hard, my dear. Roarke does not appear to be a man who would respond to force."

"I don't intend to do anything of the sort. I'm merely going to show him the pictures and ask him what they mean," insisted Elizabeth. "If he has nothing to hide, he will tell me."

"If he had wanted you to know, he would have told you long before now," said Louisa. "I'm sure he has his own reasons for keeping silent, and you should hold that in consideration when you speak to him."

"I'll be cautious," promised Elizabeth impatiently. "Stirring up his anger until he refuses to talk to me will do me no good. I need to know for certain that the child is Helen's."

"And if she is?"

"Then I intend to bring my stepsister to live with me."

"You cannot just steal the girl away and introduce her into the household," Louisa objected. "There are other matters to consider. Your father, for example, knows nothing of this, I'm sure. He will need to be advised and consulted. Also, the father of the child may have other plans entirely for her. As you well know, he has complete control over her."

"The father is Roarke," declared Elizabeth, anger sparking in her eyes. "And he is hiding her away in the country, keeping her from the life and family she should have."

"You don't know for certain that she's Roarke's daughter," argued Louisa. "And if she is, he has the right to have her live wherever he desires."

"Perhaps so, but I will not allow him to deny me access to Helen's child. No matter who the father is, she remains my stepsister."

"That makes no difference at all in the eyes of the law," reasoned Louisa.

"Then I will threaten to make such a public outcry he will be forced to permit her to know her family."

"Once Roarke makes up his mind, I doubt anything will change it. You had better approach him carefully, or you may never see the child again."

Louisa's remark caused Elizabeth to curb her temper. She was right, of course. Elizabeth had no right to demand anything of Roarke and expect him to acquiesce. Their relationship had been entirely too uneven since her recovery to count on a positive response from him.

"I'll do whatever it takes to find out what I need to know," said Elizabeth.

It was at that instant she spied Roarke with Lady Anne, and all her good intentions nearly disappeared in the heat of her irritability at seeing him with that woman again. Breathing deeply, she spent a few moments regaining her composure.

Smiling amicably, Elizabeth approached Roarke and Lady Anne. Louisa stayed by her side, determined to guard her as closely as possible. Greetings were exchanged, and all the while Lady Anne clung to Roarke's arm as if she would drown once she released it.

"Lady Anne, I understand you enjoy rose gardening," said Louisa.

"It's my passion. I am attempting to produce some new strains at our country estate," responded Lady Anne, loosening her hold on Roarke and moving closer to Louisa in order to converse more easily.

Did Elizabeth merely imagine it, or had an expression of relief pass quickly across Roarke's face as Anne's grip slipped from his arm?

"A thorny passion," murmured Elizabeth to herself.

"You mustn't overlook the blossoms and the scent," replied Roarke, restraining a smile.

Drat! Thought Elizabeth. Could the man hear everything? And just when she wanted his goodwill. "It looks as if Louisa and Lady Anne will be involved for some time. I'm told there's a lovely fountain just beyond the terrace. Would you care to view it with me?"

Roarke glanced at the two women who were conversing intently. "I don't think I'll be missed," he said, offering her his arm.

What was she up to? wondered Roarke, as they strolled past the terrace and down the path toward a fountain spraying into the air in the middle of a pool. He must remember to keep from thinking about anything he wanted to keep secret from her. He did not know whether Elizabeth had perfected her talent any farther since he had last seen her, but he did not wish his every thought to be known.

"It's lovely," said Elizabeth, watching the golden flashes of fish in the pool.

"Let's sit for a while," suggested Roarke, motioning toward a bench nearby. He might as well give her an opportunity to discuss whatever it was that was bothering her. He would have no peace until she did. He only hoped it would not seriously test his control, for Lady Anne had already stretched it to the limit with her endless chatter.

Elizabeth was pleased that Roarke was unknowingly offering her the perfect opportunity to approach him with her drawings. "Will you feel neglected if I make a few sketches of the fountain?" she asked.

"Not at all, I enjoy seeing a drawing take form. It's a talent I would like to possess myself."

"But not with the ability to see," Elizabeth qualified.

"I would imagine that might be an asset."

"You probably won't believe me, but it isn't as much of an advantage as it sounds. I don't want to know what everyone is thinking or what is going to happen. For one thing, it ruins the spontaneity of everyday life. For another, it can bring so much distress into a person's life that it is no longer enjoyable. I remember my mother saying that I would need to learn how to block the thoughts when I didn't want to draw them. I suppose when I grow adept, I'll be able to control them as ably as she must have."

"I hadn't considered it in that way," replied Roarke. "I suppose I thought of it as an endless source of gossip."

"Oh, I won't deny it can be diverting at times," said Elizabeth, smiling at him. "But I didn't know there could be so much misery and sadness, and anger and jealousy, trapped in one small space, until I began using my talent and walked into a ballroom one evening. I was forced to leave that night because I couldn't control it, and it nearly drove me mad until I was out of the room. I practiced at home, and didn't go out again until I was able to avoid the unwanted thoughts."

"So it isn't such a gift after all?" he said.

"Things are seldom all good or all bad. For example, I've been able to find out more about Helen through my drawings."

Roarke stiffened. So they were finally getting to the reason she had dragged him away from Lady Anne. He had begun to hope she felt a bit of jealousy, but should have known better.

"I assume you have them with you," he said, nodding toward her sketchbook, "and wish me to take a look at them."

"If you wouldn't mind," said Elizabeth, blushing faintly because he had guessed her intention so easily.

"Even if I did mind, you wouldn't let me rest until I saw them. So show them, and be done with it."

Elizabeth opened her sketchbook to a series of drawings she had rendered in contemplation of this very moment. But now that it had arrived, she found herself hesitating. Gathering her courage, she displayed a picture of Alexandra in the garden behind her house.

Relief swept through Roarke. Elizabeth had already furnished the explanation for this one. "It is another drawing of Helen as a child."

"I don't think so," said Elizabeth.

"And just who do you think it is?" he asked, a small knot of dread forming in his chest.

"I think it is a young girl who is very much alive; I think she is Helen's daughter."

"Preposterous! You said yourself that you sometimes had to interpret a drawing. Well, you've made an error with this one."

"I don't think so. In fact, I know someone who has seen her," Elizabeth revealed.

The afternoon sunshine beat down on Roarke, but he felt cold to the bone. "Who?" he demanded hoarsley.

"There's something you don't know," she said, instead of answering him directly. "When I first began using my talent, it was slow going. I couldn't wait for it to develop to do something about learning who had killed Helen, so I hired a Bow Street Runner."

Roarke groaned. "Tell me you didn't," he begged.

"I have nothing for which to apologize," replied Elizabeth indignantly before continuing. "The Runner located Alexandra."

"You know her name?"

"Mr. Warren is a very good Bow Street Runner," Elizabeth explained patiently.

"What else did he discover?" Roarke asked through clenched teeth.

"He found her in a village outside of London, living with a housekeeper of sorts. She is well provided for, and wants for nothing."

"And how do you know she is Helen's?"

"Just look at her," said Elizabeth, displaying her drawing again. "She is the exact image of Helen."

"There are many people who look alike, but are not kin," he argued.

"When Helen returned from the continent," Elizabeth said, "she disappeared for several weeks. Mr. Warren could find no trace of her. It's my contention she spent the time establishing a safe place for her child. I think this was it," she said, holding up a drawing of the house with the garden at the back.

"You've shown that to me before."

"And you said you didn't know where it was."

"What does this have to do with the girl? You don't have proof that is Helen's child."

Her voice was soft as silk when she answered. "Yes, I do."

He rose on legs that suddenly felt weak and walked unsteadily to the pool, gazing blindly down into the water.

When he didn't turn, she continued. "Mr. Warren observed you entering the house that is in this drawing."

"You had me followed?" he demanded, wheeling angrily to face her.

Elizabeth rose to meet him on as even a footing as she could. "You gave me no other choice. I knew you were hiding something from me, but you refused to reveal it."

"My business is my own and no one else's unless I choose to tell it." His voice was strictly controlled, but anger vibrated through it. "I did not choose to tell you then, nor am I choosing it now."

"You would only be affirming it, for I know it to be true."

"You are taking the word of a man you barely know over mine?"

Elizabeth had hoped to avoid telling him of her part in the matter, but could do so no longer. "It is not only that, Roarke. You see, I observed you, also. I was waiting nearby and watched you leave the house and drive away. At first, I only knew that a woman with a child lived there, and I thought she was your mistress."

"Dear God! What an imagination you have."

"Do not think me totally witless, Roarke. It is not unheard of. There are more men than not who have mistresses, and you are certainly a man of the world."

"I don't know whether to be flattered or insulted."

"It doesn't matter. What does matter is Alexandra."

"We are in agreement on one point at least."

"Then, as her father, allow her to come live with me."

"Her father!" he roared, outrage altering the planes of his face. "What the devil makes you think that Alexandra is mine?"

"Why, I thought . . ."

"No, the trouble is that you don't think," he raged. "I should leave you without a clue in your head as to the real story, but I know it would only bring me more grief, and possibly harm Alexandra."

"I would never—"

"Perhaps not intentionally," he interrupted. "But you are blundering around in something you know nothing about," he accused.

Elizabeth was unwilling to be bullied any longer. "Then tell me," she said, her voice rising in volume to meet his.

Two long strides brought Roarke to Elizabeth. He clenched his fists and a fine trembling swept over him. She realized he was using every bit of energy he possessed to keep himself under control. Elizabeth attempted to step backwards, but the bench hit the back of her knees and she could go no further.

Roarke reached out, and Elizabeth flinched away from him. His large hands closed over her upper arms and he drew her close. The heat of his anger burned through the thin material of her gown as he pulled her tight against his body. Her fear gave way to an emotion that was just as frightening to her as his anger. Elizabeth knew from their past encounters that it was desire.

She could feel the hard length of his body against hers and wanted never to step away. If he were not holding her arms, she was certain they would be entwined around his neck by now.

Closing her eyes, she imagined for a moment that his was a gesture of passion, not anger.

Roarke looked down at Elizabeth. Her eyes were closed and her face was pale. He cursed himself inwardly. She was not long recovered from a serious illness, and here he was wanting to shake her until her teeth rattled. He would not do so, of course. He had never hurt a woman in his life and he wouldn't start now, although he was mightily tempted.

As his rage diminished, he felt the sweet softness of Elizabeth pressed against him. He leaned over her, and her silvery curls brushed his cheek. His hold loosened and his hands soothed the red marks his fingers had left on her delicate skin. Anger and passion must certainly be closely related, thought Roarke, for he quickly moved from one to the other when around Elizabeth.

"Don't be frightened," he murmured, as his lips brushed her ear, then traveled to her cheek.

She didn't answer, but leaned against him, fitting her body to his, as his arms encircled her, holding her close. His lips continued their course until he reached the beauty mark at the corner of her lips. He paid special attention to that spot before finally placing his lips over hers.

All thoughts of Roarke's duplicity were wiped from her mind by his touch. Elizabeth was guided by physical urges alone. She could not free her arms to encircle Roarke's neck, but she could slip them beneath his jacket and wrap them around his body. She spread her hands on his back, tracing the muscles beneath the linen of his shirt.

Roarke groaned deep in his throat and tightened his hold, slipping one hand down her hips and pulling her even closer still. She did not object to his touch, and he wondered whether she would stop him if he took their lovemaking further. But once again they were in a public place. Anyone could come by at any moment and discover them. However, that might not be such a bad thing; Elizabeth would be compromised and they would be forced to wed. Strangely enough, the thought of marriage to Elizabeth did not alarm him. He could become accustomed to having her in his arms every night.

Even though her lips tasted sweet beneath his own, a semblance of sanity broke through his inflamed senses. Elizabeth's father thought Roarke had killed his wife. He would not be in the same building with him, and would certainly never approve of his marriage to his daughter. No, there was far too much keeping them apart for them to be compromised and forced into something her father wouldn't sanction.

Roarke reluctantly lifted his lips from hers, and set her away from him. Her eyes were still closed, but there was far more color in her face now, and her breath was coming as rapidly as his own. Roarke well knew the signs of passion, but he wondered what Elizabeth was thinking of her reaction to him. He tipped up her chin.

"Open your eyes, my love," he urged, in a voice far removed from the tone he had last used. She did as he asked, and he was almost sorry she had. Her eyes were deep blue and languorous, more suited to the bedroom than a goldfish pool. Desire rippled through him again, but he was the more experienced and it was up to him to bring a stop to this pleasurable, but dangerous experience, before it went any further.

"It's time we discussed this reasonably," he said.

"Umm," was Elizabeth's only reply.

Roarke smiled at her confusion. "Why don't we sit down," he suggested. Elizabeth sat where he indicated, and he took a seat beside her, still holding her hand.

"Are you ready to listen?" he asked.

"Yes." Her voice was soft and wispy, as insubstantial as the air about them.

"Are you certain?"

She sat a little straighter and turned toward him. Roarke was relieved she didn't remove her hand from his grasp.

"What I have to say is not to become an on-dit," he warned.

"I would never . . ."

"All right," he said, holding up his hand. "I've been cautious so long it has become second nature to me." He leaned forward and placed another light kiss on her lips, silencing any further protests she might have.

"As you so rightly assumed, Alexandra is Helen's child. However, I am not the father."

"But you visit her every week," protested Elizabeth.

"I promised Helen that if anything happened to her, I would watch over Alexandra. It was a promise I didn't need to make, because I would have taken care of her no matter whether I had given my word or not. You see, although Alexandra isn't my child by blood, she is in my heart.

"Helen was increasing when I met her in Paris. She was terribly lonely and homesick, and very badly needed a friend. I offered to be one. Our friendship developed before she gave birth to Alexandra. I was there when the child was born and was the first to hold her. I had never been around children, particularly a baby so dependent on the goodwill of others. I swore that she would never want for anything. Alexandra was the bond that held me to Helen—not an affair."

"You should have told someone."

"I couldn't. Helen swore me to secrecy."

A great feeling of relief swept over Elizabeth. Perhaps she shouldn't believe Roarke so easily, but she wanted to so badly, she couldn't refuse her own predilection. "If you're not the father, then who is?"

"I don't know. While Helen confided many things to me, that is one she kept to herself. Your aunt would object to my telling you this, but I see no way around it." He paused, and Elizabeth gave a tug on his hand, urging Roarke to continue his story. "Helen said Alexandra's father had forced himself on her. When she found herself increasing, she ran away from home rather than become a source of gossip for the neighborhood."

"How terrible for her," said Elizabeth.

"I was returning from the Congress of Vienna and had stopped in Paris on my way home. It was there I first met Helen. She was close to giving birth, and I helped her with some packages one day. From there our friendship grew. The story of an elderly aunt is true. The woman died shortly after Alexandra was born. She had left her small estate to Helen, which enabled her to return to England with Alexandra."

"But what of her own funds?"

"She said she didn't want her family to know where she was."

"She would have been terribly lonely without you," observed Elizabeth.

"I did what I could," Roarke admitted. "I assisted her with the legalities of settling the estate and arranged for passage across the channel. It was then I learned of the fear Helen lived with. She told me that Alexandra's father had warned her not to tell anyone of what had happened between them. If she did, he said he would kill her and anyone else near to her. Even though Alexandra had been conceived from such brutality, Helen loved her. She would not take any chances that might put the child in danger. She took great care to keep Alexandra's birth secret."

"But how could she hide a baby?"

"We hired Mrs. Marybourn in Paris. She had been there with an English family whose children had grown old enough that they did not need caring for any longer. She was returning home, and I met her when I was purchasing our tickets. She agreed to look after Alexandra on the trip to England. Helen insisted upon Mrs. Marybourn and Alexandra boarding separately, and while she kept a close eye on them, she did not approach them while we crossed the channel.

"Helen was convinced Alexandra's father was lurking around every corner, just waiting for her to reappear so he could take her child away. He would have that right, you know, even though he had forced himself on Helen."

"Yes, and it is a ludicrous law," objected Elizabeth.

"That it is," said Roarke, nodding his agreement. "But it was there, with nothing to be done about it for the moment. So we crossed the channel, acting as if Alexandra and Mrs. Marybourn were strangers. When we reached England, we left Mrs. Marybourn with the child while we located a suitable place for them to live."

"Why would she leave her?"

"By then, Helen had come up with an idea, and it meant parting with Alexandra until she completed it."

"And what was her plan?"

"She believed that if she were to marry, Alexandra's father wouldn't be brave enough to approach her. So she planned to go

to Bath or London, find a respectable husband, and then bring
Alexandra to live with her."

"Do you mean she used my father as part of her plan?"

"Let me finish before you judge her," said Roarke. "Helen
went to Bath first, but found no one she could bear to live with
the rest of her life. Then she asked if I would introduce her to
London society. I agreed."

"But why didn't you and she . . . ?" Elizabeth could not utter
the words.

Eleven

"Get married?" Roarke smiled. "I offered. As I mentioned, by then I had fallen in love with Alexandra. I had heard her first cry, had held her immediately after she was born, and she had stolen my heart. But Helen refused my offer."

Roarke looked so sad that Elizabeth wanted to comfort him. She knew the pain of loving and not being loved in return. She found herself angry at Helen for hurting Roarke.

"I told her I would keep my offer open until she was safe and secure in a good marriage."

"And she found my father."

"She fell in love with your father," he corrected. "Don't forget that. Helen could have married before she met him, but she kept hoping for a deep, abiding love. She found that with Lord Carvey."

"Then why did she keep Alexandra hidden away? Why didn't she tell my father the truth?"

"She was ready to. She had been talking about it the last few months of her life. She said she felt safe enough to tell Lord Carvey about Alexandra. That the man who attacked her would never have enough courage to go up against your father.

"I thought that was what she wanted to discuss when I received her note; that she had made up her mind to carry through with it, and wanted my advice and help. It seemed a little strange to ask me to meet her in rented rooms, but then Helen always had a flair for the dramatic. That's why my defenses were down, and why I was overcome so easily."

Elizabeth's head was spinning with receiving so much information at one time. "But after Helen's death, why didn't you tell Father about Alexandra and allow him to bring her home?"

"Elizabeth, think about what you're suggesting. Your father had just lost the woman he loved. He thought, and still does think, that I murdered her. How was I to tell him about Helen and Alexandra so that he would accept it? He would more than likely presume Alexandra was mine and Helen's, just as you did, before he would believe a word out of my mouth.

"Then there was the element of Alexandra's safety. Helen feared for the child so, I had to lend some credibility to her story. If Alexandra's father learned of Helen's death, he might consider Alexandra's age and make a correct assumption. At the time, I doubt Lord Carvey would have resisted a father claiming his child. I thought it best to keep quiet until I could prove who killed Helen, and until I could keep Alexandra safe from her father."

"Everything is such a mess," complained Elizabeth.

"That it is," agreed Roarke.

"What were you planning on doing next?" she asked.

"First I'm going to find the man who forced himself on Helen, and discover whether he had anything to do with her murder. Then I'm going to make sure he never bothers Alexandra."

"How will you do that?"

"I'm not certain, but I'll figure out something before I find him."

"I'm going to help you," said Elizabeth, a look of determination crossing her face. "If he is guilty of killing Helen, I'll find him."

"I don't know that he is," said Roarke. "He is merely the most likely suspect."

"No matter. He won't escape me."

"This is too dangerous for you to become involved in," said Roarke. "Why not leave it to me?"

"You sound like Aunt Louisa, and I will answer you the same. Little has been accomplished since Helen's death, and I intend to change that."

Elizabeth could not be convinced to sit back and do nothing, of that Roarke was certain. But he could not allow her to continue on her own. It was possible she might blunder into a dangerous situation. There was only one thing to do. "Let us join forces," he suggested.

She found herself ready to refuse his offer, then looked down at their clasped hands. Remembering the passionate moments they had shared, she found herself unable to believe any longer that he would harm Helen. "All right, but we must be equal partners. I will not be left behind to sit and wait."

"I would never suggest it," he said solemnly, raising her hand to his lips. "But what of your suspicion of me? There's no use denying it; it's been quite obvious that you've doubted my innocence from the beginning."

Elizabeth was confused and embarrassed in being confronted by Roarke, but she could not remain silent forever. By the time she had gathered her thoughts, he had risen and taken several paces away from her. The short space between them seemed enormous, and she left the bench to be near him once again.

"I never even considered you guilty when I first awakened," she confessed, unable to meet his gaze. "I was appalled when my father suggested it."

Roarke lifted her hands and pressed them to his chest, holding them there in his warm grasp. "What changed your mind?" he asked softly.

"During the two months I was recovering, my father and I discussed what had happened. He convinced me that his version of the murder was true. Although it isn't an excuse, I think I was terribly susceptible to his suggestions during that time. I was weak, I had lost Helen to violence, and I was being told that you were the reason."

The heat of his body penetrated his shirt, warming her hands which he still held tight. Elizabeth's concentration wavered, and she moved her fingers in a caressing motion.

"Keep doing that and this conversation will end abruptly," he warned, the tenseness of his body substantiating his words.

Heat bloomed in Elizabeth's cheeks as she remembered the drawings she had made of the two of them together. "I don't think I ever completely believed you were guilty," she said, "but I did allow myself to be convinced you were highly suspect.

However, there was always a part of me that said you couldn't do such a dastardly thing."

"Thank God for that," he replied. Leaning down he brushed his lips across hers, lingering a moment before releasing her.

Roarke's kiss caused Elizabeth to lose all thought of anything but his nearness. She had never experienced such happiness as she did when she was in his arms.

Roarke released her hands and stepped away. "There are several things to consider, if you have any remaining doubts," he said. Roarke hesitated before continuing. At first, he had expected Elizabeth to believe him without any need on his part to prove his innocence. That had been foolish thinking, particularly with the evidence pointing toward him.

"You don't need to explain anything," said Elizabeth. "I should have followed my initial feelings."

"You had every right to question me. If I had been forthcoming, then we might have avoided all this confusion. Now, I want to insure that there is not a question in your mind." Roarke moved a few more steps away to keep her nearness from distracting him. "Do you remember what everyone said about the scene when we were found?"

"I believe so."

"They said I was in a drunken stupor; that I held an empty bottle of brandy, and that another full one was on the table in the sitting room."

Elizabeth's brow wrinkled in concentration. "That's true," she agreed.

"I know you've been through a lot, and my drinking habits were probably never of prime importance to you, but—"

"You never drink brandy!" exclaimed Elizabeth. "I don't know how I could have forgotten that. You once told me you drank too much of it when you were young, and could not tolerate it any longer."

"That's true," Roarke said, pleased she had remembered after all.

Although Elizabeth had accepted he was innocent of any part in Helen's murder, she felt incredibly weightless upon hearing his proof. "But why didn't you mention this before?"

"Who would believe me? The people who were accusing me didn't know I never drink brandy. I could have been making up the story as far as they were concerned. No, only my closest friends would have known it was true; there was no way to prove it."

"That means the guilty person doesn't know you well."

"Exactly, but that's hardly a helpful clue to lead us to the real culprit. There's something else you wouldn't have known about. You saw roses on the table with the brandy. Everyone assumed I had brought both the brandy and the roses for my tryst with Helen, but I would never have brought roses to Helen. While she was increasing, she expressed an admiration for lilacs. I sent her those whenever possible, never roses."

"And the rose she was holding?"

"I know nothing about it. It wasn't there when I saw her, so whoever set the scene must have placed it there after I was unconscious. He had to have put me on the bed and poured brandy on me, too."

"Or she," said Elizabeth.

"I don't think a woman could have moved me without help."

"Perhaps you're right," mused Elizabeth, "but that doesn't mean a woman wasn't involved."

Roarke's eyes narrowed, and he watched her closely. "What makes you say that? What are you keeping from me, Elizabeth?"

Elizabeth did not know whether to tell him about the drawing she had made of the ball. He might shrug it aside as the product of an overly active imagination. But the dark figure had hovered over everyone. It had not differentiated between male and female. If her drawing was to be believed, she could not rule out a person simply because of their gender.

"If we are to succeed, you must be honest with me, Elizabeth."

"I've drawn something else, and I don't quite know what to make of it," she confessed. "At least, I don't like the conclusion I've come to. I haven't shown it to anyone. It may be best to keep it to myself."

"If you are this unsettled about it, there must be some semblance of truth in it. Show me, Elizabeth," he coaxed. "I promise

I will not laugh or make fun of you in any way. You should know by now I take your gift seriously."

Elizabeth studied his face, and could find nothing but sincerity there. "I first drew a picture some time ago. It was of the room where we were found. Behind the door was a dark figure. I couldn't recognize anything about it, but I thought it proved there was someone else in the room; perhaps the murderer."

"Why didn't you tell me before?" he asked.

"Because my father said my mind could be playing tricks on me. He suggested perhaps I hadn't really seen you on the bed; that I had overheard discussions while I was unconscious and accepted them as my own memory. He thought you had struck me down that day, and I . . . and I guess I still had doubts at that time." Elizabeth kept her eyes lowered, she could not meet his gaze and see the hurt she knew she would find there.

"It's all right," he said, tipping her chin up with one finger. "I can't blame you for anything you thought. I was less than forthcoming with you, and I'm sorry for that. But I will tell you now that I never hid behind the door; I never struck you from behind. Now what of this new drawing?"

If Elizabeth thought him innocent, then she must trust him completely. "At the ball the other evening," she began. "The night you escorted me to the carriage."

Roarke nodded in acknowledgment.

"That was the night I drew the picture. The whole evening I was haunted by a vision of darkness. By the time I met you, I was becoming frantic to escape the confines of the ballroom."

"I could tell you were distressed, but I was afraid you wouldn't allow me to help," he commented.

"I drew the picture after I returned home," said Elizabeth, turning the pages in her sketchbook. "This is what I drew." She held the book out to him.

The drawing chilled Roarke. An ominous black figure overshadowed the entire ballroom, seeming to threaten their very lives.

"What do you make of it?" he asked, carefully keeping his voice neutral.

"I can only assume that the figure is the murderer. He must

have been extremely close to have affected me so strongly. I don't want to believe anyone present that evening could have done such a thing to Helen, to all of us," she said, her voice such a mere whisper that Roarke had to lean forward to hear her last words.

"It isn't a pleasant thought, but one we must consider."

She was pleased he had included her in his comment. "Then we will work together?"

"I thought we had already decided that," he replied, looking up from the drawing.

"What do you propose we do next?" she asked.

"I think we should meet with your Bow Street Runner and compare notes."

"I will send him a note asking him to call tomorrow, if it will suit your schedule."

"You want to meet at your home?" he said, surprised at her suggestion.

"It's the only way we may be assured of privacy."

"And your father?" he asked.

"I hope this will be over and done with before he returns from the country," she replied.

"Let us hope so," he murmured, pulling her into his arms for one last kiss.

"I assume you and Roarke came to an understanding," remarked Louise, as their carriage rolled down the Duchess of Claiborne's drive on its way back to town.

"Of a sort." Elizabeth went on to tell Louisa the story Roarke had related to her.

"I would never have believed Helen had such a background. She was such a controlled person; she never seemed the least bit afraid or concerned during the time I knew her."

"She was a strong person," Elizabeth replied. "But for all her caution, something went wrong. Alexandra's father must have found her."

"But why would he go to such far reaches to kill her and

implicate Roarke? And what of the drawing?" she asked, indicating the sketchbook on the seat between them. "The people in the ballroom hardly seem like murderers to me."

"I don't know. I suppose no one will understand until we find him. Or her," she added after a brief pause. "Perhaps he was jealous of Roarke and decided to have his revenge on both of them at one time. As far as the drawing goes, if we could tell what a person has done by his outward appearance, life would be much more simple. If the person who killed Helen is there, then they have done an excellent job of covering up."

"What will you do now?"

Elizabeth smiled. "Roarke and I are going to join forces to find Alexandra's father."

"What? You and Roarke? Elizabeth, you will be the death of me and your father yet."

"You look as if you're holding up very well," teased Elizabeth. "Rest assured, I hope to have accomplished our goal before Father returns from the country. Then I will be able to present him with the full story."

"And a stepdaughter, I presume?"

"That might be difficult for him to accept," Elizabeth acknowledged. "But as soon as he sees her, he will love her as much as he did Helen."

"You don't know that. His reaction could be just the opposite. No matter how much Alexandra looks like Helen, another man is her father, one that forced himself on Helen."

"Surely he can be convinced to forget all of that for the child's sake," reasoned Elizabeth.

"I pray that you're right," said Louisa, a worried look on her face. "Do you have a plan?"

"Roarke and I are going to meet with Mr. Warren and see if he's made any progress on finding Helen's home. Roarke has had men searching, but they haven't made any headway." Elizabeth paused for a moment, then decided she might as well tell everything to her aunt. "I have invited Roarke to call on me tomorrow. I intend to have Mr. Warren there also." She held her breath waiting for Louisa's reply.

"You know how your father feels about Roarke."

"I believe it's unwarranted," replied Elizabeth obstinately.

"Perhaps so, but remember Roarke has only been allowed in the house once since Helen's death, and that was because Dr. James felt it might bring you back to us. William would not even stay in the house while Roarke was there."

"I know all that, Aunt Louisa, but I'm convinced he's wrong about Roarke. After hearing his story, I don't believe he harmed either Helen or me. I think you would feel the same if you would only give him a chance."

"Don't drag me any farther into this than I already am. I will not sit as judge and jury for Roarke. While I have always liked him, your father, and others, continue to think him guilty."

"That is what the real murderer is hoping for," said Elizabeth. "As long as Roarke is suspect, he will be safe."

"And how do you know there is someone else?" asked Louisa.

Elizabeth's chin lifted stubbornly. "There are my drawings."

"Which you tend to doubt yourself."

"Not as much as I did at first. I've always questioned Roarke's guilt," she admitted, "but the evidence seemed so overwhelming, and Father was so determined about the matter, that I accepted everything that was being said. However, when I began looking into it myself, I could not help but question Roarke's part in the whole thing."

"And I'm certain he told you a very convincing story today, didn't he?"

Elizabeth blushed, thinking of the kiss they had shared. "It's the truth, I'm certain of it," she replied evenly.

Louisa sighed. If she wasn't mistaken her niece's heart was involved, and it would be senseless to fight that emotion. Far better that Elizabeth still trust her enough to tell her what she was doing, than attempt to keep her away from the earl and force her to meet him in secret.

"I will not forbid Roarke entry," she said. "But I don't like this at all. You are flying in the face of your father's wishes, and you should be ready for whatever reaction he has."

"It will all be over by the time he returns," promised Elizabeth.

"I will be present at your meeting," declared Louisa.

"Aunt Louisa," Elizabeth nearly wailed.

"It is that or nothing. I can go only so far without being completely derelict in my duty toward you. I promise not to interfere, but I must be there," she announced obdurately.

"If you wish," Elizabeth remarked casually. She had lived with her aunt too long not to know when further argument would be useless. If she wanted to continue the search with Roarke, she must accept Louisa's presence at the meeting.

Elizabeth was up early the next morning. She had spent a restless night thinking of Roarke and their meeting the day before. She felt like an intruder, but before she had gone to bed, she had drawn his thoughts from their time together. The sketches of his story about Helen matched what he had told her, and she was more confident than ever that he was telling her the truth. The drawings of his thoughts when he was kissing her brought heat to her face and a yearning to her body. She wondered if there was something deviant in her behavior, for she had to force herself to burn the pictures in the fireplace, while she would much rather have kept them.

As early as possible, Elizabeth sent a message to Mr. Warren asking him to call on her at ten that morning. She toyed with her breakfast until she could no longer sit still, then arranged for refreshments to be brought to the drawing room when Roarke and Warren arrived. She ran out of things to do and turned to her sketchbook; but the only image that appeared on the paper was Roarke's.

When they arrived, both Roarke and Warren appeared surprised that Louisa remained in the room with them.

"I felt Elizabeth should not be alone with the two of you. She is a young unmarried woman, and we must keep up appearances," she explained casually, taking up the embroidery on her lap.

Elizabeth turned her attention to Warren, who had also covered his surprise at Roarke's presence very well indeed. "Lord Roarke has also been investigating Lady Carvey's past," she explained to the Runner. "He has a theory about who killed her, and we decided to join our investigations. I had hoped you would be willing to stay on and help us."

"I would be happy to, my lady. I never like leaving a job unfinished."

"Good," said Roarke. "Lady Elizabeth has nothing but praise for your work. Now, let me tell you what I know." Roarke revealed what he had learned about Alexandra's father.

From the corner of her eye, Elizabeth could see Louisa had lost all interest in her sewing and was devoting her attention to Roarke. She hoped her aunt would believe what he said. In the meantime, Warren was listening closely to Roarke's account of what he knew about Helen.

"When I was last in Bath," revealed Warren, "I was told there was an elderly woman who said she had been acquainted with Helen's mother. I attempted to call on her, but she was extremely ill and could not have visitors. She was there to take the waters and consult a doctor. It's possible I might be able to see her now."

"That's more than I have," said Roarke.

"You must return at once," urged Elizabeth. "I pray she is still there and that her health has improved."

"I will leave in the morning," said Warren.

They spoke a little longer, then the Runner departed to prepare for his journey.

"I suppose I should take my leave also," said Roarke, his attention fastened on Elizabeth until she lowered her eyes before his regard.

"I believe you've said everything there is to say," remarked Louisa, which caused a streak of color to appear high on the ridge of his cheekbones.

Roarke bid Louisa good day, and Elizabeth walked with him to the door. "Will you be going out this evening?" he asked, thinking her reply would answer many questions for him.

"Yes, we are engaged for the evening," she said. She hesitated, and his heart dropped, until she spoke again. "We will be at the Farnleys' ball."

"Perhaps I shall see you there," he said, lifting her hand, and allowing his lips to rest against the softness of her skin just a little longer than was considered proper.

* * *

"You are not being very wise," remarked Louisa, several days later.

"What do you mean?" asked Elizabeth innocently.

"You know very well what I mean. You and Roarke have been the object of gossip for the past two days."

"We've done nothing wrong. We have danced only two dances each evening."

"That is more than enough to raise eyebrows. Everyone knows how your father feels about Roarke; it's only a matter of time before word gets back to him."

"If Roarke is innocent, Father cannot object to him," argued Elizabeth.

"So far you only have conjecture and Roarke's word about what happened," maintained Louisa.

"You forget Mr. Warren has verified much of what Roarke has said."

"But not enough to convince your father should he demand proof. The child would only persuade him that something had been going on between Roarke and Helen."

Elizabeth knew her aunt was right, but she hated to admit it. They must find out about Helen's background before her father returned to town. Elizabeth rubbed her fingers together; they were itching again, a sign for her to pick up her sketchbook.

A house first appeared on the page. It was a respectable size and seemed to be well cared for, but Elizabeth did not recognize it. A woman was walking away from it; only her back was visible in the drawing.

"What do you think of this?" she asked Louisa.

"I've never seen the house before," murmured Louisa, studying the drawing. "But from the back the woman looks somewhat like Helen."

Elizabeth took the sketchbook back. "It could be," she said dubiously. Turning the page she began drawing again. This time the likeness to Helen was unmistakable, and she was climbing into a crowded coach.

"It is Helen," confirmed Elizabeth. "This must have been the day she left home."

Louisa came to sit beside Elizabeth as she continued to draw. When she finished, they looked at one another.

"He has a familiar look about him," commented Louisa. "But I can't place him."

"He certainly does," Elizabeth agreed.

The man she had drawn was outside the same house Helen had been walking away from in the first drawing. His face was contorted with anger, his hands clenched into fists held stiffly by his side.

"I think we're looking at the man who frightened Helen so much," said Elizabeth. "Which could mean we are looking at the father of her child, and her murderer." Both women silently stared at the drawing.

"But how will you ever find him?" asked Louisa.

"I will copy this, and have Warren ask in the villages whether the house and man are known."

"It could take forever. Only sheer good fortune will allow you to find him anytime soon."

"Then I shall have Warren hire more men. I am determined to find out what happened to Helen no matter how long it takes."

"You don't have time," Louisa reminded her. "Your father could return home any day now."

"Have you heard from him?" Elizabeth asked.

"A few days ago. At that time he didn't seem to be in any hurry to return to town, but that is no guarantee."

"Then as soon as Mr. Warren returns from Bath, we shall begin."

"And if we are wrong about the picture?"

"I will not even consider it," said Elizabeth stubbornly. "We must conclude this, and do it quickly. None of us can have the matter drawn out any longer; it has ruined too many lives for far too long already.

Fortunately, Elizabeth did not have long to wait, for Mr. Warren appeared on her doorstep that very afternoon with news from Bath.

* * *

That evening, Elizabeth's excitement stemmed more from the details Mr. Warren brought back from his trip.

"I must talk with you," said Elizabeth, before Roarke had time to greet her.

"What has happened?"

"Don't be alarmed; it's good news for a change. Come with me," she said, leading him toward a massive flower arrangement.

"You don't think we'll attract attention hiding behind a pot of flowers?" he asked, a smile spreading across his face.

"In this crush? No one would notice if we *ate* the flowers," she retorted.

"What is it then?" He was so taken by Elizabeth in her black dress surrounded by a bower of blossoms that at first he did not hear the words that tumbled from her lips. What she was saying finally reached his mind, and she had his full attention.

"Slow down," he said, reaching for her hands. "Tell me again."

"Will you listen this time?" she said with a smidgeon of exasperation.

"I apologize; I was distracted for a moment."

"Mr. Warren returned this afternoon. He found the woman who knew Helen's mother. She told him what she remembered about whom she married and where they lived. It isn't exact, but Mr. Warren feels he can at least locate the area. And that is not all," she continued excitedly. "Just before Mr. Warren arrived, I drew a house. There was a woman walking away who looked remarkably like Helen. Then I drew her again getting on a coach, and we were able to definitely identify her as Helen. Aunt Louisa and I thought it might depict her on the day she ran away."

"Did anything in the picture indicate the location?"

"No," groaned Elizabeth, vexed by her inability to draw something more explicit.

"Don't blame yourself," said Roarke, clasping her hands between his. "You are doing more than we have any right to expect."

Elizabeth had kept the most exciting news for last. "There is one thing though; I think I have a picture of the murderer."

"You what?"

"Well, perhaps he isn't the murderer," admitted Elizabeth, "but I suspect he's the man Helen was running from." She went on the describe the other drawing she had made.

"I must see it," said Roarke

"And you will," replied Elizabeth. "Mr. Warren is coming to call in the morning. He's going to travel to the area where he thinks Helen's home is located, and I'm going with him."

"No, you aren't," Roarke said firmly. "It's too dangerous."

"I don't need your permission," shot back Elizabeth. "And my father is away, so he cannot object."

"What of your aunt Louisa?"

Elizabeth smiled, and he knew he wouldn't like what she was going to say at all. "She's going with me."

Of all the words he was thinking, "Dear Lord," was the only thing fit to say in front of a lady. "Then I am going, too."

"I was hoping you would say that," she confessed.

Roarke's eyes narrowed as he stared down at her, feeling she had gotten exactly what she had wanted. "But I still want to see that drawing tonight. I'll leave immediately after you this evening, and come to your house. Tell your aunt I only intend to stay a few minutes. We can make arrangements for tomorrow then. Now, much as I hate to lose your company, if we stay hidden in this rosebush much longer, there will certainly be an interesting on-dit about us making the rounds tomorrow."

Elizabeth laughed, something she had done very little lately. Roarke offered his arm and they joined the crush of people.

Twelve

"I am going up to bed," said Louisa when they reached home. "I know I shouldn't, but if I'm to be ready for our trip in the morning, I need some sleep."

"Roarke said he would stay only long enough to view the drawing," Elizabeth assured her. "I promise to come straight upstairs as soon as he leaves."

"See that you do," replied Louisa, covering a yawn with her gloved hand. "I still worry about you, even though you look much stronger these days. Marston will be in the hall if you need him."

"I have long gotten over the idea that Roarke is going to strike me over the head to see whether he can finish the job."

"But it is not yet proven," warned Louisa. "And if it is not, and if your father finds out you have not only been socializing with Roarke, but that he has been in our home on several occasions, we will be in more trouble than I care to think about. So make his visit short; you will see him again in a few hours."

Louisa had no more than disappeared up the stairs when Roarke arrived. Elizabeth felt a rush of delight that except for Marston waiting in the hall, Louisa upstairs, and several maids and footmen somewhere in the house, they were alone.

Elizabeth showed him the drawing of the man. Roarke spent several minutes studying it before raising his eyes, disappointment clearly written on his face.

"Although there is something familiar about him, I'm certain I've never seen him before."

Elizabeth released the breath she had been holding. "That is exactly how Aunt Louisa and I feel. Perhaps it's only because we want to recognize him so badly that we believe he's someone we know."

"Possibly," he said, looking at the drawing again before laying it down. "What time should I be here in the morning?"

"Mr. Warren is coming at eight. We are taking a change of clothing in case we're forced to stay overnight at an inn."

"Splendid idea. We'll take my traveling coach, it will be far more comfortable than anything Warren can come up with."

Elizabeth could not keep the excitement from her eyes. "We are going to be successful this time," she said. "I just know it."

"I hope you're right," he replied, smiling at her enthusiasm. "I must go. Marston is probably in the hall with his ear pressed against the door waiting to rush to your rescue."

"Aunt Louisa has already retired, so I expect Marston would take that as a sign you can be trusted."

"It's good to hear those words again," said Roarke.

They had been standing close together in order to view the drawings, and he stared down at her in the candlelight. Time, illness, and bereavement had changed her, and while she had gained back much of the weight she had lost, her features were still delicately defined, wiping away the last traces of her childhood.

But it was not merely the physical changes that attracted him. During the months they had been separated, Elizabeth had matured, her individuality had asserted itself, and he no longer thought of her as a young girl to be taken about as much for convenience's sake as for her company. She had defied everyone in searching for an explanation for Helen's death, and had been more successful than he had ever imagined.

No matter how fragile she looked standing before him this evening, she was a strong woman, with a will of her own, and he admired her for it. When she married, she would not be content to live her life in the shadow of her husband. It would take an understanding man to accept a woman of such fortitude.

Then there was the small matter of her talent. A man could easily be charmed by Elizabeth's looks and manner, but how many would want a wife who could draw what he was thinking? Not many, he would wager.

Elizabeth placed the drawings on the small desk, then turned to him. The light scent of her perfume rose to tease his senses. He knew better than to catch the deep blue of her gaze, but he could not help seeking it out, and then it was too late. He reached out and traced the planes of her face with the gentlest touch he could manage. Her skin was soft beneath his fingertips as he tipped up her chin. His thumb caressed her full lower lip, and he bent to let his lips follow the same path. She tasted as sweet as her scent, and Roarke was enthralled as he had never been before. There was no rush of desire that urged him to pull her close. There was only the sweetness of Elizabeth, and the joy of being near her.

"I must go," he murmured, his lips brushing hers.

"Must you?" she whispered, her eyes still closed.

"Yes, or else I'll have no time to change, and I wouldn't want to begin our trip in evening clothes."

"You would be a very well-dressed traveler," she replied, opening her eyes and smiling.

"You should try to get a little rest; we will probably have a long day tomorrow, or perhaps I should say today."

"I shall," she promised.

He gave her one last touch of his lips, then left without looking back. If he saw her standing there watching him, he would never leave.

Even though she had gotten very little sleep, Elizabeth felt alert and ready for their trip the next morning. Roarke's coach was at the door, and the small group of travelers were gathered in the hall ready to depart earlier than was planned. It was true Louisa looked tired, but she had assured Elizabeth she could rest in the coach.

The streets of London were nearly deserted as the coach rolled over damp cobblestones, and into the dew-fresh countryside. The occupants were silent, all of them involved with their own thoughts on how the day might change their lives.

It was late afternoon by the time they reached Little Burnham, where Mr. Warren believed Helen's home was located. It seemed prosperous, with a busy coaching inn at the outskirts.

"We will stop at the inn for refreshment, and ask if anyone is familiar with the house in your drawing," said Roarke.

The coach pulled into the inn's yard. Roarke gave instruction on the horses' care while the others entered the inn. It was a well-kept establishment, clean and with appetizing odors drifting out of the kitchen. They settled into a private parlor, and ordered a light repast.

"I hope this is not all for nothing," commented Louisa, removing her bonnet and spencer.

"We should know before long," replied Elizabeth, crossing to the window and looking out.

"I'm fairly certain this is the area which Mrs. Townsley described," commented Mr. Warren in an encouraging tone. "I was here once years ago, and it hasn't changed much since then. The inn has been rebuilt and is much better run, but I would still recognize the village."

Roarke swung open the door and stepped through, bringing a new vitality to the room. He glanced quickly at Elizabeth, then removed his hat and placed it on a table by Mr. Warren's. "I've asked that the innkeeper attend us. I'm hoping he will be able to identify either the sketch you made of the house, or the Northrup name."

"It's strange to think that after all this time we might be near an answer," remarked Elizabeth pensively.

"Don't get your hopes up," warned Louisa. "This could yet prove to be all for nothing."

"I don't think so," replied Elizabeth. "I have a strong feeling we are near the solution to Helen's demise."

"I pray you are right," said her aunt, taking a seat and smoothing the skirt of her gown around her.

"We should know soon enough," Roarke said shortly.

Elizabeth noted Roarke's face was expressionless as he paced the floor in front of the empty fireplace. He was more restless than she had ever seen him, and she was reminded how much today meant to him.

The tension in the room was broken as a maid and the innkeeper appeared carrying trays laden with food and drink. The table was soon arranged, and they were all seated around it.

"Will that be all, my lord?" asked the innkeeper.

"There is something more you can do," said Roarke.

"However I can be of service."

"I'd like you to look at a drawing and see whether you recognize the house in it."

Elizabeth opened her sketchbook to the drawing and showed it to the innkeeper.

"Why that's the Northrup house," he said without hesitating. "Of course, after Mr. Northrup died, Mrs. Northrup married a Mr. Raymond Gilbert, but it's still called the Northrup house. The daughter, Miss Helen—Mrs. Thornton, I should rightly call her—lives there now."

"Helen?" gasped Elizabeth. While the innkeeper had been talking, her fingers had begun the familiar itch and she had begun a new sketch. The shock of hearing Helen's name made her stop drawing and stare up at him in dismay. Helen had been dead for nearly eight months, how could she be at Northrup House?

"Yes, my lady," replied the innkeeper, enjoying his role of storyteller. "All grown up she is now. When she left she was just a bit of a girl, slipping in and out like a shadow. After her mother died, it was said she had gone to live with a relative."

The innkeeper glanced down at the sketchbook that lay near Elizabeth's hand. "You must know Mrs. Thornton right well," he said.

"Why do you say that?" she asked.

"Because that's Mr. and Mrs. Thornton right there," he said, pointing at Elizabeth's drawing.

Elizabeth gazed down in undisguised confusion at her sketchbook. She had paid no attention to what she had drawn until the innkeeper had pointed it out to her. An excellent likeness of George and Sylvia Wendell filled the whiteness of the page.

Roarke, Louisa, and Warren rose from their seats and gathered around her.

"I can't believe it," said Louisa.

"Are you certain that this is Helen Northrup, now Mrs. Thornton?" asked Roarke.

"As sure as my own name," replied the innkeeper, a puzzled look appearing on his face. "You can ask anyone in the village, and they'll tell you the same."

Roarke said nothing, but a tight, angry look transformed his usual genial features. "When did you last see Mr. and Mrs. Thornton?"

"Back in March, it must have been. Mr. Thornton stopped by for a pint of ale, and told me they were going to London for the Season."

"Is there anyone in the house now?" asked Roarke.

"Only a couple who keeps the place up while the Thorntons are away. First thing they did was pension off the old servants and bring in new ones. They aren't too friendly, so I can't tell you much about them."

"I want you to look at another drawing," said Roarke, nodding at Elizabeth.

Elizabeth turned the pages until she came to the one of the man in front of Northrup House.

"Do you know this man?" questioned Roarke.

The innkeeper stared intently at the drawing. He was answering questions beyond his personal knowledge. He had only bought the inn close to the time of Michaelmas the year before, and had no firsthand knowledge of what had occurred in the community before September. However, nothing remained secret long in a small village, and the lives of the people in the larger houses were the source of gossip after a few pints of ale in the tavern room.

Much of what the innkeeper had passed along to the ladies and gentlemen concerning Northrup House and its inhabitants had been hearsay gathered while he served the locals. However, he had met the new Mr. Thornton, as he had claimed.

But now, the gentleman was asking him to identify a man he didn't know. The innkeeper knew he could expect a generous sum for his answers. Rather than call in someone who had been in the area longer, he decided to give what answers he could and keep the entire reward for himself. How much could a small distortion of the truth matter? he asked himself.

"Well, what say you?" pressed Roarke.

The innkeeper had never seen the man before, but there was no one in the room to question his word. "It looks like one of the men who was let go when Mr. and Mrs. Northrup returned. He looks mad as hops. Don't reckon I can blame him if he just lost his job."

The tension in the room dissipated with his answer.

"Thank you," said Roarke. "You've been extremely helpful." He slipped some coins into the innkeeper's hand, and the man bowed until he was out of the room.

"What is going on?" asked Elizabeth, her thoughts in too much disarray to think clearly.

Roarke stated the obvious, as if saying it out loud would make it more palatable. "It seems we were wrong; the man in the picture is not Helen's murderer. Unless you can believe a servant conceived the plot and had the means to travel to London and carry it through."

"Even if he had, he would have known the difference between Helen and Sylvia," remarked Louisa.

"My drawing of the two Helens," murmured Elizabeth.

"This is what it was all about," added Roarke, following her thoughts. "It represented Helen and Sylvia, who has been impersonating Helen."

"But why would I have drawn someone who worked at Northrup House if he had nothing to do with the murder?" asked Elizabeth.

"Perhaps his anger brought him to your attention," suggested Mr. Warren.

"It's possible, I suppose. I am still not completely confident when deciphering my drawings," confessed Elizabeth.

"I wonder how the Wendells found their way here, and whatever possessed them to attempt such a scheme?" said Louisa.

"Your guess is as good as any," remarked Roarke. "We know for certain that George and Sylvia have convinced the locals they are Helen and her husband. They're certainly living here when need be, and are probably bleeding the estate for as much as possible. How they came upon enough details to successfully deceive everyone is difficult to say."

"Perhaps they knew Helen before you met her," said Elizabeth.

"Perhaps," agreed Roarke.

"With the right hairstyle and clothes, Sylvia could certainly look a great deal like Helen, but she would have required a certain knowledge of Helen to carry it off," added Louisa.

"Would it do any good to visit Northrup House?" asked Elizabeth.

"Probably not," said Mr. Warren. "But if we stay the night here, I will ride out to the house and find out what I can."

"I think we should stay," said Roarke. "It's getting late and we've had a tiring day. It's been too long and too full of surprises to anticipate spending additional time in the coach today."

"I agree," said Louisa. "I was tired before we began this morning. An early night sounds welcome to me."

"I'll see to the rooms," said Roarke, going in search of the innkeeper.

Dinner was past when Elizabeth mentioned the need to stretch her legs after the hours spent confined in the coach that day.

"You must do it without me," said Louisa. "The only walking I want to do is upstairs to my room."

"I'll go with you," said Roarke to Elizabeth.

The two left the inn and took a road leading away from the inn. It was still light enough to clearly see the way, and although Elizabeth enjoyed the beauty of the countryside, she could not keep from thinking about George and Sylvia.

"Do you think they were responsible for Helen's death?" she asked.

"It's possible," replied Roarke, knowing whom she was talking about without asking. "They certainly could have had the opportunity. They knew all of us, and would probably know that Helen and I would follow the directions in a note without question. Whether Helen's estate is large enough to warrant murder is another thing altogether. Sometimes it takes very little greed to bring about horrendous deeds. However, we won't know about that until we talk to either Helen's solicitor or the Wendells."

"I wonder whether they will be forthcoming with us?"

"They will if they expect any mercy at all in this matter. Lord Carvey has friends in high places. I should know. It took all the influence I could gather to keep myself free."

Elizabeth wanted to apologize, but realized it was neither the time nor the place to do so. They needed to wait until the complete mystery was revealed before amends could be made, and it must come from her father as well as her.

"We should soon know about Helen's death," mused Elizabeth. "I have thought about how I would feel, but it was never like this. I am not at all joyful and, although I feel a sense of relief, I'm filled with a terrible sadness that people are brought to this."

Roarke placed his hand over hers as it rested on his arm. His warmth comforted her and she drew a bit closer.

"Unfortunately, it happens all too often. We will settle this the best we can, then we will go on with our lives; there is nothing more we can do."

Elizabeth wondered whether his life and hers would be linked, or whether once Helen's death was solved, he would want anything more to do with her. If she believed his kisses, she could foresee a future. However, kisses sometimes came far too easy for gentlemen, and were soon forgotten. Then there was always the possibility Roarke had been turning her up sweet to gain access to what her drawings had shown. She imagined he was desperate to solve the mystery of Helen's death and regain his family's good name. Elizabeth glanced up at the man who walked by her side. She would enjoy his company while she could, for once he was free of suspicion, she might not have his company again.

* * *

The trip back to London was quiet. There was sporadic discussion on the possibilities of how to use what they had learned, and when to approach the Wendells.

"We should deal with the Wendells as quickly as possible," urged Elizabeth. "Father could return from the country at any time, and I must have this settled before then."

"I agree," added Louisa, "for I don't know how I will explain everything unless it is."

"If we have not yet confronted George and Sylvia by the time Lord Carvey returns, I'll talk to him," volunteered Roarke.

"William will not even be in the same building with you, let alone the same room. And long enough for you to discuss the death of his wife for which he blames you? I think not," said Louisa.

"Then it will be as Elizabeth says. We will finish with this before he returns," replied Roarke with enough assurance that Elizabeth believed him.

"Where and when would you like to face them?" asked Warren.

"They will be at the Finchleys' ball tomorrow evening," contributed Elizabeth. "Sylvia and I discussed it the last time I saw her." It felt odd, suspecting Sylvia might have had a hand in killing Helen. They had spent hours together at various entertainments; she had invited her into her home, and they had gossiped like best friends. That this same person could have held a satin pillow over Helen's face, or stood by while it was being done, was nearly unbelievable.

"I dislike waiting even that long, for we must do this quickly," said Roarke. "It wouldn't do for them to get wind of our trip and escape. Warren, as soon as we reach town, we'll go to the Finchleys' house. Finchley is still a friend of mine, and will cooperate with us. I'll introduce you, and you will arrange to be at the house tomorrow before the ball begins. You will wait in the library until we arrive. We'll get the Wendells to the library and confront them there."

"What if they attempt to escape?" asked Elizabeth.

"I'll bring a man with me to guard the door," said Warren, "but I don't think it likely they'll try anything."

"If they do, we can handle it," Roarke remarked grimly.

"I intend to be there," said Elizabeth.

Roarke started to object, but the stubborn tilt to her chin proclaimed it would be useless.

"As do I," added Louisa.

If they had not been in the close confines of the coach, Roarke would have thrown up his hands and walked away. However, he could do nothing but agree with both women, knowing that refusing them would do no good at all.

"We will need to arrive earlier than the Wendells," said Roarke. "If they see us all file into the library, they might suspect something. The two of you will wait with Warren. I will ask George and Sylvia to join me to discuss some private piece of business. Once we are in the library, they'll be caught."

"It makes them sound like animals," said Elizabeth.

"If they're guilty of what we think, they are," said Louisa, with unaccustomed contempt.

"Then we're agreed?" asked Roarke, looking at each of them in turn until he received unanimous consent.

"We are just coming into London," observed Warren. "It won't be long now."

"Scarcely seen you the past few days," remarked Drew when he called the next day.

"I've . . . I've been busy," replied Elizabeth, disliking to be less than forthright with her friend.

"Heard you've been seen with Roarke quite often."

"Gammon! We've shared a few dances, that's all."

"Took an early morning drive yesterday," said Drew. "Happened to see Roarke helping you into his traveling coach."

Elizabeth's face flamed. "We were not alone," she burst out.

"Never thought you'd do anything inappropriate."

"Aunt Louisa accompanied us," said Elizabeth.

"Roarke must have redeemed himself," observed Drew.

"Drew." Elizabeth stopped. She did not know how to explain without revealing everything, and that she could not do until after their meeting with the Wendells. "Let's just say that I no longer suspect him of being involved in Helen's murder. I can't explain right now, but you must believe me, Roarke is innocent of the deed."

"Have never completely believed the gossip making the rounds," admitted Drew. "But would warn you to be careful until the real culprit is revealed."

"I hope that will be soon," she said. "Now, tell me how you and Jeanette are getting along." She was less than subtle in changing the direction of their conversation, but she knew Drew was too much of a gentleman to make an issue of it.

"We are dealing very well with one another," replied Drew. "But she's just a child."

"I assure you, Drew, Jeanette is no longer a girl, and her feelings toward you are not childlike. You mustn't say I told you, for she would never speak to me again."

"Would never do so."

"There is one thing that bothers me, and that is Alura. I would deplore it if you allowed Jeanette to think there was more than friendship on your part, then turned all your attention to Alura when she returns from her trip."

"Elizabeth," said Drew, looking truly hurt. "Surely you've known me long enough to think better of me than that."

"I'm sorry," said Elizabeth, sighing. "I do, but I can't help but be concerned. Jeanette is such a soft-hearted person, and I would do anything to keep her from being hurt."

"Don't know what's going to happen between us when Alura returns. Don't even know how I feel about her anymore; she's been gone quite some time. And Jeanette is quite a taking young thing. Do you think she really thinks of me as more than a friend?"

"I know so, and that is what has me worried. Don't do anything that will encourage her unless you're sincere," she begged.

"Promise I'll be careful," said Drew, a thoughtful expression on his face.

"Will you be at the Finchleys' ball tonight?" asked Elizabeth.

"Yes, and you?"

"Aunt Louisa and I will both be there, but it may be late." She did not reveal they would be concealed in the library for most of the evening.

"I may have something to tell you after tonight that will explain everything," she said.

"Will look forward to it. Now, must go. Have promised to take Jeanette riding in the park this afternoon."

Elizabeth watched him leave, hoping his engagement with Jeanette boded well for their relationship. Not that she wished Alura any ill will; she only wanted what was best for everyone involved. Which made her think of Roarke and herself, and whether Helen's death would stand between them forever.

Elizabeth breathed deeply and rose from her seat. She would rest for a while this afternoon. The specter of the evening's activities loomed over her, and she felt she would need all the energy she could muster.

Thirteen

The ballroom was sparsely populated when Elizabeth, Louisa, and Roarke arrived at the Finchleys' that evening. They quickly passed it by and hurried into the library.

"My reputation will be ruined if anyone sees me arrive so early," complained Louisa.

"I have complete faith you will come up with something ingenious should that occur," replied Roarke, an amused expression passing across his face.

"I'll be glad when this is over," remarked Elizabeth, her voice a little higher than usual.

"Would you rather stay in the ballroom?" Roarke asked. "I can guarantee this won't be pleasant."

"It isn't pleasant thinking about what happened to Helen either, but I need to know. It would be even worse waiting for you and attempting to carry on in a normal manner. Drew and Jeanette would immediately notice something was wrong."

"Then it's probably best you stay with us," said Roarke. "You need only sit and listen." He turned toward the Runner. "Are you ready, Warren?"

The man had risen to his feet as they entered the room. "Ready as I'll ever be, my lord. I'd suggest we do this quickly."

"I'll wait near the door; as soon as the Wendells arrive, I'll bring them here." Roarke turned to Elizabeth and Louisa. "If you want to leave, now's the time to say so," he warned, giving them one last chance to change their minds.

"We'll stay," said Elizabeth, as Louisa nodded in agreement.

Roarke hesitated a moment longer, then left the room. The waiting had begun.

It seemed like hours, but could have been no more than one, before the latch on the door moved. Elizabeth held her breath and glanced at her aunt. Louisa was staring at the door as if it were a cobra weaving its spell. Warren had taken up a post beside the door.

Sylvia and George entered first, with Roarke close behind.

"Elizabeth, Lady Louisa, how good to see you," said Sylvia, upon entering. When the women did not answer, her expression changed. "What is wrong?" she asked, her voice quivering. She turned to the man just behind her. "George?"

"Who's this?" said George, as Warren stepped from the shadows to stand in front of the door. "What's going on, Roarke? Why did you ask us here?"

"You'll know in a few minutes, Wendell; or should I call you Thornton?"

Sylvia gasped, and stepped closer to George, taking his arm.

"I don't know what you mean," blustered George. "We're going to leave and forget this ever happened. When you come to your senses, I'll expect your apology."

"And will you apologize for murdering Helen?" This was not the way Roarke had planned on questioning George, but he had spent too many months being blamed for an action for which this man was most likely responsible.

"You are insane!" accused George. "What reason would I have for causing Helen harm?"

"Her family home and most probably her money," charged Roarke.

"You're mad," replied George, taking Sylvia's arm. "We're leaving here."

"Give it up," said Roarke, harshly. "We know you and Sylvia are masquerading as Helen and Richard Thornton. You are living at Helen's home, and when we reach her solicitor, I'm certain we'll find you've been helping yourself to what funds were left her."

"I told you it would never work," cried Sylvia.

"Be quiet!" ordered George. He stared at Roarke for a moment. "You have no proof of anything."

"We have people from the village who can identify both of you as Helen and Richard Thornton. They will say that you have been living at Northrup House for months."

"We've been there," said Elizabeth, unable to keep silent. "We talked to the people, and they recognized both of you from a drawing."

George's shoulders sagged, and his belligerence changed to resignation as he realized they had been well and truly caught. "We've done little harm except live in a house that was deserted," claimed George.

"You wanted the entire estate," accused Roarke. "If Helen had found out, she would have stopped you. You killed her before she had the chance."

"We did nothing of the sort," blustered George. "I will take the punishment for stealing, but not for murder."

"Your choice of Helen could not have been random. You must have been knowledgeable about her background, how else would you know how to go about stealing from her?"

"She didn't need what we took," said George.

"Tell us your story," demanded Roarke, weary of hearing his useless denials of guilt. "Convince us you didn't kill Helen, for at this point everything points to you."

"Tell them," urged Sylvia, "or I will."

George looked down at her, then gave a reassuring smile and patted her hand. "Everything will be all right." He guided her to a nearby chair, and stood beside her after she was seated.

"You're right, our names are not George and Sylvia Wendell; nor are they Helen and Richard Thornton. I am George Gilbert and this is Rose Sutton. I am the elder son of Raymond Gilbert, Helen's stepfather."

Elizabeth and Louisa looked at one another in disbelief. "I had forgotten all about her stepfather," whispered Elizabeth.

"None of us remembered until now," replied Louisa in a low voice. "Do not take on any extra guilt because of this."

Surprise had rendered Roarke momentarily silent. He absorbed what George had told him, taking himself to task for overlooking such an obvious answer. "Let me have your sketchbook," he said, holding out his hand to Elizabeth.

He turned through the pages until he came to the drawing of the angry man in front of Northrup House. "Do you know this man?" he asked, showing the drawing to George.

"That's my younger brother, Edward," he admitted, with a shake of his head. "He has brought me nothing but trouble my entire life."

Roarke returned the sketchbook to Elizabeth. "That's why your drawing seemed so familiar to all of us. Once you know to look for it, there are similarities between George and his brother."

Elizabeth stared at the sketch, then turned her gaze to George. "You're right," she said, chagrined she hadn't noticed it previously. "But why didn't the innkeeper tell us who he was?"

"The innkeeper in the village near Northrup House?" inquired George.

"Yes," said Roarke shortly.

George's laugh was brief and bitter. "He never saw Edward or Raymond. He only came into possession of the inn sometime last September. I imagine he didn't want to lose a reward for his information."

"I may have to pay him a visit after all this is cleared up," remarked Roarke. But George came first, and his patience with the man was rapidly dwindling. "Let's hear your story," he demanded.

"I've been on my own from a very young age," said George. "And while I kept in touch with my father and brother, I seldom saw them since I was out of the country a great deal of the time. I received a letter from my brother Edward, saying our father had married a woman by the name of Eileen Northrup, and that they had both moved into her home upon her marriage to Raymond."

"He had no home of his own?" asked Elizabeth.

George's smile was mocking. "My father never owned anything; at least, not for long. He soon squandered what little my mother had and, after her death, her family would no longer support him.

"You must understand my father could be extremely charming as long as he remained sober, but he turned into something quite different with the first drink. That's the main reason I left home at such an early age. Edward, on the other hand, had followed in our father's footsteps. His love of the bottle equaled Raymond's, and the two remained completely castaway whenever they had the funds. They made a career of living off women or anyone else they could dupe. However, Helen's mother was by far the best endowed of the lot. There's no question in my mind that as soon as the marriage vows were said, both my father and Edward returned to their drunken ways."

"Couldn't anything be done about them?" asked Louisa.

"And what would that be?" he asked. Receiving no reply, he went on with his story. "I went to see them once after Raymond married Helen's mother. Edward got me out of the house before I could even meet my new stepmother. He was jittery and I recognized the symptoms. He would react that way every time he got into trouble. Most of the time our father didn't care what we did, but upon occasion he would beat us just to have someone to vent his spleen upon." George's face was bitter with unwanted memories.

Sylvia looked up at him, tears filling her eyes.

"Don't cry, my dear, it isn't worth it."

"Get on with it," said Roarke, brusquely.

"Don't rush me," replied George. "These are probably my last few hours as a free man."

"I might feel sorry for you if you hadn't had a choice," replied Roarke, his voice harsh with anger.

George rubbed his hand over his face, as if wishing he might erase the scene from his sight. When he removed his hand, he seemed surprised they were still there. Giving a shrug, he began again. "Edward insisted I try the inn's ale while we waited for the coach. He had scratches on his face, and I asked him how he got them. He had already been drinking that day, and his tongue was loose. That was when I learned we had a stepsister. Edward said she was a fancy piece and that the scratches had come from his first taste of her. While Edward sat bragging, he looked out the window, and pointed to a woman passing by on the street. She was really no more than a girl; slight in build, and looking as if she would like to hide from everyone's eyes.

"Edward said that was our stepsister, Helen. He swore it wouldn't be long before she was begging him to bed her again. I'm far from perfect," admitted George, with a quick glance around the room. "But this was the first time I could not sit at the same table with my own brother. Perhaps I should have done more, but I was a stranger, and I doubt I could have changed things. Who would have believed me? I couldn't wait to get away that day, and I vowed never to return."

Roarke's eyes were full of dark anger. "Where are they now," he demanded, with clenched fists. "Where are your father and brother?"

"They are both dead," announced George, in the silence that had enveloped the room.

"Dead?" echoed Roarke, as if he could not believe what he had heard.

"From what little I've learned, Helen's mother died rather suddenly. There was no viewing of the body, and it's my opinion that she may have died at my father's hand. He had a reputation for beating women when he was drunk.

"Soon after that Edward wrote to tell me that Helen had run away. He bragged he and Raymond now had the estate all to themselves. Our father convinced the solicitor that Helen had gone to live with a relative until she got over the loss of her mother. The solicitor agreed to furnish funds to keep the estate running, and an allowance to send to Helen. They had never had it so good," said George, disgust fairly dripping from his words.

"Poor Helen, how frightened she must have been," murmured Louisa.

"What she did was better than staying with my family," remarked George. "But you may take some solace that my father and Edward didn't get to enjoy the fruits of their destruction for long. That winter they had been at the inn drinking. Barely able to climb on their horses, they started home in a blinding snowstorm. The next morning, the stable boy found their horses by the barn, still saddled. He went searching and found them by the side of the road. My father was dead; Edward lived only a few days afterwards."

"I was in London when I saw the notice of Helen's marriage to Lord Carvey. I went to the church and watched as they came out. Although she looked healthier and happier, I could still recognize her as the girl Edward had pointed out on the street. I was still puzzling about how she had come to be Lady Carvey when I received notice of my father's and brother's death from the Northrup solicitor. At the same time, he asked whether I had any knowledge of Helen's whereabouts.

"I had hit hard times, and as I thought about the house standing empty, a plan began to form in my mind. I knew Helen didn't need the estate; Lord Carvey would give her everything she could ever want. So I began to search for a woman who looked similar to Helen. I found Sylvia; or perhaps I should say Rose, for that was what she was known as at the time." His expression softened as he looked down at the woman who sat quietly beside him.

"I was not what you think," Sylvia protested. "I was respectable, but poor. I had a widowed mother and two sisters, with no way to support them. When I met George, I couldn't refuse his offer."

"I dressed her as a lady," said George, taking over the story again, "and hired a woman to teach her the finer points of etiquette. I acquired some false documents to introduce me to London society, and we came to town to allow Sylvia a firsthand look at Helen. She studied her mannerisms and dress until she could act very much like her if she chose."

"Remember the smudge on my bonnet?" asked Sylvia, looking toward Elizabeth. "I thought you had found us out then. I had just colored my hair and didn't notice it had rubbed off."

"Betsy told me you dyed your hair, but I asked her not to mention it because I didn't want to embarrass you," said Elizabeth. "The night I found you in Helen's room; was that another part of your plot?"

"I was looking for anything that might connect Helen with her home. You said the room hadn't been touched except for cleaning. I thought if there was anything that could lead to

Northrup House, I could remove it, and no one would be the wiser. I'm sorry, Elizabeth, I didn't like deceiving you, but we had to protect ourselves."

George placed his hand on her shoulder, and continued his story. "As soon as Sylvia felt confident in her role, we returned to Northrup House as the newly married Helen and Richard Thornton.

"I was counting on the fact that Helen hadn't been allowed far from home before she ran away. She was also an unformed girl when she left. It had been several years, and there was no family left to question her identity. Anyone would expect to see changes in the mature woman, and since time dulls the memory, I was hoping that Sylvia's similarity to Helen would be strong enough to fool everyone.

"We were more successful than I ever imagined. No one questioned whether she was Helen. Then we found Eileen's and Helen's diaries, and by the time Sylvia finished reading them, the transformation was complete. Sylvia was altogether convincing as Helen.

"After living at Northrup House for a time, I suppose we became too confident in our roles. We had not planned on coming back to London, but after Helen's death, we decided there was nothing to stop us. When we came to town, we would be George and Sylvia Wendell; when we returned to Northrup House, we would once again be Helen and Richard Thornton. Sylvia had never experienced many pleasures in life, and I wanted to give her as much as I could."

George's hand tightened on Sylvia's shoulder, and it was then Elizabeth realized he truly loved the woman who was known in London as his sister.

"But Helen caught you, didn't she?" asked Roarke bitterly. "You had to keep her quiet or she would ruin everything, and both of you would be back on the streets where you belong."

"She didn't even know my father was dead, and she had never even met me. Why would she suspect us of anything?" asked George.

"Helen felt safe in her marriage with Lord Carvey," said

Roarke. "Shortly before her death, she had decided to tell him everything."

Sylvia gave a small cry of alarm and buried her face in her hands. George remained standing stiffly by her side, frozen in a vignette of despair.

"I think you found out what she was going to do," pressed Roarke, giving George no time to refute his allegations. "She may have even discussed it with you; I know she felt close to Sylvia. You plotted to kill her and cast the blame on me. Except for some reason Elizabeth showed up and stopped you before you could finish me off. If your plan had succeeded, you could have continued living off Helen's estate. Helen had kept her secret too well for anyone to question you."

"We had nothing to do with Helen's death," blustered George, fear showing in his eyes.

"What had you planned on doing if Helen ever returned?" asked Elizabeth.

"We prayed it wouldn't happen," said Sylvia, regaining some of her composure. "We thought she would be satisfied with what Lord Carvey could give her. There were so many unpleasant memories attached to Northrup House, we hoped she would forget all about her mother's estate."

"And if she did return, we hoped to have put away enough by that time so we could continue living well," added George.

"But we didn't kill her," said Sylvia.

"Let me show you something," said Elizabeth, opening her sketchbook to the drawings of Alexandra, and the house in which she lived. Neither Sylvia nor George exhibited any recognition or surprise upon seeing them. "Are you familiar with either the child or the house?"

"I've never seen either," said Sylvia.

"Nor have I," agreed George.

"The girl does bears a resemblance to Helen," commented Sylvia.

Elizabeth looked at Roarke, uncertain how much to reveal.

"The child is Helen's," confirmed Roarke. He fastened his gaze on George. "And most likely your niece."

George blanched. "You mean when Edward forced himself on her?"

"Exactly," said Roarke grimly. "He had also threatened to kill her if she ever told anyone what had happened between them. The only way Helen knew to protect herself and her child was to run away and hide from your brother. You knew who Helen was, and perhaps you even knew about her child."

"But we didn't," interjected Sylvia desperately.

"You were close, and she could have confided in you."

"No," cried Sylvia again.

"If you did," continued Roarke, as if she had never spoken, "it's possible you also saw Alexandra as a threat. Helen might want to reclaim the estate for her daughter. Since no one knew about the child, perhaps you chose to silence Helen for good in order to retain Northrup House and the money."

Silence fell over the room as George and Sylvia stood accused of taking part in Helen's death.

"Surely you know me better than that," said George.

"After what you have just told me, I don't think I know you at all," replied Roarke.

"Sylvia, if you know anything about this; if you are involved in any way, now is the time to say so," pleaded Elizabeth.

"I only know what George has told you," said Sylvia, her voice choked with emotion. "We had no thought of bringing harm to anyone. We were to attend the theater with you that evening. As far as we knew, everything was going as planned. You must believe us, Elizabeth, we never even saw Helen that day."

If she had not had a hand in Helen's murder, Elizabeth could feel pity for the woman. Sylvia was merely attempting to provide for her mother and sisters. What she had done was wrong, but was it any more than anyone else would do if faced with being destitute? Elizabeth hoped she would never have to make such a decision.

"George," cried Sylvia, her face suddenly filled with relief. "It would have been impossible for either of us to have harmed Helen; we were attending Lady Mattheson's card party that afternoon. I remember it well, because I thought later that while

we were enjoying ourselves, poor Helen . . ." She could not finish the statement.

"I think you're right," said George, hope registering on his
face.

"Are you certain it was that day?" asked Elizabeth.

"Yes, and I'm also certain several people could remember we
were present for the very reason that I remember it."

Roarke and Elizabeth looked at one another. If Sylvia was
telling the truth, then she and George could not have been in two
places at once.

"You could have hired someone," said Roarke, loath to let
them off so easily.

"And risk being blackmailed for the rest of my life?" said
George with a dry laugh. "No, if I were going to do it, I would
have done it myself; but as Sylvia said, we could not have been
there. We will give you a list of people to question."

"Even if you are innocent of Helen's death, you still have a
great deal to answer for," said Roarke.

"I'm willing to face up to what I've done as long as it doesn't
include murder," replied George.

He was so adamant that Elizabeth tended to believe him. She
would never admit it, but she was relieved that George and Sylvia
were not involved in the murder.

Roarke made several restless circuits of the room, then con-
ferred in low tones with Mr. Warren. Warren left the room, returning some minutes later and nodding to Roarke.

"It seems we cannot prove you had a hand in Helen's murder
at present, but you are guilty of defrauding her estate, and that
you must answer to. I am going to allow you to leave, but you
are to remain in town. I have arranged for you to be watched
every hour of every day. If you make so much as a move to run,
I'll have you apprehended and restrained. Do I make myself
clear?"

"Of course, but we won't run away," George assured him.
Sylvia stood and moved closer to him. He put his arm around
her. "We will right what we did wrong. We only want an opportunity to build a life together."

"But not at anyone else's expense," added Sylvia. "We've learned our lesson."

"Don't become too happy," warned Roarke. "This doesn't mean you've been cleared of murder, only that I can't prove it yet. We will check out your alibi to make certain you were at the party. In the meantime, it's best you go home and stay there."

George and Sylvia hurried out of the room, and disappeared into the throng of people who were arriving.

"Dammit!" exclaimed Roarke, slamming his fist onto the nearby desk, causing Elizabeth and Louisa to jump. "I'm sorry. I can't stand to think of Helen's murderer walking free. If the Wendells, or the Thorntons, or whoever they are, aren't to blame, then who is?"

No one had an answer, so he began pacing the floor again. The very air in the room hung heavy with disappointment and discouragement. Elizabeth closed her eyes and began to rapidly review what she knew about Helen's murder.

One consistent factor had been the absence of the notes that had brought everyone together at the rented rooms. Elizabeth had found Helen's in the hall where she had dropped it, but Roarke's and her father's had disappeared.

"Elizabeth? Are you all right?" asked Louisa anxiously.

"Yes. I'm merely attempting to concentrate on the day of Helen's murder, thinking I might remember something."

"And have you?" asked Roarke.

"I was thinking about the notes, which have all seemed to have mysteriously disappeared," she replied. "Someone first wrote to my father, telling him Helen was betraying him with you."

"Good Lord!" exclaimed Roarke. "No wonder Lord Carvey can't stand the sight of me."

"Then you and Helen each received a note which I assume gave the directions and the appointed time for the meeting."

"That's right," agreed Roarke.

"The same person had to have then arranged for the boy to lure my father to the rooms immediately after you and Helen were scheduled to arrive. That my father was meant to catch you with his wife is obvious."

"But what does that tell us?" asked Louisa.

"The notes all disappeared. If I had not seen Helen's note, I might have been convinced that they never existed," Elizabeth said.

"You saw her note? I thought you didn't remember how you came to be there," Roarke said angrily.

"I couldn't tell anyone I had found it, not even my father. It was signed by you, and I couldn't say whether or not it was your handwriting. It would have only built a stronger case against you if I had mentioned it. I felt it wiser to keep the information to myself until I knew more about what had happened."

Roarke's expression remained angry, and she wondered whether they would be speaking when this night was over.

Elizabeth concentrated on each person who was known to have come to the rooms that day. Her fingers began to itch; she rose and moved to the desk searching for something with which to draw. The pen she found was not suitable for sketching, but she would make do.

"What is it?" asked Roarke, joining her at the desk.

"I need to draw," she replied shortly, sitting at the desk with the paper in front of her.

As soon as she took pen in hand, she began to sketch. She was relieved when the first drawing showed her father and a young boy on the steps of her house. The boy was pointing down the street and her father's carriage still waited at the bottom of the steps.

"It looks as if Lord Carvey told the truth about how he came to be at the rooms," said Roarke, looking over her shoulder.

Louisa joined them at the desk, and even Mr. Warren drew near.

Next, Elizabeth directed her thoughts to the day of the murder when she was leaving her room to go shopping. She drew a quick sketch of herself picking up the note on the floor in the upper hallway. She clearly remembered retrieving it, and noticing the dark slash of Roarke's signature on the bottom. She remembered wondering why Helen and Roarke had to meet in such secrecy. At the time, she had not been proud of the fact that she was following them, but she had done so nevertheless.

"So you found it in the hall," said Roarke. "Helen was forever losing things, but I suppose it was for the best this time."

"But what happened to the note?" murmured Elizabeth as she stared at the drawing. "The last I remember is having it in my hand when I reached the house, then I put it in my reticule. Did Betsy mention finding it?" asked Elizabeth, turning toward her aunt.

"Not a word," answered Louisa.

"She didn't bring it up with me either, and she's inquisitive enough to ask or at least show it to me, even if she had to wait until after I had recovered from my illness."

"So if Betsy did not find it, someone else must have taken it," surmised Roarke. "But who?"

Elizabeth concentrated more intently, and her hand began to move again. When it ceased, she looked down and saw herself lying on the floor of the rented rooms. Part of a hand also appeared in the picture.

"What does it mean?" asked Louisa.

"It means my drawing of the figure behind the door was right," said Elizabeth.

"What figure?" asked Louisa.

"I'll show it to you later," replied Elizabeth, staring at the drawing in front of her.

"This proves there was a man in the room that day," said Roarke. "That's easy to determine by the size of the hand, and the end of the jacket sleeve and shirt cuff. He's rifling Elizabeth's reticule."

"But I can't tell who it is," cried Elizabeth, nearly gnashing her teeth in frustration.

"Don't fly into a frenzy," said Roarke, attempting to soothe her. "Keep calm, concentrate, and try again."

Taking a deep breath, she did as he said, and intensified her deliberations. She barely knew when she began drawing, but she heard Roarke's swift intake of breath, and an incoherent murmur from Louisa.

Opening her eyes she looked down. The drawing again showed a masculine hand. This time it was lifting a piece of paper from Roarke's coat pocket. The detail was amazing for such a quick sketch. Helen's signature was plainly visible on the note. The small portion of the man's clothing was again unremarkable.

"Don't you see it?" asked Roarke.

Elizabeth examined the drawing again, then discovered what had caught Roarke's attention. The man was using the opposite hand from what he had used to search Elizabeth's reticule, and a crested ring—extremely precise in detail—was clearly discernible on one finger.

Elizabeth's heart gave a leap. She had seen the ring too often not to know it. She turned to Roarke, but he was already gone.

Fourteen

The door to the hall stood open, attesting to the haste with which Roarke had hurried from the room. "Shouldn't you go with him?" asked Elizabeth of Mr. Warren.

"I would probably attract more attention than Lord Roarke will. He'll be back soon with the gentleman we're looking for if I'm any judge," said Warren.

"Who is he going after?" asked Louisa.

Before Elizabeth could answer, Roarke was back. She had been hoping she was wrong, but he was accompanied by Lord Westbrook. As soon as the two men were through the door, Warren closed it, and stationed himself before it as he had done when George and Sylvia had entered the room. When the earl saw the gathering, his face assumed an expression of resignation.

"I've been found out, haven't I?" he asked, an amazing innocence in his voice. "How long have you known?"

"Not until a few moments ago, when Elizabeth completed a drawing."

"Ah, the gift," Westbrook acknowledged. "Your lovely mother had the same talent. I should have known she would have passed it down to you."

"Take a seat, Westbrook. You have a story to tell," said Roarke.

Westbrook took his time in selecting a chair and seating himself in it. "Could I have something to drink? I find my throat is extremely dry." Elizabeth's nerves were stretched to the limit by the time Roarke had poured a drink from a bottle on a small table in the corner of the room.

Westbrook took a sip, savored it, then took a longer swallow.

"You know how much I loved your mother," he began, looking at Elizabeth, and waiting until she had nodded in agreement with him. "I'm not saying anything your father doesn't know, but Jane would have been my wife if he hadn't interfered. She was a beautiful woman, and any man would have fallen in love with her. I only wish she had committed to me before Carvey set his sights on her. She considered me her friend, but I wanted more than that." His face was a mask of sadness.

"I had long desired to make Carvey pay for taking Jane from me, but in deference first to her, then to her memory, I did nothing. As long as your father treated her properly, and she was happy, I hid my animosity toward him." Westbrook emptied his glass and held it out to Roarke. When it was once more full, he spoke.

"Everything would have continued as it always had, if Carvey hadn't remarried." Westbrook's voice had grown stronger, and he gripped the glass so tightly his knuckles turned white from the strain. Elizabeth wondered what kept it from shattering in his hand.

"What was so wrong about that?" questioned Roarke.

"He demeaned her memory," snarled Westbrook, showing more emotion than he had since entering the room. "I decided to get revenge for myself and for Jane."

"My mother would have wanted him to be happy," said Elizabeth.

"Poor, dear Elizabeth. I know you mean no disrespect for your mother, but you—above all others—must see the iniquity in what he did. How could a man who had been married to such a woman as Jane, ever put anyone in her place?"

Elizabeth quickly realized there would be no reasoning with Lord Westbrook, and remained silent.

"Tell us how you avenged yourself," said Roarke.

"You probably know most of it by now, but I suppose you want to hear me confess it. Well, I will," he announced proudly, "and I will not bow my head in shame nor apologize to anyone."

"We do not expect it," replied Roarke calmly.

"It was rather a clever plan," bragged Westbrook. "I planted a seed of doubt in Lord Carvey's mind by sending him a note warning him that his wife was having an affair, then I let him simmer for a few weeks." He shifted his gaze to Roarke. "The next step was to set up a meeting between you and the new Lady Carvey," he said with a sneer.

Elizabeth marveled at Roarke's ability to restrain his anger.

"I wanted Carvey to assume the worst," continued Westbrook, "so I rented the rooms, and sent a note to both you and Lady Carvey. The timing had to be precise. Carvey couldn't arrive until the two of you were in the room, but it couldn't be too late or else you might decide someone was pulling a sham and be gone before he appeared."

"So you sent the boy to lead him there at the precise time," said Roarke.

"I warned him I'd thrash him within an inch of his life if he failed me," remarked Westbrook. "I got there early, bringing flowers and several bottles of brandy. I wanted it to look as if two lovers were having a secret tryst. I was in the rooms at the time Lady Carvey arrived. My plan was to surprise her and force enough laudanum down her throat to render her senseless, then put her on the bed. I knew, when you came into the room, you would rush to see what was wrong with her," he said, looking at Roarke. "Carvey was scheduled to arrive and find Helen in bed, with you bending over her."

"What ruined it?" asked Elizabeth. "Lady Carvey called out when she entered, just as I thought she would," explained Westbrook. "When no one answered, she stepped into the bedroom; that's when I grabbed her. But I had underestimated her; she fought. We struggled silently for a few moments, then I pushed her down on the bed. She drew a breath to scream, and I snatched a pillow from the bed, pressing it across her mouth to keep her quiet. Looking down at her, I saw recognition dawn in her eyes, and knew I had no choice but to make certain she never revealed my identity to anyone."

The room had become entirely silent. Not even an intake of breath could be heard.

"I couldn't allow her to tell anyone what had happened, so I covered her entire face with the pillow, and pressed as hard as I could. It didn't take long until she stopped struggling." Westbrook recounted the story as if it were a casual conversation that had nothing to do with death and deception.

Roarke uttered a curse and slammed his fist down on the desk. Warren stepped between him and Westbrook.

"Sorry," said Westbrook, looking at Roarke in surprise. "I had thought you would have been over it by now."

Warren murmured a few words, and Roarke slowly composed himself. When he had his rage under control, Warren returned to his post at the door.

"Continue," ordered Roarke brusquely.

"Time was growing short. I knew you would be arriving soon, and I couldn't risk being in the room much longer. I had to continue with the plan, except now Carvey would find you bending over his *murdered* wife instead of catching you in a romantic liaison. When I thought about it, it seemed appropriate. The woman who took my dear Jane's place was gone; you would stand accused of murder, and Carvey would suffer as I had over the years. I hastily arranged Lady Carvey, but had lingered too long. I heard you enter the rooms, and then continue toward the bedroom.

"I hid behind the door, and when you entered, I struck you from behind with a candle holder from a nearby table. I was still working against time for Carvey would be arriving within minutes. I dragged you to the bed, doused you with brandy, and poured as much down your throat as I could. I had removed your jacket and shirt and arranged you on the bed when I heard another sound. I suspected Carvey had arrived early and cursed the messenger boy for being too eager to perform his duties. Once again, I hid behind the door, hoping that when Carvey saw what had happened, he would rush to the bed, and I could slip out without being seen. But, once again, I was in for a surprise.

"I heard a woman call out, and recognized Elizabeth's voice. I had no idea how she came to be there. It was the hardest thing I've ever had to do, but I had no choice. When you entered the room," he said, looking at Elizabeth, "I also hit you with the same candle holder." Tears rose to his eyes, something that hadn't happened when he had described killing Helen.

"You were breathing evenly, and I prayed you would not suffer too greatly. I checked my watch, and realized I must leave or else be caught by Carvey. If everything went as planned, he was due any second. I had no time to finish undressing Roarke, nor to check on your condition again. I started out of the room, then remembered the notes. I found Roarke's in his jacket pocket, then saw the edge of a paper sticking out of your reticule where it had fallen open. Much to my relief, it was Helen's note. I could hear the front door of the house opening, and men's voices. Leaving you both as you were, I rushed out the back entrance, and escaped."

He remained silent for a moment, staring down into his brandy glass. "It was too bad you had to follow her," Westbrook chided Elizabeth. "None of this would have happened, if you hadn't shown up." He looked at her crossly for a moment, before giving her a smile of forgiveness. "You should have been my daughter, you know."

A heavy silence hung over the room. The pain of love and hate, jealousy and murder, kept everyone immobile. The loss of a woman's love years before had finally come to its tragic conclusion.

Westbrook cleared his throat. "I know what you must do," he said, looking at Roarke. "But I would ask for a few minutes privacy to write instructions for my solicitor and staff, before we continue."

Roarke deliberated for a long moment. "We will give you the time you need," he said. Warren started to object, but Roarke nodded sharply. He ushered everyone from the room, and walked a few paces away with Elizabeth and Louisa, while Warren stationed himself outside the library door.

"Do you think we should be doing this?" protested Elizabeth. Roarke merely took a tighter hold on her arm, and urged her and Louisa farther down the hall.

Before Elizabeth could again complain about his tactics, a muffled shot was heard from behind the library door.

"Oh, no," cried Elizabeth, turning to run back toward the library, but Roarke held her firmly, not allowing her to move. "You knew this would happen, didn't you?" she accused him, raising her fist to strike him on the chest.

"It was the best way," said Roarke, attempting to reason with her.

"Hasn't there been enough killing? Enough pain and suffering?" demanded Elizabeth, a small sob escaping from her lips.

He did not answer, but pulled her against him and held her tightly; but Elizabeth fought free, and ran down the hall and out into the night.

"I should think we would have seen Roarke by now," said Louisa. She sat with her embroidery in her lap, but doing very little to complete the design.

"He has what he wanted," Elizabeth replied stiffly. "The real murderer has been revealed, and his family's honor is restored. He has probably been celebrating his good fortune."

"You don't sound happy about it," remarked Louisa.

"Why shouldn't I be? Now he can offer for Lady Anne without worrying about a rejection. Although I doubt she would have turned him down even with murder hanging over his head. She is uncommonly concerned about marrying, and I don't wonder why."

"Elizabeth! That isn't worthy of you."

"Perhaps not," said Elizabeth, sniffing in disdain, "but she is a clinging woman, who is too roundly fashioned for Roarke."

Louisa smiled. "I believe gentlemen like roundly fashioned ladies; or at least that has been my observation."

"Then he is welcome to her," declared Elizabeth, rising from her chair in a huff and walking around the room, picking up one object, then another.

"I thought you no longer cared what he did," said Louisa. "You have not even let me speak his name since the Finchleys' ball."

"I was shocked, that is all. I thought him cruel to allow Lord Westbrook an opportunity to . . . to put an end to his life."

"And now you have a change of heart?"

"Drew explained it was the most honorable course he could have taken," replied Elizabeth. "He made me see that Lord Westbrook could never have borne the scandal his confession would have brought. He would probably have done it sooner or later, whether we had found him out or not. It was too much for him to live with, and I think he wanted to join my mother." Elizabeth dashed a hand across her eyes.

"Come sit down, my dear, I have something I want to tell you," said Louisa, laying aside her sewing. "It will take your mind off all this talk of death."

Elizabeth returned to her seat across from her aunt, and looked at her inquiringly.

"I have some happy news," announced Louisa. "Lord Chesterfield has asked me to marry him." Her usually pale cheeks turned pink as she waited for Elizabeth's reaction.

"Oh, Aunt Louisa," said Elizabeth, rising to give her a hug. "I'm so happy. I think you make the most attractive couple, and he is so attentive to you. I know you'll be happy. You did say yes, didn't you?"

"Of course, I did. Not immediately though; I didn't want to seem too eager. By the time I answered, he vowed he was the happiest man alive." Louisa's laugh sounded like that of a young girl.

"And he's lucky," agreed Elizabeth. "When will you marry? And where? Does Father know yet?"

Louisa was caught up in Elizabeth's excitement. "You're asking too many questions. We haven't decided on a date yet, or a place. I thought I'd wait until William returned and tell him in person."

"Do you know when that will be? Have you heard from him?"

"I've sent a letter telling him he should come home, but I haven't heard anything from him yet. Of course, he might have decided to return without sending a message. I imagine he could leave at very short notice since he has been in the country so long. Surely he has solved every problem that could have occurred by now."

"I dread explaining Helen's death to him," said Elizabeth with a shiver.

"Don't worry, my dear, I'm certain Roarke will take care of that."

Elizabeth looked at Louisa suspiciously. "What do you mean by that?"

"Why nothing more than I'm sure Roarke will want to prove to your father he had nothing to do with Helen's murder. He deserves that at the very least, don't you think?"

"I suppose so," Elizabeth agreed grudgingly. "But I refuse to see him if he comes to the house."

"I'm confident he will be far too busy with your father to annoy you in any way," remarked Louisa, taking up her embroidery again. Elizabeth did not look at all happy with her last remark.

Two days later, Roarke entered Elizabeth's small sitting room. Her appearance brought him to a halt, for she had put aside her black and wore a blue dress that he knew would match the color of her eyes. He had not seen her since she had run away from him at the Finchleys' ball, and did not know what sort of reception to expect. He had been busy since Lord Westbrook's death; determined to settle all question of his guilt before seeing her again.

He had left for Lord Carvey's estate as soon as he could pull himself free from all that surrounded Westbrook's suicide. He was thankful that he had the foresight to ask Viscount Stanford to accompany him. Even with the viscount at his side, his reception had been a heated one, and it had taken some time to persuade Carvey to listen to their story. It was another long argument to convince him of the truth of the matter.

Once his skepticism had been overcome, Lord Carvey packed quickly and left immediately for London, instructing Roarke to be at his town house the next morning. Roarke and Drew ate a quick meal and then began the return journey. As requested, Roarke had presented himself early that morning. The meeting had gone far better than he expected, and now he only had Elizabeth to face.

Elizabeth had not heard him enter the room. As usual, she had her sketchbook in hand. She still looked a little pale, he thought, hoping that when she did discover him she would not immediately order him from the room.

Upon arising that morning, Elizabeth learned that her father had arrived in London a short time earlier. When she had come down for breakfast, he was already sequestered in the library with Roarke, or so Marston told her. She would have entered but he stayed her hand, and advised her it might be better if she waited until her father and Lord Roarke were finished with their business. Unable to eat, she had retired to her sitting room. Taking up her sketchbook, she stared down at the empty page, waiting for the gift to inspire her. Nothing happened, and she was left to imagine all manner of things taking place behind the closed door of the library.

Elizabeth knew immediately when Roarke stepped into the room, but she chose to ignore him, gathering the courage to face whatever he might have to say. He did not speak, and after a few tense moments had passed, she could no longer bear the silence.

"Do you mean to stand there forever without speaking?" she asked contentiously.

Roarke moved farther into the room. "I didn't want to interrupt. I was also momentarily surprised at seeing you in something other than black."

"It was time," she replied simply. "You met with my father?" she asked suddenly, giving Roarke a sideways glance.

At least she was speaking to him, he thought, with relief. "Actually, I went to the country and took him the news about Westbrook. I don't think he would have even seen me if Louisa hadn't sent a note, and if Viscount Stanford hadn't been with me."

"You went to the estate and no one told me?"

"I thought it best, in case Lord Carvey wouldn't listen to me. Even with the note, and with Stanford at my side, it took some doing to get him to listen. I related the entire story, which sounded pretty farfetched even to my own ears. I told him he could talk to Warren when he reached London, but I don't think he would have believed any of it if I hadn't taken Westbrook's note for proof."

"What . . . What did the note say," she asked.

"Westbrook confessed to setting up the entire scheme and to murdering Helen. At the end, he asked for forgiveness."

"He was a sad man," commented Elizabeth. "I hope he's happier now."

"I'm certain he is," said Roarke gently.

"Did you and my father made amends?" she asked as casually as she could manage.

"I think it will take time for us to be on good footing again, but he offered me his hand, and his apology."

Elizabeth smiled. "I consider that a very good beginning, knowing my father as I do."

"I told him about Alexandra. He asked if I would bring her to town as soon as possible. He means for her to reside with the family. The only thing that anyone need know is that she is a child from a previous marriage that ended in the death of Helen's first husband."

"Do you think the story will be believed?" asked Elizabeth.

Roarke shrugged his shoulders. "Who can dispute it?"

"What of George and Sylvia?"

"Your father is inclined to be lenient with them for Alexandra's sake. After all, he is her uncle."

"I'm so happy. I don't think they're bad people, just desperate ones."

"Well, you needn't feel sorry for them any longer. Lord Carvey is considering allowing them to stay on at Northrup House, since someone needs to be there to oversee it. He will no doubt be generous enough that they will live a very comfortable life, and also be able to support Sylvia's family."

"Everything seems to be working out, doesn't it?"

"It does," agreed Roarke, moving closer and looking over her shoulder at her drawing. The sketch was of Elizabeth sitting at a desk writing. "Does this mean you're going to change from being an artist to a writer?"

"If I did, I don't know what I would write. Helen's story would be far too sad to put down on paper."

"You could tell what a good wife and mother and friend she was. You could explain how much joy a new sister has brought to this house."

"She will, won't she?" said Elizabeth, looking up at him. Her eyes were bright with excitement, and some color had crept into her face. He wanted to hold her, not as a friend, but as a lover, and future husband.

"And I know just how to end it," he said, holding her gaze.

"You do," she whispered.

"I do," he replied, sounding as if he were already repeating his vows. "End it with a wedding," he suggested. "Weddings always make for a happy ending."

Elizabeth merely stared at him, until he pulled her up into his arms. "Your father has given me permission to ask you to marry me," he said, straining to keep his voice steady.

Elizabeth remained speechless.

"Well, aren't you going to say anything at all?" he asked, wondering if he had made a mistake.

"I've waited years to hear those words," she confessed. "Now, I can't believe they've been spoken. Are you certain you're over your love for Helen? I swear to you, Roarke," she said fiercely, "I won't accept being second best."

"Second best!" exclaimed Roarke, holding her away from him so he could look directly into her eyes. "How can you even suggest that?" Then he realized how she might very well imagine that he had been in love with Helen. "Elizabeth, Helen and I were good friends, but never lovers. I loved Alexandra, and was committed to keeping them both safe until Helen found someone to protect her and the child. I know that many people thought there was more between us, but I swear to you there wasn't."

Elizabeth looked as if she wanted to believe him, but wasn't quite convinced.

"I will admit to stupidity," he said with a wry smile. "I was a fool to wait so long to offer for you. But I didn't realize I loved you until I nearly lost you. After the incident, I thought I was missing Helen; that the emptiness in my life was due to her death. I'm not saying I didn't miss Helen, but when you returned, when I saw you all silver curls and black gown, I realized *you* were the one I had missed most. *You* were the one I loved." He released her arms and took her hands in his.

"Now, in case you've forgotten the question, let me ask it again. Will you be my bride, Lady Elizabeth? I've loved you so long without admitting it to myself, that I wonder at your patience," he murmured, bringing her hand to his lips. "Please, Elizabeth, don't keep me waiting any longer. Say you'll marry me."

"Yes! Yes, yes, and yes," she repeated, throwing her arms around his neck and laughing with joy. "Is that enough yeses?"

"For the moment," he replied, catching her in his arms and pulling her close.

Sometime later, Elizabeth stirred from her place in his arms. "Perhaps I *will* write our story, since it has ended so well."

"It hasn't ended, my love," Roarke replied, brushing his lips against hers. "It has only begun."

"I could write about my gift and what has happened thus far," she reflected.

Roarke pulled her back into his arms. "Even if you were to craft it into an excellent tale, it would be far too unbelievable for any publisher in England to print."

"But it would all be true," she protested weakly, as his lips worked their magic.

"We shall think on it," he replied, hoping she would forget about it until they were both old and gray.

BOOK YOUR PLACE ON OUR WEBSITE
AND MAKE THE
READING CONNECTION!

We've created a customized website just for our very special readers, where you can get the inside scoop on everything that's going on with Zebra, Pinnacle and Kensington books.

When you come online, you'll have the exciting opportunity to:

- View covers of upcoming books
- Read sample chapters
- Learn about our future publishing schedule (listed by publication month *and author*)
- Find out when your favorite authors will be visiting a city near you
- Search for and order backlist books from our online catalog
- Check out author bios and background information
- Send e-mail to your favorite authors
- Meet the Kensington staff online
- Join us in weekly chats with authors, readers and other guests
- Get writing guidelines
- AND MUCH MORE!

Visit our website at
http://www.zebrabooks.com